Friends Forever

Kate Vale

Published by North Cascades Press

Copyright 2018 - Kathleen Auerbach

ISBN: 978-17321082-2-6

Cover Artist: LLPix Designs

Discover other titles by the author at: http://katevale.com

Other Titles by Kate Vale

Single Titles
Where This Goes
Gillian's Do-Over
Package Deal
Dream Chaser

On Geneva Shores
Safe Beside You
Choices
Just Friends
Granddad's House
Crossing Paths
Family Bonds

Cedar Island Tales
Secrets Revealed
Her Daughter's Father
Heartstrings
Concealed Attractions

The Lamberts of Pacific Knoll
Only You
Chance Encounter

Short Stories
The Christmas Car

PUBLISHED BY PROMONTORY PRESS
Destiny's Second Chance

Dear Reader:

I knew before page one that Chris would be a rebel among the Lambert siblings. He refuses to go to college, unlike his older brother and all of his sisters. Furthermore, he has no interest in settling down with a wife and making grandbabies for his oh-so-proper mother to spoil. And his relationship with his retired professor father could best be called stiff.

Although he intends to show his parents that he can make a success of his construction business, one disaster after another dogs him—in the guise of an accusation by a former one-off, and a fire that destroys his workshop, turning to ash several recently refurbished furniture pieces. How to recover from all this?

His construction crew steps up, led by the woman he's been friends with since they were pre-schoolers. Teddy has always been just one of the guys—until he's forced to acknowledge that he might want to date her. But he hits a major snag when he asks her out—right after he offers her a partnership in his construction firm.

Teddy is a woman who knows her own mind and she shocks Chris in re-examining everything he's held dear when she turns him down, incensed that he also assumes that her growing carving and stained-glass artwork will become part of his business. He wants to change her "no!" to "yes." She'd like to agree, but there's that Lambert family thing: his parents' view of who Chris *shouldn't* associate with, and why.

Special thanks to contractor Mike Wallace, Dr. John Raduege, PT Keith Kline and Nurse Jeanne Brotherton. Any errors of certain tech-nical details are all mine.

I love hearing from readers. Contact me at katevale@sent.com.

Enjoy!

One

Chris Lambert studied the recently planed leg of the dining table he was building. He shifted his stance slightly and slowly cut the fourth leg with his band saw, following the curve he'd drawn on the wood. He turned off the saw and the whine ebbed to a throaty gurgle as he removed his noise-reduction earmuffs and protective glasses.

His workshop sat on a one-acre parcel holding a left-leaning one-car garage practically begging to be replaced, and the 40s-era Craftsman he called home. Despite the age of the buildings, he'd bought the property for the workshop. Then he discovered that the dated house with faded wallpaper and leaky fixtures could be made livable. Which soaked up whatever time he could spare after working all day at the construction site he was managing. He'd upgraded the kitchen and uncovered the carpeted oak floors badly in need of patching before he sanded and sealed them.

Lately, he'd spent most evenings in his workshop, filling orders from people interested in him refurbishing antique and damaged furniture or buying the custom furniture Chris made.

He ran his fingers over the wood and looked up when the overhead lights flashed off and on several times, a signal that someone had opened the door to the outside. His sidelong glance revealed a woman in a red dress and matching stilettos.

"Bambi?" Her curvy body in an outfit that was more fitting for a fancy dinner than a late afternoon visit to his dusty work area was a surprise. But her presence generated barely a hint of the lust he'd acted on weeks earlier. Hadn't he said he didn't expect to see her again?

"You've got sawdust all over you, sweet thing," she drawled. "And you need a haircut. Want me to take care of that for you? Privately?" She gave him a slow-motion wink and reached for him.

Chris backed up before Bambi, with her bleached blond hair piled high on her head, could brush her blood-red nails through his hair.

The woman had never before shown interest in his construction site, or his shop. And now she was interrupting his concentration on his customer's table?

"What are you doing here, Bambi?"

Dust motes danced in the air as Chris pulled a handkerchief from his pocket and ran it across his forehead and along his nape, swiping the sweat along the neckline of his T-shirt. *She's right. I do need a cut.*

The woman he'd slept with several weeks earlier—a mistake he'd regretted shortly after the fact— pouted. As if her ex-pression would alter Chris's feelings. "Why are you here?" he repeated. Something had to be amiss. "Don't come any closer. Your dress might get messed up."

"We need to talk, honey-pie."

Words Chris had never associated with a woman who claimed to want nothing more than a no-strings-attached night with him.

"The other day, you said we might go to lunch." She stepped closer and grasped his arm. "I guess you forgot." Her lips puffed out again into an expression Chris no longer thought cute. After seeing Bambi's faux pouts too many times, he felt only irritation.

"Your idea, not mine. And that was weeks ago. Besides, I don't break for lunch when I'm in the middle of a job. Which I am. Gotta get these legs finished." He turned away from the band saw and scanned for tiny nicks requiring extra fine sanding before setting all four table legs on his late grandfather's workbench. Next step after that? Oiling the wood to bring out the grain. "Did you skip out of work early? Going somewhere?"

"I'm meeting the girls for drinks after they get off." Her pout returned, joined by a hurt-little-girl whine and a lengthy sigh. "I got fired. My boss just doesn't understand that I need more out of life than work work work. Especially now." She stamped one foot, raising dust that rose above her ankles before settling onto the floor. "We need to talk."

He'd heard that before, and didn't like what it might portend. "Yeah, well. I need to get back to what pays my bills." Chris plucked his buzzing phone from the workbench, relieved when he recognized the number and pointed. "This call? It's business." He raised the phone to his ear. "Mr. MacIntire. Hello!"

Chris turned his back and hunched his shoulders forward, as if doing so provided him a modicum of privacy.

"Yes, sir. Table top's about ready for a final coat and the legs are ready to be sanded. Right on schedule." He ran a hand through his hair and a cloud of sawdust drifted past his shoulders. "You want it when? But that's a week earlier than we agreed."

Chris squinted at the calendar tacked to the wall above the workbench, its penciled-in date squares denoting several customer deadlines. He took a step closer to the table legs and reached for the nearest one. "Okay. A bonus. I understand. I'll do my best. Yes, thanks."

He slid his phone into his pocket. "Damn!"

"Trouble?" Bambi drawled as she slid her hands down the front of her dress, as if to call attention to her ample breasts.

"Nothing I can't handle. But you need to leave. I've got work to do." Chris picked up another chair leg and examined it. *Smooth. Good.*

He glanced at her as she wandered around the limited free space in the shop. "Last time we … talked, I said we were done, had our fun. Remember that, Bambi? And you agreed."

"That was then. This is now," she whined.

"Not for me." But he felt a twinge of guilt, even though he'd been crystal clear about his rules. He enjoyed fun dates, even dates that ended in sex. But no commitment. And Bambi hadn't argued the point.

Chris wasn't changing his mind, acknowledging to himself that he'd made a mistake ending up in curvy Bambi's bed a third time. Two times too many, he now concluded. He should have broken it off with her after that first date, when she'd said she was just looking for a good time, a way to forget her last boyfriend.

Chris barely recalled her words. Wasn't that months ago? His first night with her, the sex had been great. He'd made sure it was good for her, too. Was that why he'd taken her out a second and then a third time?

Chris reached for a can of wood oil and a screw driver to open the container.

What was Bambi saying? Chris half turned in her direction, aware that he'd tuned her out.

"… but you changed your mind? Is that it? I thought you really liked me, Chris."

He set down the can, determined to send Bambi home so he could get back to work. He'd let her down gently before. Maybe he needed to be more forceful, reminding her that he'd moved on, that he thought she had, too. Not that he was seeing anyone at the moment. In fact, since Bambi, he'd decided to focus on his furniture business even after putting in long hours at the construction site. Weekends, too, when he wasn't taking baby steps in home improvement.

"I like you just fine, Bambi, but you agreed. No commitment. Remember?" For the first time in months, he debated whether he'd lost his touch as a maximum two-date, one-night-of-sex man.

He'd broken that rule with Bambi. Had sex with her three times. Even though she wasn't his type. Not that he was sure what that type was. He had yet to meet a woman who *was* his type, the reason he gave his older brother for sampling as many women as possible. It was his preferred M.O., one he had no intention of changing until he met that elusive *right* one.

He wiped his hands on a nearby rag and faced Bambi, frowning. "Look, I like you well enough. But if you're looking for a regular boyfriend, he's not me." He paused. "Didn't you say you wanted to get back with your ex, the one you were mad at when we met?"

"You just wanted to get in my panties," she accused, her lower lip protruding again.

"Maybe I did. The sex we had was good. Great, even. But I'm not into settling down. Which I told you."

"Even if—" Her face reddened and she looked as if she was going to burst into tears.

Chris brushed a hand down the front of her dress, ignoring the press of her breasts against his palm. "I got sawdust on you. Which proves you shouldn't have come here. I have to get back to work."

Bambi glanced around the building, as if taking in what he'd been working on, the lumber drying in stacks along one wall. "You care more about all this stuff than you do about me."

Chris mentally counted to ten, wishing she would take his hint. "Like I said, what we did, it was short-term fun, but that's all. End of story." Chris waited for a sign that Bambi had heard him, then turned back to the table legs on his workbench.

But instead of leaving, she pressed her chest up against Chris's backside as he leaned over the work table. Her hands slid past Chris's chest, the edge of the table preventing her from reaching what she seemed to be seeking below his belt. "But Chris. I *need* you."

Chris jerked upright, knocking Bambi backward.

"Oh!" She exclaimed as she lost her footing and landed on her butt in the sawdust covering the floor. "Damn it, Christopher!"

"Sorry. I didn't mean to knock you down." Chris offered her a hand then leaned down again and snatched up one of her shoes, its four-inch stiletto hanging off the shoe. "Maybe this is why you fell?"

Bambi jerked her arm out of Chris's grasp, turned and limped out the door. She glanced over her shoulder at him. "I should have listened to Ursula. She warned me, said you almost never do more than one date, but I thought … when we …" Her voice trailed off into a barely discernible squeak. "You led me on, Chris."

"No, I didn't." Was she going to keep eating into his work time? Chris unclamped his jaw. "Go home, Bambi. Or do you want me to drive you, since your shoe is wrecked?"

She shook her head and walked away, her gait lopsided. "I can drive myself home," she fumed. "Even if I have to do it barefooted," she declared, then yelped when her bare foot encountered something in the driveway that caused her to take two hops. She leaned against her car and pulled off the remaining shoe, then slid behind the wheel. "This isn't the last you've seen of me, Christopher Lambert," she declared, her angry squint emphasizing her words.

Just because I broke your shoe? "Want me to pay to fix your shoe?"

"Don't bother!" Bambi slammed her car door and backed out of his driveway, clipping the neighbor's hedge as she did so.

Under his breath, Chris mumbled, "And good riddance to you, too." But he wondered what she meant that she might be back. He hadn't wanted to hurt her, but he breathed a relieved sigh at having escaped an encounter that could have become testier.

Unlike his three older siblings, commitment wasn't his gig. Not like Fletcher, married again after the death of his first wife and baby daughter. Not like Deb, either, who'd married Fletcher's law partner, Todd Prescott, eighteen months ago. Even his two-minutes-older twin, Elaine, was engaged. Had been for almost four years. What was holding her and Norm back from setting a date?

Chris glanced at his watch. Two hours. He'd work on the table legs, take a quick break for dinner and then come back to clean up. Tomorrow, after work at the jobsite, he'd apply a final seal to another project, the last step before delivering that piece of furniture to its owner.

Chris resumed his work on the table legs.

Ten minutes later, his phone interrupted him. He debated letting it go to voice mail until he saw who was calling. *Ah, my bestie, a woman I'll always talk to.*

"Hey, Teddy. What's up?"

"Do me a favor?" She coughed.

"Sure. What do you need?"

"That fireplace surround. The owners are coming over this weekend."

Teddy Jameson blew her nose. After her raspy voice sounded.

"And you're worried about all the drywall dust. I'll stop over and run a cloth over your masterpiece."

"Would you, Chris? I—" Teddy coughed again.

"Soon as I get these table legs sanded. Want me to stop by, maybe make you a hot toddy? My mom swears by them. Later, Teddy." Before she could reply, he slid his phone into his pocket.

Unlike Bambi, Teddy was a long-time friend, just not a *girl*friend. A pal, more like a guy. All through school. Part of his construction crew, too. In the past six months, she'd also begun using a corner of his workshop for her stained-glass work.

"I don't need much space, but I can't do it at home," she'd explained when he'd asked why she was looking for space downtown. "I insist on paying rent. What I'd be doing at any other place."

"You don't have to, but if you insist." Chris had grinned as he removed stacks of wood along the far wall, shoving the pieces he'd selected for future furniture projects into the rafters of the old building. "You're welcome to this space. Look! You'll even have a window so you can check the glass colors even if the lights go out. I need that electrician back here to check on that switch."

"You're a peach, Chris." Teddy had playfully punched him on the shoulder. Like a guy.

Since using that space, she'd sold several stained-glass windows and a collection of holiday ornaments. Teddy wanted to build her work into a fulltime business along with carving wood sculptures and other specialty pieces, like that fireplace surround she'd been working on. Until she could make a living at it, she was using her construction skills on Chris's crew to pay the bills.

Ironic that they'd both started as house painters and worked their way up in the trades, eventually handling larger projects. Chris now ran his own construction crew. Teddy had gained her skills while putting herself through college, something Chris hadn't known about until she came home to take responsibility for Yancy, her kid brother.

She'd contracted out with several different construction crews as a painter and layer of tile. She was conscientious and careful, did a better job supervising new guys, especially on the painting crews, than other people Chris had hired. And her tile work, on floors, and on back splashes, was first-rate and creative. After Chris had shown pictures of her work to the owner of the custom home he was building, that man had hired her to create the fancy fireplace surround his wife wanted. Chris was certain completion of that job would generate more carving work for Teddy.

He returned to examining the table legs. *Time to sand,* he decided, and picked up his noise reduction earphones after flipping the switch so that he could listen to music while he sanded. Maybe he'd grab a burger. Then he'd head for the house under construction and check Teddy's fireplace. And he'd drop by and let her know how it looked, so she wouldn't worry about what the judge and his wife were likely to see in her absence.

~ ~ ~

"You look sick, kid." Chris grinned at Teddy as she huddled under two blankets on the couch of her tiny two-bedroom bungalow.

Chris sniffed. "Whatever Yancy's cooking smells good."

"Soup," she croaked. Teddy's long red hair, usually captured in a braid that she pinned under her hat, flopped over her shoulders. "Not that hungry. I could use some ice to suck on."

Chris nodded at Teddy's lanky seventeen-year-old brother. "How ya doing, Yance? Has she been cranky like this all day? Good thing it's the weekend and you can take care of her. Make sure she doesn't do anything except rest."

"I tried to get her to go to the doctor, but she wouldn't. Maybe you can talk her into it." The teen ran first one hand and then the other through his dark auburn hair then pulled it into a man bun and tightened the rubber band holding it in place near his nape.

Yancy handed Chris a glass filled with ice cubes and water. "She's been sucking on these all day, in between complaints."

"Maybe I can put her in a better mood."

Chris sat down next to Teddy. "Let me look at your throat."

Teddy shook her head. "You're as bad as Yancy. Tell him he shouldn't have skipped school on Friday. I don't need him hanging around telling me what to do." But she sounded more like a whipped puppy than the always-on-the-job big sister who'd assumed custody of Yancy after their mother's death almost a year earlier.

"Suck and chill, Ted." Chris retreated to the kitchen. "Mind if I taste that soup, Yance?" He reached for a bowl and glanced at the boy as he buttered a piece of toast. "Teddy says you stayed home from school yesterday."

"So?" Teenage attitude coated the word.

"How're you going to graduate if you don't show up?"

"I didn't like how weak she was. Barely made it to the couch before practically falling down. She hasn't been much better today, either." The boy crunched on the toast and reached for another piece.

Chris finished slurping up the soup. "You made this? From scratch?"

Yancy frowned. "Of course, from scratch. You think Teddy would let me open up a can of crap?"

Chris chuckled. "Stay in school, kid. If you can make soup this good, I'll bet you could become a chef at a fancy restaurant. You should talk to Lexi, my sister-in-law. She's a baker. Just graduated from the Culinary Academy. Partners with Monet Durham now."

"Oh, yeah?"

"Lexi's cool. Makes fabulous desserts. She could tell you all about the Academy, but I'm guessing they only take people who've graduated high school. Which means you should stop skipping school, especially your senior year."

"Yeah, yeah." Yancy frowned.

"Think past your nose, kid. You want a future where you can have some of the finer things? Like a place to live, and I don't mean mooching off your sister. Maybe even a nice ride? You have to finish high school. Maybe even go to college or the tech school or a place like the Culinary Academy."

"You didn't go to college and you're doing okay," Yancy argued.

"No, but I apprenticed. Maybe you could do that, too."

Chris walked back into the living room. The glass of ice cubes was empty and Teddy's eyes were closed. She was breathing out of her mouth, and her cheeks looked more like pale marble than their usual healthy patina. Her pale lashes, usually darkened by mascara, reminded Chris of untrimmed brushes as they lay against her skin, hiding the dark blue eyes that flashed with lightning sparks whenever she argued with him.

He reached for Teddy's hand. Her fingers were cool. At his touch, they curled slightly. "Hey, Ted." After a pause, "Calling Theodora. Is Theodora Jameson in here?"

Use of her full name seemed to rouse her. "Don't call me that." Teddy opened one eye to stare balefully at him.

"Come on. We're going to the doctor."

She groaned under her breath.

He grinned at her and pointed to her flannel pajama bottoms. They sported puppy dogs and kittens. "Want me to help you get dressed or can you do it yourself? Unless you want to go in your PJs." He made a show of glancing at the wall clock. "I'll give you five minutes. Have a wad of stuff to finish tonight and time's a'wastin.'" The phrase Teddy and Yancy's late grandfather had used so often was sure to spur her to action. Too bad Mrs. Jameson had died and forced Teddy to quit school to keep Yancy out of foster care.

"I'll change." Teddy struggled to sit up and finally, reluctantly, accepted Chris's hand to stand. She grabbed the top blanket off the couch and wrapped it around her shoulders. "No help needed." She walked unsteadily past Yancy toward her bedroom.

Chris flopped onto the couch cushions that held the warmth of Teddy's body. He glanced toward the kitchen, pleased to see that Yancy was wiping down the stove top. The dishes, previously piled in the sink, now formed a sparkling pyramid on the counter, under a draped dish towel.

Minutes later, Teddy emerged from her room in a sweatshirt and a pair of jeans that had seen better days. She'd shoved her feet into a pair of Uggs and shivered as she returned to the living room.

"Where's your jacket?"

She pointed to the side of the living room window.

Chris opened the door of a tiny closet and pulled out a high school letter jacket. It reminded him of Teddy's years on the girls' basketball team. By ninth grade, she was taller than the rest of the girls and many of the boys. By their senior year, she could look directly into six-foot Chris's eyes. She'd earned a spot on the girl's team during tryouts by scoring more three-pointers, more jump shots, and more free-throw points than even the captain of the boy's team. That kid's nose had remained stubbornly out of joint for half the season when Teddy's scoring highs were pointed out at an all-school assembly touting the girl's team's winning record that year.

"You still have this jacket?" he asked. "After all the shit you put up with in high school?"

"You seem to forget they left me alone after you tackled Nels. That crybaby."

Chris nodded. "You're right. Forgot about that little scene outside the locker room."

Teddy rewarded him with a wry grin. "Come on. Let's get this over with." She grabbed her purse.

An hour later, Chris parked in front of Teddy's little house and helped her out of his truck. "Who knew medicine could be so expensive? Good thing the doctor gave you some freebies."

"One reason I didn't want to go in the first place." She coughed into her sleeve.

"At least the doc said that shot he gave you would kill the germs eating up the back of your throat."

"Not an image I want to think about, if it's all the same to you."

"Now that you're home, you should try Yancy's soup. It was really good. Like the doc said, to keep up your strength. Fight those germs."

"I do feel hungry now," she admitted. "Sorry I was so grouchy before."

"Hey, gotta keep you alive so you'll keep paying rent," he countered with a grin. He tromped up the porch steps and banged on the door. When Yancy let them in, Chris watched the boy bring a steaming bowl of soup to the table.

"Points for you, Yance. Make sure she takes her pills, too. Before she goes to bed. No later than ten."

"I can take care of myself," Teddy assured him. "Besides, I want Yance to pick up some of my wood projects. Even sick, I can finish those eagles I'm carving for the mayor's office."

"As long as you rest, too."

~ ~ ~

Chris wiped his arm across his face, glad he'd worn a sweatband. His crew had turned up the heat in the custom house to aid in drying the mudded-up drywall. He turned up the music in his boom box, determined to finish rubbing the sculpted design Teddy had created in the family room fireplace surround. If the homeowners stopped by and saw the newly cleaned wood, he knew they'd be pleased.

"Chris!" His sister, Debra, called out, her voice overwhelming the sound of symphonic music wafting through the house. "Todd. Here he is!"

Debra's husband grinned and waved at Chris as he entered the front door. "Hope we aren't disturbing you. Deb wanted to check out what you're working on."

Debra and Todd stopped next to the fireplace where Chris was crouched.

"Because you're interested in something like this?" He stood up and pointed to the frieze and the pattern that continued down the extra wide legs of the surround.

Debra nodded. "You said you thought my fireplace could use a carved surround. But Teddy never came over to talk to us."

"She's sick. That's why I'm here, to spiff this up for when the owners come by." He ran a soft cloth over the wood then backed away. "What do you think?"

Todd leaned closer. "She's a real artist. And we're happy to pay her usual rate, if she's willing to do the work. But no rush."

"We collaborated on another design that might work as an inset for a table top or maybe a door. After we add pictures to the website, Teddy's betting it'll bring in more business for both of us. The owner of this place wants front door panels, too. Teddy was going to start them next week."

Deb grinned. "So, she's doing more carving? Stained-glass work, too?"

"Only between regular construction jobs."

Todd laughed. "Back to the carving. Except for the door panels, all the customizing Teddy's doing here is interior work?"

"Yep. And only for this house. The rest of these places"— he motioned down the street at two other structures in varying stages of completion—"and those lots on the other side, too, will look pretty much like the others when they're finished. All about the same size, same number of beds and baths, that sort of thing, even though the exteriors will vary along with the paint colors required by the neighborhood association. You know, cedar roofs, no exceeding of the established height limits, no fences except in the back yard. Yada yada." He glanced at his sister.

"Teddy's sketch of the front door panels is at my shop if you want to check them out."

Todd glanced at Debra. "What do you think? Should we consider a new door? New panels anyway?"

"I'd like to see what she's planning for this house. Have you had dinner yet, Chris? Or do you have a hot date, since it's Saturday?"

"Just came from Teddy's where I grabbed a bowl of soup before I took her to the doctor, but I could still eat something." He glanced sidelong at Debra. "Who's cooking?"

Todd chuckled. "That would be me."

"Then I'm in." Chris avoided a playful swat from his sister. "Not that I won't eat whatever you fix, sis, but Todd's meals are more my style."

Deb gave him a wry smile. "I'm getting better. Haven't burned anything in at least a month."

Todd leaned over and kissed her. "She's right. We were planning to sit down around eight. Does that give you enough time to get cleaned up?"

Chris nodded. "Sure." He returned to wiping down the fireplace surround. "See you in an hour."

He watched as his brother-in-law and sister departed, hand-in-hand. Chris imagined how his custom furnishings might look in this family room. He'd use wood complementing the moldings, the doors and their framing. But this place wasn't his home. He didn't need a five-bedroom place with three and a half baths. He was happily single. Free of the encumbrances of other people. Free to date anyone, work anywhere. And build his furniture business into a success where he could choose between contracts and not have to squeeze it in between construction work.

Thank you, Teddy, he thought. Who'd have guessed when he offered to share his workshop space that he'd also gain an expert in websites? Teddy was a whiz at slapping pictures on the web and generating inquiries Chris had never expected to receive.

He'd missed her when she'd left Pacific Knoll for college, surprising everyone who'd known the red-haired rebel back in the day. He suspected circumstances had settled her down, made her take things seriously. Because now she was responsible for Yancy.

Chris gave the fireplace mantel a final swipe before shutting the front door. He tromped across the dusty yard to his truck. *Gotta email these pictures to Teddy.* Proof he'd cleaned off her carving. After that, he'd jump in the shower and head over to his sister's place.

~ ~ ~

Chris grabbed two six-packs of beer and walked toward the side yard of his sister's home. Todd, bundled against the late-January cold, waved from the patio where he was turning what smelled like steaks on the grill.

"Looks like I made it just in time. Want a beer?"

Todd handed a covered bowl to Chris. "Potatoes are done. If you'll take them inside, I'll trade you for one of those beers."

Chris entered the kitchen and handed the bowl to his sister. "Todd says the steaks are almost done."

Debra nodded. "He insisted on trying out the new grill. What do you think of how I added more garden space around the patio you helped him pour?"

"Looks good. Especially with those big pots on the corners. They should look nice full of flowers come spring. Too bad it's not warm enough yet to eat outside."

"I'm hoping it will be after school's out. My second year as assistant principal, aka disciplinarian, has been exhausting and I still have months to go before we say good-bye to the seniors."

Chris gave his sister a bemused stare. "You don't look all that tired. I'm betting the kids who end up in your office would say they got it worse."

"Leave it to you to take their side," she scoffed, and glanced up when Todd entered, the steaks sizzling on a platter.

Over dinner, Chris answered Todd's questions about his furniture business and his goal of gradually easing out of general contracting jobs to focus exclusively on furniture. "I got a taste of what I can make when I did all those pieces last year for that guy Fletcher knows, the one who was willing to pay top dollar."

"I heard he was very happy with your work," Debra added.

Chris nodded. "If only I had more clients like him. Things really slowed down over the winter. And haven't picked back up again, although with the new construction, I'm staying busy."

"I checked out your website," Debra enthused. "I hope you're giving Teddy free rent at the shop. She deserves it for how she's improved your online presence."

"I offered, but she insisted on paying," Chris countered. "Yancy skipped school yesterday. Is he doing that a lot?"

Debra frowned. "Several times this past month, which has me worried. After Teddy came home last year, Yancy seemed to be doing okay. Now he's reverted to what he was doing right before his mother died. I left her a message." She set down her fork and reached for her phone to thumb in a quick note. "Since she's been sick, I'll call her again."

"What'd he do, other than skip, that you need to talk about with her?"

"Confidential, bro. And you know better than to ask."

"You're getting uppity now that you're assistant principal," Chris hooted. "Okay, I won't ask. I'm guessing he's like she was in high school. In and out of trouble, at least when she wasn't wiping the basketball court with other teams." He raised an arm as if to deflect a blow. "Just sayin', sis. And he had an excuse yesterday. He was taking care of Teddy."

"You've known them a long time?" Todd asked.

"Teddy and I have been friends forever. Her grandfather signed her up for soccer when we were in first grade. She was the only one who begged to be goalie. In middle school, no one else wanted her for a lab partner in science, or chemistry in high school. She was smarter'n me in those classes, so I took advantage."

"And you stood up for her when those boys on the basketball team weren't so nice," Debra added.

"They didn't like looking bad. But since I had a tomboy sister" —Chris pointed to Deb and smirked— "I didn't mind that she was so good. Now that she's back home, it's worked out great that she needed shop space. And I can use the rent she's paying."

"Doesn't that make things crowded?" Todd asked.

"A little, but she doesn't take up much space and she's rarely there when I am."

"Probably a good thing, since I don't recall she's into classical music," Debra said. "Isn't she more a country music fan?"

Chris scowled. "I'm working on her to use ear buds. That way, she can listen to what she likes, and I can chill out with what I enjoy."

Todd added, "And she carves. I'd think someone doing that would want to be soothed by beautiful music, not blasted by guitar riffs."

"You don't know Teddy. Her taste in music fits perfectly with her temper. And hair—fire-engine red." Chris pushed his plate away. "But I don't call her Tomato Head anymore. She threatened to make me into a girl the last time I called her that."

"In high school?" Todd asked.

"I think it was middle school." Chris grinned. "Teddy's not at all like me, is she, sis? She's fiery, while I'm calm, easy-going."

Debra snorted. "Yeah, right."

"I need soothing music to help me chill."

"You mean bring out the artist in you," Debra added. "That's how Mom would explain it."

"Another beer, Todd?" Chris stood up to retrieve two cans from the refrigerator. He tossed one to his brother-in-law and was about to pull the pop-top when his cell rang.

Caller ID told him it was Yancy.

"Yo, what's up, kid?"

"Chris, you better get over here. Your shop's on fire!"

"Jesus! I've got finished pieces in there." Chris jumped to his feet and clicked off his phone.

"Deb, call the fire department," he shouted over his shoulder. "My shop's burning. Tell them to hurry."

Todd ran after him, toward the front door. "I'm coming, too."

Chris dove into his truck, started it up and hit the accelerator before Todd had closed the passenger door.

Two

Chris gulped as he made a two-wheeled turn into his driveway. Black smoke hid the moon, turning the night darker, and the smell of burning wood coated his throat. How could this have happened? He hit the brakes and slid out of his seat as the truck bumped forward a few feet before stopping.

"Got a hose?" Todd shouted as his feet hit the ground.

Chris pointed toward the garage. "Not sure it will reach, but it's worth a try." He headed for the large shop doors, intent on hauling out his finished work before those pieces were lost. Sirens sounded and the long beep of a horn on a fire truck signaled that a car might have blocked the nearest intersection as the big rig barreled toward his business.

He grabbed the metal handle of the right side of the double doors and let go with a hiss at the heat of the metal. Was the interior already engulfed? Smoke spiraled between the big doors, choking him. Using the hem of his shirt, he tried again and managed to pull open one of the doors just as water doused his head and neck. Chris glanced over his shoulder and saw that Todd was aiming a stream of water through a nearby window, the splashes soaking him.

He hauled open the other door. Flames burst out to meet him, as if intent on crisping his skin. In the light from the flames, he could see a tall thin figure pulling on a pallet laden with completed furniture.

"Yancy?"

"Help me get this away from Teddy's space!"

Chris angled past the boy and took his place. "Go around the back side."

Minutes later, Yancy carried two large sculptures of eagles in midflight and dropped them onto the grass between Chris's garage and his home.

The roar of the fire reminded Chris of a jet engine. The heat of the flames singed his shirt and the skin of his neck and face. He hefted a table top he'd just finished for Mr. MacIntire, ignoring the pain in his right hand. Yancy edged past him, a soaked shirt covering his head and shoulders, his chest bare, and grabbed the other end of the table. Just as they reached the open doors of the workshop, a stream of water aimed at the building bounced off the smoking walls and knocked them to the ground. *Firemen?* Chris and Yancy scrambled to their feet and hauled two more finished pieces outside as water arced over a stack of blazing wood that hissed angrily and sent more smoke billowing.

Ignoring shouts from a firefighter, Chris ran back into the building, intent on rescuing more of the furniture he'd been restoring.

"Right behind you, Chris," Yancy yelled.

Chris could barely see the hundred-year-old dresser. If only he could get it out. "Over here!" he shouted at Yancy. Together, they pulled the heavy dresser away from the flames.

Through the billowing smoke, flames angled up the long western wall of the shop like so many orange and red serpents creeping along the rafters. Pieces of burning wood fell from a storage area high on the wall. Chris ducked as the first of several long pieces of smoking lumber fell to the workshop floor.

Todd grabbed Yancy's arm and pulled him toward the door. "Chris! Give it up."

"Get back! Now!" came a muffled order from the nearest firefighter. He grabbed Chris's arm, yanking him away from the flames. "Out!" he repeated, pointing.

Chris started to protest when something knocked him backwards and pain seared his right shoulder.

The first responder took advantage of Chris's fall to shove him outside. Chris stumbled toward Yancy, who was on his hands and knees, coughing. The boy's shirt, previously soaked, now seemed to be smoking. A blue-shirted EMT picked up Yancy, his arms around the boy's chest and hauled him closer to their rig, gesturing for Chris to follow.

Chris heard a crash and then another, and turned back toward the sound. The roof? If it collapsed, he'd lose everything.

Cinders and pieces of flaming roof rained into the yard. "Get back, Chris! The roof's going! Let the pros do their job." Todd backed away from the firefighters as they moved closer to the building.

One first responder in a mask manhandled Chris away from the building, dragging him when he failed to respond. Todd followed and reached for Chris as he fell to his knees, his eyes burning, his chest on fire, the front of his jeans and shirt searing his skin.

Chris coughed and stopped pushing against the arms that held him away from the flames, away from his business that was no more. Suddenly, Debra's face came into focus.

"Chris! You're hurt! Stop fighting. You're more important than the building." Tears ran down her cheeks. She moved between him and Todd, who was sucking oxygen from a mask as he sat nearby. Todd's eyes streamed black streaks, a sign he had braved the smoke and flames to help, though his efforts hadn't been enough to save his brother-in-law's business. Or Teddy's, Chris reminded himself. Yancy's big feet were all that Chris could see as he lay next to one of the fire trucks, an EMT bending over the teen.

How many minutes elapsed before the building collapsed in on itself, Chris couldn't say. He refused a ride to the hospital, telling the EMTs he'd get a ride with Todd, who assured the first responders that he would follow them in his own car. Debra left in the ambulance with Yancy, assuring the boy she'd call his sister. Todd and Chris stood back as two firefighters continued to stream water on the hissing pile of debris where his workshop had stood.

The fire chief approached. "Any idea what might have caused the fire?"

"No idea. I wasn't here." Chris coughed before answering. "Yancy called me at my sister's place. It was pretty far gone by the time I got here."

"Well, the fire investigator will be here in the morning. Don't go tromping around. Not for any reason. You'll only mess up evidence that your insurance adjuster will want. My men—" he pointed to the firefighters still dousing the smoking debris—"will stick around, make sure nothing starts up again. You're lucky your house was far enough away to avoid becoming collateral damage. And the garage.

"I called for another rig to take you to the hospital." The chief's gaze roamed over Chris and then Todd. "You both look like you could use some help. What's with your arm, Chris?"

"Got hit by some debris. I'm okay." But he flinched when Chief Donovan placed a hand on his shoulder.

"You're not fine, and both of you are coughing. You're going in as soon as more EMT's get here." The chief pulled off his hat and ran a smoke-streaked hand through his hair. "While we're waiting, tell me about your business. The kind of equipment you use. That sort of thing."

Chris nodded, his throat feeling too sore to form words. "We have all the usual stuff."

"We? You have a partner?"

"Teddy Jameson makes stained glass."

"Was she working today? Uses a blow torch? She's the one who did that piece I saw at the craft fair last month? Maybe she forgot to unplug her equipment."

"She'd never do that. She's extra careful. And she's been sick the last couple days. Only one here today was me."

"Is that old mountain bike yours?" the chief pointed to the corner of the garage where a bike leaned against the building.

"Yancy's. He came over to pick up some work for Teddy. The doctor said she was supposed to stay home and rest." He grimaced. "Which she probably won't do if Yancy's at the hospital."

Todd glanced at the fire chief. "What're you thinking, Chief?"

The older man shuffled a boot in the blackened mud. "Just trying to tie up loose ends. No one else was around besides that kid?"

Chris shook his head. "No. After I finished up, I saw Teddy, then stopped by the jobsite to check her latest project. Had dinner with my sister and Todd, why I was at their place when Yancy called."

"Where do you keep your flammables? In the shop?"

Chris shook his head. "Do I look stupid? No, I stow them in closed cans in the garage. Near the wall farthest from the shop. On some low shelves. In fact, that wall closest to my garage is the only one still standing. Maybe because my granddad's workbench is holding it up." He pointed to what remained of the old shop. The ancient workbench was made of eight-inch thick boards hewn out of huge old growth cedar logs. A legacy of his paternal grandfather's days when he'd worked in the woods, before going to college at Chris's great-grandfather's urging.

Chris felt numb. His work was gone. Two dining room tables and six chairs, assorted other tables, the frame for the old-fashioned mirror he'd been restoring. Only its matching dresser and MacIntire's table top and some miscellaneous pieces had been saved. He rose unsteadily from where he'd been sitting and slowly approached what was left of his shop.

"Hey!" The chief started after him. "What'd I tell you?"

Chris stepped around a large puddle. "Look there, Chief. See that old workbench? Looks like I might be able to salvage it. About the only thing that isn't totally destroyed."

The chief stepped closer and placed a hand on Chris's uninjured shoulder. "Where's your power saw, other equipment like it?"

"Along the back wall. Unplugged. Near the door." He pointed toward the pile of blackened material. "That lump of melted metal? Probably some of my tools."

He glanced at the fire chief. "How is it this one wall of my shop didn't get totally destroyed?"

"There's no accounting for what fire does, where it goes," the chief replied. "Could be a breeze kept the flames away. Good thing, too, as that wall is closest to your garage and the house. But like I said. Don't touch anything. Your insurance adjuster will want to see what we're looking at. And he'll want our investigator's report, too. You have insurance?"

Chris nodded. "But I've lost at least six months' worth of work, most of it ready to be delivered, and half of those jobs prepaid at least fifty percent. I was going to deliver them tomorrow or the next day."

Todd asked, "You think it was arson, Chief?"

Chris stared at the chief. Who would want to hurt him that way? His mind whirled at the thought.

"No way to know yet. We'll let the investigators do their job. When they talk to you, be sure and tell them what you told me. Who was here, when, what you were doing. That sort of thing."

An EMT rig pulled into the yard. Two men in blue uniforms approached Todd and Chris.

The chief nodded in their direction. "Chris, you're favoring that shoulder. Let these men do their job. You could probably use some oxygen, too, after all that coughing." He waved the EMTs closer. They placed oxygen masks on Chris and Todd.

Chief Donovan stood by while the EMTs assessed for other injuries. "They'll take you to the ER and get you checked out. Whatever they say to do, do it. I don't want to end up in holy hell from your mother if she suspects we didn't take proper care of you."

He spoke briefly to the men continuing to spray water on the smoking remains of Chris's shop, then approached the red SUV parked crookedly on Chris's lawn.

~ ~ ~

At the hospital, Chris and Todd met Debra in the ER after they were treated for smoke inhalation. Chris was then sent up to x-ray to verify that his aching shoulder wasn't broken. Only after a second slathering of cream onto his skin did the burning along his collarbone finally settle enough that he could ignore it. Mostly. The medicated wash for his eyes also helped, although when he looked in the mirror, their redness testified to his fight to rescue furniture from the flames.

But what hurt worse were his right palm and fingers, which had sustained second-degree burns. With his hand bandaged, he wouldn't be restoring or building anything for a while. He hated to have to tell old man MacIntire about the delay in finishing his dining table. *Maybe he'll understand.*

While Chris sat, his eyes closed against the bright lights of the ER, Todd's eyes were washed out and he was given a prescription for more of the same, to be used should he feel the need. When the nurse finished, he took a seat next to his wife.

Chris approached Debra and Todd. "Know anything about Yancy?"

Debra spoke up. "I heard they're keeping him overnight."

"Why?"

"He has a concussion."

"Then no school on Monday." Chris grimaced. "Something he and I talked about."

Deb raised her chin and looked at her brother.

"We had a little talk about skipping school," he explained.

She nodded. "I'll check with his teachers and pick up the assignments he's missed."

Chris huffed out a cough. "Shouldn't you leave that to Teddy?"

"You said she's sick, and I'm assistant principal. Which makes me entitled to help him out. Let's go see him before we leave."

Chris and Todd followed Debra down a long hall into Yancy's room.

"Let me go in first," Chris insisted.

The boy lay in bed, his head bandaged, and one arm held across his chest in a shoulder brace similar to the one Chris now sported. Only the hand lying on top of the sheet moved, randomly jerking as if to music only Yancy could hear. But the boy sported no ear plugs and Chris saw no evidence of the teen's ever-present cell phone.

"Hey, Yance."

The teen opened his eyes, their rims looking as irritated as Chris's felt.

"How are you feeling?"

Yancy's hand waggled back and forth.

"I guess you're not going to school unless they let you out before Monday."

He rasped out, "Rather be there than here."

"Deb here—er, Ms. Lambert, to you. She's threatening to bring you the assignments you missed on Friday. Any others, too."

Yancy grimaced, looking past Chris toward the half-open doorway. "She doesn't have to do that."

Debra spoke up before entering. "I don't have to, but I will. The doctor wasn't sure how long you might have to stay."

"Teddy's going to have a fit. Hospitals cost money. Something we don't have much of." Yancy's hand rose then fell back onto the sheet.

As if conjured by his words, Yancy's sister swept into the room, her flip-flops smacking. She was wearing the same clothes she'd donned when Yancy took her to the clinic. "Don't worry about the bill, you little twerp." Her voice broke. "Getting you well is what's important." She leaned over the bed and grasped her kid brother in a hug made awkward by the bandages on his face and the brace holding his arm across his chest.

"How'd you know I was here?" Yancy asked.

"Deb called. You shouldn't have tried to get my stuff out of the fire. What were you thinking? I'll bet the firemen told you not to." Her words dissolved into watery sobs.

Chris turned toward his sister and lowered his voice. "What did you tell her?"

"Teddy must have called the chief, demanded details. I only mentioned the fire and that you two were here being checked out."

Chris listened as Teddy talked to Yancy.

Her eyes still welling with tears, she turned toward Chris and hugged him tightly. "Thank goodness you got him out of there." The strength of her arms belied how sick she'd seemed only hours earlier, though her hair was mussed as if she'd been sleeping before coming to the hospital.

"Aren't you supposed to be in bed?" he asked, awkwardly patting her back before she released him. "How's your throat?"

She swallowed and grimaced. "Doesn't matter. I had to see Yance." She looked around the room. "I guess all my pieces are burned up?"

"I got the eagles out," Yancy croaked. "Left them by Chris's garage. The stained-glass windows, too."

"We'll go back and get them," Debra offered. "Come on, Todd. Yancy needs to rest. Chris, you coming?"

"In a minute." He pulled a chair closer to the bed, thought better of sitting down and offered it to Teddy.

"I guess you'll want to stay with him for a while."

Without glancing his way, Teddy nodded and reached for Yancy's uninjured hand.

Chris backed out of the room. Now was not the time to talk to Teddy about what she'd lost. A place to work, her supplies, and the special wood she'd reserved for the door insets.

~ ~ ~

While Todd drove, Chris closed his eyes and tried not to think about what he'd lost, how he was going to recover. What worried him most was the furniture so near to completion, the finished pieces that would have netted him a tidy profit and pictures to put up on his website, pictures Teddy had said would generate new commissions.

Todd stopped the car well away from Chris's house and what was left of the workshop. Two firemen were still soaking the smoking wood pile.

"Oh, my," Debra exclaimed softly.

Todd opened her door, and they walked well away from the muddy area surrounding the scene of the fire. He flipped on the flashlight he'd plucked from Deb's trunk and scanned the grassy area between the garage and Chris's house. Three passes, no luck.

Debra pointed, "Over there, honey. Closer to the lilac tree. Not quite at its base. It was singed, too. Look at those curled up leaves on the upper branches."

Todd aimed the light where she pointed, and the glint of something shiny caught Chris's eye. He trotted closer. Teddy's stained-glass windows. Four of them. They looked unscathed. Yancy must have been extra careful laying them on the grass. Next to them, almost touching the base of the lilac tree were the two eagle sculptures destined for the mayor's office. They needed only a final coat of varnish.

"Those stained-glass pieces probably should go in the backseat." Todd picked up one of the windows. "Deb, could you grab the eagles?"

"Sure."

"Should we take them to her, Chris?" Todd asked. "Or leave them with you?"

"She'll probably want to see them. I don't know what varnish she was planning to use. It'll make her feel better if she can see what Yancy saved."

Todd nodded. He retrieved the other windows and they drove to Teddy's house.

"Do you have a key?" Debra asked.

"I think she hides one under a rock like Mom used to." Chris smiled, in spite of the pulling sensation around his mouth and under his eyes from the singeing his skin had endured.

"Or she left without locking up," Debra offered.

Todd nodded when he tried the front door and discovered it unlocked.

They placed the sculptures on the counter. Todd brought the four stained-glass windows into the house, carefully placing them on the kitchen table. Debra rummaged in a linen closet and pulled out several towels to serve as cushioning between the windows.

"Okay, guys. Time to go home," Deb declared. "Chris, you're staying at our place tonight. So I can make sure you take your medicine like the doctor said."

"Oh, come on. I'm not a baby." He grimaced.

"No, but it'll be easier for me to apply the salve to your face and hands."

Todd waved Chris toward Debra's car. "No sense arguing, bro. She might sic your mom on you if you don't go along."

Chris conceded the point and climbed into the back seat, careful to avoid bumping his sore shoulder.

He'd have to make calls. Or maybe he would wait until Monday. After all, what was the weekend going to change? He still had his construction crew, but what he most regretted was the major setback to his furniture-making business and what Teddy had lost.

Three

Teddy climbed out of her car, her burning throat a reminder that it was past time for the medicine the doctor had given her. She slipped her key into the front door and stepped inside the house, its warmth welcoming her.

"Oh!" The eagles she'd carved from a single cedar post stood guard on the kitchen counter. She stepped closer, shrugged out of her jean jacket and dropped her purse onto the nearest chair, her heart climbing into her throat when she spotted the stack of stained-glass windows on the table. Her latest projects. Yancy had saved them, too? Her heart swelled with love for her kid brother. As much as she often resented him and his acting-out, he'd cared enough to save her artwork.

Her phone buzzed in her pocket and she pulled it out. "Hi, Deb. I'm guessing you brought my eagles and other artwork home?"

"Yes. We knew you'd want them in a safe place. I hope Yancy's feeling better."

"He was sleeping when I left the hospital." She glanced again at the eagles. "What about Chris? The fire chief told me the shop was a total loss." Her mind skittered back to the chief's remarks when he'd broken the news, along with the police officer, that her late mother had died in an explosion that had leveled her home. The chief had warned her against going into what was left of the building, that it was toxic.

Now a second fire had dealt her and Yancy another blow. And Chris, too: losing the building he'd been so thrilled to find.

"You know Chris. He'll rebuild. After he replaces the furniture he lost."

Deb was being deliberately upbeat, Teddy thought. "All those contracts he had …"

She exchanged a few more words with Debra before hanging up. She brushed her fingers over the eagles, as if to reassure herself that they hadn't been damaged. When she passed her fingers lightly over one spread wing, she decided they needed another oiling. The rest of her stash of similar woods was probably gone, along with the boxes of colored glass she used to make her stained glass. Like Chris, she'd have to start over. At least she could photograph what Yancy had saved and use those pictures to generate new business via her website. But she could ill afford to lose her other projects, or the money they represented.

The thought that Yancy could have died in that fire sent Teddy's pulse racing. But maybe his injury would force him to get caught up with the schoolwork Teddy suspected he hadn't been completing. Not just one day, more like a few weeks' worth. *I should have paid more attention, not just taken his word for it,* she decided.

As for Chris? He'd need help with his construction business. *I can do more than paint or oversee the other painters,* she thought. *Or lay tile.* She'd increase her involvement at the jobsite during the day and oversee Yancy's homework at night. It would make for exhausting days, but she'd step up.

She headed for her bedroom, turning off lights as she approached the back of the bungalow she and Yancy occupied. Teddy climbed into bed and lay there, staring at the ceiling she couldn't discern in the dark, aware that tears slid down her cheeks, dampening her pillow.

She wiped a hand across her face. What she'd lost was nothing compared with Chris. But would he accept her help? He was one of those guys who rarely accepted assistance from others. It had taken her weeks to convince him to charge her rent after she'd begun using space in his building. Even though she knew he could use the money.

What was it about guys who assumed that girls couldn't do what guys could do? Even though she'd shown him she could do as much as the men in his crew. She had the muscles and the strength. She'd already demonstrated that she could handle sprayers and brushes as well as—or even better than—the other painters he'd hired. Which was why he'd put her in charge of them. And he mostly left her alone when she laid tile, too, trusting that she would get it right. Because she'd shown him she could.

She rolled over and clutched the extra pillow to her chest. Chris Lambert, her BFF. He'd grown into such a handsome man. Had remained a friend in spite of his mother's comments over the years. Even after she'd left home and never bothered to talk to him or tell him what she was doing, until she'd come home to take care of Yancy.

Chris had acted as if the years she'd been gone never happened. He'd greeted her like he always had, with a flip remark about the brightness of her hair. Had only teased her once about fleeing Pacific Knoll to attend college on an art scholarship, which was how she'd dreamed of making a living. As an artist, creating sculptures. And as a creator of one-of-a-kind stained-glass pieces, a medium she'd added to her repertoire at the urging of one of her instructors. Who knew she'd enjoy creating beauty with colored glass?

But her artwork would have to wait. Maybe she'd put her lamp, occupying pride of place in the living room, up for sale. It was the first prize-winning piece she'd made, the one she'd entered a month before she quit school to assume responsibility for Yancy. Her art instructor had insisted she leave the lamp in the show, and it had won the grand prize.

That check for one hundred dollars had become her first investment in the wood she used for her first small carvings after coming home. She'd been asked to sell the lamp, but had refused. She'd kept it as a reminder of what she'd learned, what she wanted to get back to when putting food on the table and clothes on Yancy's back didn't take every penny she earned.

Her little brother needed her, and now he was injured. She'd have to concentrate on construction. Even though she'd begun to develop a following among people who had the extra cash to buy her custom creations, she'd have to set her carving and stained-glass work aside until she had more time.

Starting over. Again. Just like after their mother's death, when she'd found a job doing construction for Pacific Knoll builders to pay the bills.

Only after she was getting regular jobs did she begin carving again, using what little free time she found—usually after midnight—to do what made her heart sing when she closed her fingers around a piece of wood, and listened to it tell her what was captured inside.

Another breakthrough occurred when one of her friends from high school saw the portfolio she'd put together of the stained-glass pieces she'd created while in college. Corinne had married a man with tons of inherited money, and she wanted something special for the house they'd renovated.

Teddy's first stained-glass circle window had replaced one high on the second-floor landing of a mansion that overlooked Puget Sound, the afternoon and evening light casting swaths of color on the curved staircase that was a centerpiece in that home.

Teddy smiled in remembrance when Corrine had insisted on paying her double what she'd asked. After that first piece, she featured both her lamp and that window in her website. She'd never have guessed when she was in college that it would be her glass projects that brought in more requests for sculpting, too.

But her artwork had yet to pay very much. Until it did, she and Yancy would have to stay in a house barely big enough for them. Without a basement or even a garage, she'd been grateful when Chris made room for her.

Of all the builders in the area, Teddy preferred to work with Chris. He was a gentleman, as evidenced by his insistence that F-bombs on the jobsite weren't tolerated. Chris treated everyone in his crew respectfully. He treated her the same as his male crew members. Although she resented when he'd stepped in once and stopped a couple guys who'd badmouthed her, she chose not to complain until everyone except Chris had left the jobsite. And he was as likely to correct her as anyone else if something wasn't up to his standards. But he also was generous with praise when it was merited. And when a given house was finished ahead of the scheduled date of completion, he gave everyone a bonus. Those bonuses weren't always big, but they made everyone on Chris's team feel good. Probably why most of his crew stayed with him, even through the slower winter workdays.

Chris was a stand-up guy. But he was going to need help now that he was hurt. And Teddy had to make more money to cover Yancy's hospital bills. Two reasons to convince Chris to let her take on more responsibility.

Teddy rolled over and punched her pillow, wishing she could relax enough to go to sleep. Tomorrow was going to come around too soon. Tomorrow, she hoped to spring Yancy from the hospital and get on him to do his homework. *Yeah, tomorrow.*

~ ~ ~

The next morning, Teddy was told Yancy would be released later that day. She thanked the doctor for that good news. As she left her brother's room, Debra Lambert approached with an armload of books and papers.

Teddy's heart sank. "He's behind that much?"

"You'll have to ask him. I picked up everything in his locker and from the looks of the pile, he is probably behind more than a few days. How's he feeling?"

"Sore, mostly. But he's coming home this afternoon. What you brought should keep him busy for quite a while."

"I'll come by to pick up what he finishes, along with the books he doesn't need."

"You don't need to do that. I was going to stop by the school on Monday and talk to his teachers. Something I should have done weeks ago." Teddy grimaced.

"And I'll chat with him, see if we can figure out a way to motivate him."

"Are you the principal now?"

"Assistant, and still counseling." Debra grinned wryly. "Keeps me from getting bored with administrative duties, according to my husband." She pushed open the door and set the books on a nearby chair.

Under her breath, Teddy said, "Good luck getting Yance to do his work."

~ ~ ~

On Monday morning, Teddy parked her car at the jobsite. After checking on the painting crew that had begun spraying another home two doors down, she walked into the custom home. Chris must have wiped down the fireplace surround. Its wood glowed softly in the light from the windows. She touched the edge of the mantel, and wondered if the homeowner had seen it. The noises she heard indicated someone was upstairs, probably the person hanging shelves in the closets.

She proceeded across the street to a house under construction. The bulk of Chris's crew was hard at work, the sounds of hammering and sawing attesting to their activity. She looked for Chris, but he didn't appear to be on site, so she approached Val, who often supervised when Chris was elsewhere.

"What's up, TJ?" Val asked.

"You didn't hear about the fire at Chris's shop?"

Val shook his head then gave an ear-splitting whistle to get everyone's attention. Two men on the second floor trotted downstairs as a table saw on the main floor was turned off and two other workers set down the lumber they'd brought inside. "Could you guys come over here for a minute?"

"Listen up. Teddy has news."

She explained what had happened and that Chris was hurt, though she didn't know how badly. "The rest of us have to step up our game and get this house done without him. Which means working smarter so he isn't tempted to try to do his part when he comes back."

Murmurs from the men told Teddy they were considering her words.

"You told Chris I'd supervise while he's out of commission?" Val asked.

"No. But when you talk to him, ask him what he's planning once these two houses and that custom are finished." She pointed down the block. "Has he said whether he was going to hire more people this spring and summer so he could finish this neighborhood sooner?"

Val removed his cap and rubbed his hair. "It's hard finding experienced men these days. And you know Chris. He doesn't take on a lot of new guys who don't know what they're doing. I'll talk to him. Maybe you and I could take on the newbies." He grinned and set his hat back on his thinning light brown hair.

Teddy nodded. She was about to head for her team of painters when a man standing behind Val spoke up.

"Since when did Chris put *you* in charge, girl?"

Teddy looked over her shoulder at the man who reminded her of a wrestler. The muscles in his arms and shoulders suggested he could move stacks of drywall without breaking a sweat. She recalled he was a recent hire, and decided she didn't like him or his expression.

She felt her cheeks and neck heat. Her gaze skimmed past the curly haired newcomer as she tried to ignore him.

"Chris shouldn't have to worry that this job won't get done on time just because he's not here." She chose to address the other men standing nearby. "You guys all know Chris is a good boss. Let's show him we've got his back. That we won't let him down."

She shot the new guy a look, daring him to object, then raised her arm to encompass the rest of the neighborhood, as yet mostly empty lots and a few previously poured foundations. "We're close to being done with that custom job. And these other two homes are moving along. He'd expect us to keep things going. Right, Val?"

"That he would." Val pointed down the street. "What about the painting crew? How are they doing?"

"They're almost done on Number two and I sent half of them over to Number four to start taping the interior earlier this morning. They're on it."

The new guy shoved his way forward and poked Teddy's shoulder. "You never answered my question. Who made *you* boss?"

Val frowned. "She didn't, Axel. All she meant was, we work as a team around here. Chris's team. What he'd expect. I'll run the jobsite until Chris shows up—where you're supposed to be working." He crossed his arms over his chest. "Unless you prefer to find work elsewhere."

Axel rounded on Val, but seemed to think better of it and stepped back. "Yeah. Well, as long as *you're* in charge. I don't work for bitches."

Teddy's pulse started a slow trot that turned into a race as her cheeks and neck heated again. "You calling me a bitch, boy?" She took a step closer to the shorter man, almost touching his burly chest. His badly cut dirty blond bangs were plastered to his forehead, and her height forced him to angle his head back to meet her stare. She flexed her fingers, wanting to knock him down, knowing she shouldn't.

Someone behind her stage-whispered, "Oh boy. A fight Axel's gonna lose."

Out of the corner of her eye, Teddy saw several men nod. They knew her from high school, had worked with her on the job, knew she worked as hard as they did. Was careful, avoided stupid mistakes. Didn't take guff from anyone.

Axel glanced in the direction of the speaker. "Whaddaya mean by that?"

"She'll take you down, man. She's done it before," came the explanation from behind Teddy's back. Was that George Gunderson? She'd played pick-up basketball games with him after school. Which he invariably lost, though he was good-natured about it.

Val spoke up. "Everyone get back to work." He stepped between Axel and Teddy. "Picking on Teddy is a mistake you'll regret. If Chris were here, he'd fire you on the spot for talking like that. Consider this your one chance to show me you won't act stupid with her or anyone else on this crew. So I don't have to tell Chris why we're down another man when we need every one of you."

Axel dropped his gaze. Avoiding Teddy's stare, he mumbled and backed up. "Yeah, right. My mistake, girl, er, little lady," making no effort to hide his contempt.

"I'm no girl," Teddy uttered between clenched jaws. She poked his chest, hard. "No lady, either. And I happen to know your job better'n you do, so if you—"

"Stand down, Teddy," Val ordered, reverting to what he'd probably sounded like in the Marines.

She gave Val a quick nod. "Sorry, Val." She turned her fierce gaze back toward Axel. "My apologies." She held out her hand.

But Axel batted it away and strode back upstairs, muttering something under his breath.

"Show's over, guys. Back to work." Val ended the conversation by waving Teddy over to a corner of the living room.

"Your carving in the custom looks great."

"Thanks."

The table saw began to whine again.

"If it's possible, could you not get into it with Axel? He's a rookie, but we need him, even for grunt jobs, now that Chris is out of commission," Val said.

"He sounds like trouble," she countered.

"If he is, I'll handle it. Weren't you going to do something fancy with the front door on that custom job?"

"The wood I was going to use was lost in the fire." She whooshed out a puff of air.

"Too bad. The owners know?"

"Not yet. I want to talk to them if you don't mind, find out if they're willing to wait for the door work." She imagined the other option, reducing what she'd expected to be paid because only the fireplace carving had been completed.

He nodded. "Go ahead. Assure them the rest of the house will be done on time."

"I'll keep to myself that Chris is hurt. Too bad you didn't let me deck that creep."

He smirked. "I was just savin' him from a sore jaw."

They shared a quick laugh before Teddy walked back to her car. Next stop? The homeowner's office in the courthouse.

~ ~ ~

"Judge Poindexter." Teddy offered her hand. "Have you got a minute?"

"Certainly. Have a seat. My wife and I were going to stop over this afternoon to see how things are going at the new house. She's getting mighty tired living in that apartment."

"Yes, well, that's what I wanted to talk to you about."

"Is there a problem?"

"Not really. The fireplace surround is finished. Well, almost. I want to do another oiling of the wood before I seal it. And I'd like to know what you think. But, there was a fire—"

The man's smiling countenance collapsed into a look of concern.

"—at Mr. Lambert's workshop where I was storing the wood for your front door inserts. That wood was lost in the fire."

"Hmm. Does that mean the house won't be finished on time?"

"Chris won't let that happen. But unless you're willing for me to use a different wood than I was planning, I won't be able to carve your door inserts until I can find replacement wood."

"Hmm." He rubbed his chin. "Do you need a decision from me right away? I'd like to talk to my wife about this."

"Take your time. I'll refund the deposit you've already given me for the doors."

Mr. Poindexter raised a hand. "No need to do that just yet. I'd like to see what you've done with the fireplace surround. And talk to my wife," he repeated. "She was the one so intent on having special doors."

Teddy nodded and stood up. "Then I'll wait until you get back to me."

He nodded and escorted her out of his office.

~ ~ ~

Teddy breathed out a relieved sigh after tossing Yancy's books and papers into the backseat and helping him into the passenger seat.

"You're hurting?" she asked when he closed his eyes and rubbed his shoulder.

"Just sore. Can we not talk about my shoulder?"

"The doctor said you should take these pain pills."

"I will when we get home."

"Did you get any homework done? What Ms. Lambert brought over?"

"Some of it." Yancy frowned.

"What's left for you to do? I was thinking I'd drop it off at school for you." Teddy felt Yancy's gaze. "So you won't have to carry all this stuff back with your sore shoulder and all."

"What you really mean is you're going to talk to my teachers." He scowled.

"Something I should have done that night in October when they held parent-teacher conferences. Which you didn't tell me about until they were over." She glared at him while stopped at a light. "Just because I'm not Mom or Dad doesn't mean I'm not responsible for you, Yance. And you're not making it easy."

"Yeah, well, why don't you just let me take care of myself?"

"Because I'm your sister and I love you and I won't stand by and let you throw your life away." Tears she refused to shed threatened. She jerked when a car behind her honked its horn.

"Just 'cause I'm behind at school doesn't mean I'm throwing my life away. Maybe I want a different life than you. You're always working, always worried about money."

"And you think you're going to find a great job without even graduating from high school? Get real, Yancy Jameson! Dad left us when he couldn't stay out of trouble and was afraid the cops were going to throw him in jail. Which made it that much harder for Mom. And then she died, because she couldn't take all the pressure of trying to do everything herself. Which means I probably shouldn't have left when I did. Maybe then she wouldn't have started cooking meth."

She glanced at Yancy, hoping he was listening, really hearing what she was trying to say.

"Look, there's no point rehashing the past. I'm worried about today. And keeping us together is up to me. I just wish you'd help me out a little —by staying in school, getting decent grades so you can graduate and get a decent job. Then we won't have it so hard. And I won't end up yelling at you when I really don't want to!" Her voice rose with every word.

"I didn't know that," Yancy replied, his voice tinged with shocked awareness. "About Dad, I mean. He broke the law?"

"I found it out by accident. After I talked to the police. They had evidence. Thought I knew about it when I came back to get you out of foster care."

"What're you going to do, now that you've lost that shop space at Chris's? I tried to get as much out as I could."

"And you did good. Ms. Lambert and her husband brought my eagles over to the house. The windows, too." She snuck a quick peek at Yancy as she turned the corner into the driveway. "Come on. Let's get you inside so you can take that pain pill."

She helped Yancy out of the car, giving him a halfhearted hug without putting pressure on the arm in a sling, and handed him the key. "Think you could open the door while I get your books and stuff?"

Yancy nodded, turned the key and shoved the door open.

"About your schoolwork. Why don't you tell me what you still need to finish so I can take the other stuff to your teachers? It'll make them happy to know you're trying to catch up. Me, too."

Over the next several minutes, Yancy separated his completed assignments from those yet to be finished. Teddy piled three books on the table, and dumped the others in a cloth grocery bag. She hefted the bag and went back out the front door.

Four

Chris took a surprised step back at seeing Teddy at his door. He ran his free hand through his hair, certain it was now standing on end. "Come on in. Take a load off." He pointed to a chair after resuming his seat on the couch.

Teddy remained standing. "I'm here about the door carvings for the custom. Since I don't have insurance, I'll have to eat the cost of the wood."

"You talked to the owners?"

She nodded.

"Why don't you give me a receipt for the wood? I'll add it to my costs—since I'm the general on the job. My insurance should cover it. After all, you wouldn't have lost that lumber if it hadn't been stored in my shop." He cocked his head and appraised her as she went up on her toes and back down again. "You nervous, Teddy?"

"When are you coming back to work? Not that the crew can't work without you, and you probably shouldn't even try until your shoulder's healed. Yancy's shoulder isn't bad, but he has a concussion, too. What about you?"

"My headache has more to do with wanting to know how that fire got started."

"The firefighters don't know?"

"They asked if you might have left on some equipment when you worked there. I told them you always take your stuff with you. Good thing," he muttered and glanced out the window at the rubble that was his workshop. "I'll have to replace most of my tools. Only those on my belt, in the house, didn't get burned up."

Teddy pointed to the papers sitting on the table. "You're putting together a list for the insurance people?"

He nodded. "I should have taken pictures of the big stuff after I bought them. Fletcher told me to, in case anything was stolen. I was wrong not to think about fire. Every time I go outside, what's left of my building ... I keep smelling what's left."

"I'm sorry."

He glanced back at Teddy. "I was planning to hit the jobsite as soon as I finish this paperwork."

"You're not worried about the crew, are you? You should rest. Val's overseeing things. And he put me in charge of the painting crew. We're moving things along."

Chris started to stand up. "Did you tell the homeowner I was laid up?"

"No. All I said was I wouldn't be able to get the door inserts done on time. At least not until I can get the right wood."

Chris waved his uninjured arm toward the door. "Get me those numbers as soon as you can. We'll talk after I get with Val."

Without waiting to see that Teddy had driven away, Chris grabbed his jacket then tossed it back inside the house. He couldn't put it on with one arm, and wasn't interested in trying. He struggled to open the heavy truck door and then to shift it into reverse with his left hand. *Jesus!* How long would he be stuck doing things one-handed? Maybe Teddy was right, he should stay home.

There wasn't much he could do with his right arm immobilized. Even paperwork was proving to be a chore. He debated asking one of his sisters to help him. Writing with his left hand had produced more illegible scribbles than his usual right-handed scrawl. And he wasn't about to use his laptop one-handed.

After twelve minutes of careful driving, taking back streets that avoided stoplights where he might risk stalling the truck if he messed up shifting, he arrived at the jobsite. A quick scan of the places where his crew usually parked revealed that Teddy hadn't returned.

Chris slid out from behind the wheel and walked up the steps of the custom home. The owners were standing near the fireplace surround, admiring Teddy's work. Someone must have wiped the wood down again. The surround and mantel looked pristine.

Val motioned to him from near the hallway that skirted the kitchen area. "How're you doing? We didn't expect to see you for at least another week."

Chris squinted in Val's direction, keeping his voice low. "Any problems I should know about?"

"Everything's moving along on schedule. Too bad about your shop. Teddy said it might be a total loss."

"Yeah. What really hurts is all the wood Teddy lost and the lumber I'd picked out for my furniture business. And the pieces I was supposed to deliver last weekend. We saved some of them. Can't seem to get the smoke smell out of my head."

Val motioned toward the owners. "Seems they want to talk with you." He retreated up the stairs to the second floor.

Chris faced the older man, a senior judge on the state superior court. The judge's wife reminded him of his mother, smartly dressed, with gray streaks highlighting her fashionably styled auburn bob.

"You like the surround?" he asked. "Ms. Jameson does good work."

"Excellent work, I'd say," Judge Poindexter corrected. "She told us about the fire. We don't want to hold up our move-in date. We've decided to worry about the fancy doors later, after Theodora tells us she's found the right wood."

"I'll tell her that."

"Your man said the building will continue apace."

"Yes, sir. My accident isn't going to slow us down." He hitched his injured shoulder and barely avoided wincing. "I'm glad you're pleased with the fireplace surround."

"Very," the judge's wife gushed.

After the homeowners departed, Val clumped back down the stairs. "Got a minute?"

Chris left off rubbing his shoulder. "Sure."

"Shoulder bothering you?"

"Should have popped another pain pill."

"Then why don't you go home? Everything's under control here."

"What about the other two houses? And where's Teddy?"

"She said something about picking up more tile for one of the bathrooms." Val grinned. "And she split up the painting crews. Must have put a fire under them. Interior work is coming along at Number two. Taping inside Number four is almost done already. I figured it would take them two days." He grinned. "Leave it to Teddy to crack the whip."

~ ~ ~

Chris woke from an impromptu nap on his couch when someone knocked. He tripped over a shoe when he clambered upright, barely missing ramming his good arm into the wall. "Be right there!"

He opened the door to a forty-something man who flashed fire department ID badge with the name, Emery Sunosome.

"Mr. Lambert? Christopher Lambert?"

"That's me." He stepped back. "Come on in. You must be here about my shop."

"The fire, actually. How's that arm of yours?"

"Better." Chris waved the man into a nearby chair.

"Just wanted to fill you in on what my report's going to include."

"Okay."

"Firefighters on the scene noted that the fire was the hottest along that far wall before it went up into the rafters. They said you had a bunch of lumber stored there."

"Which explains why the roof went?"

"Very likely. I spotted a char pattern near the door on the back wall. It was most pronounced at an electrical plug near that door. From what was left of that wall, we discerned a heat shadow, probably from the lumber stacked nearby that actually shielded the wall from the flames until the fire really got going. Not that the wall isn't mostly gone, but from what was left. The fire turned hot from all that wood in the rafters, which caught the roof and then dropped pieces down onto you and that kid who was hurt. How's he doing?"

"He's home now, with a concussion. You think it was an electrical short?"

"Very likely. I checked what was left of the box. The outer metal part was charred, but it appears the fire began in that plug. I found a splatter pattern suggesting that the circuit may have overheated."

"But I had twenty-amp wiring installed after I bought the place, since I use some heavy-duty equipment."

"You upgraded *all* the wiring?"

Chris shook his head. "Oh. Maybe not the light switch. I don't use it to plug in my equipment. All it does is turn on the ceiling lights and it's probably connected to the switch on the outside. I have a sign there telling visitors to flip the switch a couple times to let me know someone's out there. That sign's gone now, too."

The fire inspector nodded. "Which explains what I saw of the old box."

Chris rubbed his fingers across the three-day scruff on his chin. "I just remembered something. That afternoon, when I was in the shop, I had a visitor. She flipped the switch on and off a few times to get my attention. I had my earplugs in. If she knocked, I didn't hear it." He glanced at the fire inspector. "Would several flips right in a row have caused a short?"

"Maybe. Did you notice anything about the lighting. Flickering, for example?"

He shook his head. "I went back to work. And I shut down everything when I called it a day."

"It's possible the switch might have stayed in the on position with the lights off. You wouldn't have noticed it."

"Yancy probably flipped that switch when he came for Teddy's art work. The lights above her work table are controlled by that switch. He was the one who called in the fire."

The inspector glanced down at his notes and nodded. "What do you recall of the smoke?"

"There was a shitload of it. Made it hard to breathe when I went in to rescue my stuff. What are you getting at?"

"A regular wood fire usually burns with lots of bright flame. Red, mostly, with a kind of grey or brownish smoke. Not the kind you can't see through. Thick black smoke would suggest the presence of gasoline, like from a gas-powered generator or some other gas-powered equipment. Which, according to the fire chief, doesn't appear to have been involved."

"Follow me." Chris slipped into his shoes and led the man around the side of the house to his one-car garage. "Could you get the door?"

"Sure thing." The man lifted the door and waited for it to slide upward into the tracks paralleling the ceiling.

Chris flicked on the light and walked to the back of the garage. "Here's where I keep my generators." He pointed under a shelf holding a spare truck tire and two cans of car wax.

"You have a gas can?"

Chris nodded.

"Where?"

"Other side of the truck."

Both men walked around the front of Chris's truck.

"There." Chris pointed to a spot near the driver side door next to the garage wall. "You're ruling out that gasoline started the fire?"

"Based on what I saw, I'm confident it was electrical in origin. How old was your workshop?" The inspector pulled down the garage door and the two men walked back toward Chris's house.

"House was built in the forties. Probably the shop, too, or near then."

"And you didn't upgrade all the wiring."

"When I brought in an electrician, I just asked him to get me a new box that would support my tools."

"What about the house?"

"All upgraded when I gutted the kitchen. The old stuff was in bad shape and I kept losing the lights whenever I turned on the microwave." He laughed. "When I took things down to the studs, I had all new wires strung with lots of separate plugs in the kitchen. Should have done the same in my shop." He kicked at a piece of burned wood as he headed toward the house. "When will I get your written report? One I can send to my insurance guy?"

"Soon. I'll give you a second original. Know where I can find your renter, so I can talk to her?"

Chris pulled out his phone and scanned for Teddy's address. "Here." He waited for the investigator to jot down the address. "If she's not home when you stop over, she's probably at my jobsite."

"She works for you?"

"Been on my crew in one role or another for almost a year now. One of my best workers." He squinted at the investigator as he scribbled a note.

"You should have my report by the end of the week."

~ ~ ~

Chris climbed out of his truck, aware of the throbbing in his shoulder as he headed for the custom home.

"There you are," he said when he spotted Teddy near the fireplace surround, a can of sealant in one hand, a tiny brush in the other.

"You're putting on the final coat?"

"Mrs. Poindexter called and said she loves what I did. She and the judge are happy to wait until I find new wood for their front doors. She agreed we should hang temporaries for now. We can swap them out after I carve the new doors."

"Sounds good." He walked two steps away, the better to take in the entire fireplace.

"Has the fire investigator called you?" Chris asked.

"No. Does he know what started the fire?"

"He thinks it was electrical, from an old plug that controlled the lights."

"Really?" Her face paled and her eyes widened, reminding him of bright blue marbles surrounded by her unruly red curls. "Maybe that explains why I had trouble awhile back."

"What kind of trouble?"

"When I plugged in my soldering iron, the lights flickered. I didn't think anything of it, since the sun coming through that window was more than enough light. And it only happened once. Which is why I never said anything."

"You should mention that to the inspector. He said he wanted to talk to you."

"He thinks I'm to blame for the fire?"

"No, he's just trying to cover all bases. Since you had work space there. He gave me this." From his pocket, he pulled a piece of glass that resembled a broken cup folded in on itself, its several colors blending together.

Teddy plucked it from Chris's palm. "The last of my glass pieces, right?" She sighed. "A reminder of what fire can do without my blow torch."

"Right. I'm just glad Yancy went over to get your carvings and spotted the fire. Think what else we might have lost if he hadn't been there." He upended an empty five-gallon bucket and sat down. "Is he still at home?"

"Yeah. I fed him lunch. Then I came back here after giving Yancy his meds. He said he was going to take a nap." She pushed a curl away from her cheek. "You think the fire investigator wants to talk to him?"

"Maybe."

"Yance isn't going to like that people are connecting him with the fire. I was hoping that word of him saving my finished work and your furniture means people will stop thinking he's nothing but a troublemaker. His reputation from before Mom died. After, too."

"Right. Well … when the investigator talks to you, tell him what Yancy did."

"I will. Can we talk about me doing more than overseeing the painters, doing the tile work, and finishing up this personal stuff?" She pointed to the fireplace surround and stepped closer to resume brushing the sealant onto the carving.

"What's on your mind?"

"I stepped back from everything except the painting crew and tiling so I could concentrate on my carvings. But since Yancy's accident, I was hoping you could use my help more. Like when I first came home, when I helped you hang drywall, taped and mudded it, and so on. I could use more hours."

"If you want more work, you've got it." He pointed. "I think you missed a spot, right near the deer's ear."

"Thanks." She brushed the wood where Chris pointed.

"That surround looks really great. If you take pictures, you're sure to get people asking you to do more carving work."

"I hope so."

As Chris left the custom home and headed away from the jobsite, his shoulder throbbed, reminding him to take another pill. *Jesus!* How long was he going to have to put up with the pain? How long would he need Val and his crew, including Teddy, to ensure that his work got done on time? Questions swirled in his mind as he drove home.

Five

Two days later, Chris waved cheerily at Orralee so she wouldn't ask why he was seeing Fletcher on short notice. No notice at all, actually. The letter stuffed in his pocket felt like a bomb ready to go off.

Fletcher looked up when Chris entered his office. "What's up that's so urgent? Orralee said you had to see me. Is it about the fire? Heard from the investigator yet?"

"He thinks it was an electrical short, but that's not why I'm here." Chris slumped into a seat facing his ten-years-older brother, hoping that their age difference amounted to ten years of wisdom. Which he sure as hell could use right now.

"Okay. Lay it on me."

Chris pulled out the letter crushed into a ball. He tossed it onto Fletcher's desk. "Read that."

Fletcher smoothed out the paper and took his time. The only sign he'd read certain words was the slight lifting of his right eyebrow. Twice.

Chris shifted in his seat. "Can you run a background check on her? Or have your lady associate do so? Didn't she used to be a PI or something before she joined the firm?"

"Yes and yes, but I see no reason to get Sophia involved in what looks to me like a personal *family* issue." Fletcher looked at Chris. "Why don't you tell me about the letter writer? I gather she's one of your latest one-date wonders?"

"Three dates," he corrected. "A big mistake."

Fletcher gave him a *keep talking* motion. "And?"

"I guess you could say she wanted more than my usual." Chris leaned forward to stare at the floor before glancing up into Fletcher's calm brown eyes. "What I mean is, all I wanted was a night of fun. Or three. Then good-bye, nice knowin' ya.' I should have guessed what she was trying to say the other day when she stopped by my shop."

"When was that?"

"The day of the fire."

Fletcher sat up straighter. "She had something to do with that?"

"Not according to the investigator." Chris leaned on one elbow, trying unsuccessfully to find a more comfortable position. "She acted kind of pissy, if you want to know the truth. But she never came right out and said she was pregnant. Kept saying we had to talk, but when I wouldn't drop everything and talk, she left. Never mentioned the p-word."

"Maybe she wasn't sure."

"Yeah, well, she didn't have any trouble putting it in writing." He pointed at the letter propped against Fletcher's coffee cup.

"This is her home address?"

"1219 Melrose. Site of our first date. The end of it, anyway." Chris felt his neck and cheeks heat, recalling that lust-filled night.

"It seems she's better at typing than talking," Fletcher replied, his tone dry.

"Maybe I should have been nicer to her. But she interrupted me when I was really busy."

His brother leaned back in his chair and reached for the letter again. "You kicked her out of the shop?"

"Not exactly, but I didn't encourage her to stay. How can she accuse me, Fletch? I was upfront with her from the start. And she agreed. Just fun and done."

"You didn't happen to record that, did you?" Fletcher chuckled. "Never mind."

"She said, and I quote, 'No-strings sex? Yeah, works for me.' I walked her out to my truck, drove her to where she parked her car and followed her home."

"Where did you meet her?"

"Brewskers. She was trying to play darts. Could barely hit the wall, much less the bull's eye. Too many beers. I followed her home, to make sure she got there."

But it was on him that he'd gone inside and then sought her out a second time and a third, although the sex wasn't as good. Was that why he'd put her off? She'd said they should hook up again, and he'd alluded to a lunch, its time undetermined. Because he didn't really plan to call or text her. He'd wanted to let her down easy.

Fletcher turned serious. "What do you know about her? What does she do?"

"That first date, we never did much talking. She's a hairdresser. At Trish's Tresses, I think. Or was. When she came to the shop, she said she'd been fired. Who knows where she's working now?"

"But she knows what you do. The letter said—"

"I know. She wants the kid to inherit a piece of my business. Not my dick …" His neck reddened at the thought.

"Understood." Fletcher rubbed a hand up his arm. "Okay, let me summarize. You had sex with her three times, but no other contacts, and now she says you're her baby daddy."

"She sent me a bunch of texts. About getting together. I wasn't interested. She's not exactly a conversationalist."

"And you weren't ready to make Ms. Crawford, Bailee, a regular lay? Maybe even a girlfriend, someone you'd introduce to Mom?"

Chris gawked at Fletcher. "Can you *imagine* what she or Dad would say if they met Bambi?"

"That's what she goes by? Please don't tell me she's a stripper. What's she look like?"

Chris pulled out his phone and scanned the pictures, stopping at one of the selfies he'd taken with Bambi when they'd been fooling around at the beer pub. "The curvy one, in the tight clothes. The bottle blonde."

"Hmm. I see what you mean. With or without that nickname, Mom would declare her 'unworthy,'" Fletcher air-quot-ed. He returned Chris's phone. "But the issue here isn't Mom's opinion. It's what kind of trouble you're in. I take it you don't see marriage as a logical outcome to your horizontal mambo with Bambi?"

"Hell, no!"

Fletcher reached for his legal pad and selected a pen from the collection poking out of a holder on his desk. "Keep your voice down, bro. Okay. So you're still not into commitment. It's not such a bad thing. Just because I had to find out the hard way, no reason you have to take the same road I did." He grinned.

Chris knew all about Fletch's hard road, how his first wife, Jacqui, and their baby daughter had died in a car wreck. If that hadn't happened, Fletcher wouldn't have been unhappy for such a long time. Until he met Lexi and Chance. Now he had a new family and was happy again.

Fletcher folded the letter, slid it into an envelope and placed it on the credenza behind his desk. "Step back one. You asked me to do a background check. Is that your way of saying that the alleged baby Ms. Crawford claims to be carrying might not be yours?"

"Oh, hell, Fletch. How should I know? She's no virgin, that's for sure." He recalled the woman's assured actions against the door, in the bed, how she'd grabbed the condom wrapper and ripped it open. She knew how to make a man come, wasn't put off by anything he'd suggested to her that second time, either, when he'd decided to be more adventurous, to recapture his enthusiasm from their first encounter.

"How was I to know she'd show up pregnant, or claim to be?" He mentally crossed his fingers that he wasn't the baby daddy, his heart thumping at what that might mean. Was Bambi going to sue for child support? Was she going to insist on moving in with him during her pregnancy?

"You broke your one-date rule and went bareback, Chris? Didn't Dad and I *both* talk to you about the importance of protection back when you were in high school? Why do you insist on living dangerously?"

Chris's lungs pressed uncomfortably against his heart at Fletcher's accusation. "No, Fletch, never. I *always* use a condom. And Bambi said she was on the pill. *That* I remember. 'Cause I asked. I *always* ask. Meaning we had double protection." As if to prove he was prepared, Chris hauled his wallet from a back pocket and retrieved a packet. "I keep more in my truck, too. Just in case." He wondered if that sounded as lame to Fletcher as it did to him. "Not that I make a habit of doing it there. Beds are a lot more comfortable."

Deadpan, Fletcher replied, "Spare me the details. Her letter mentions she went to a doctor, who confirmed that she's knocked up. No way the doctor can confirm that *you* did it, though."

"Which is why I want you to do a background check on her. Maybe it isn't mine. Maybe she just wants it to be, thinks I have money. You know, 'cause I'm a Lambert." Chris frowned, recalling all the problems Debra had with that nasty tool of a professor she'd almost married. Thank goodness she'd avoided that calamity and was now happily married to Todd, one of Fletcher's law partners.

"What else *do* you know about her, besides that you liked her enough to hook up with her three times? How old is she? And please don't tell me she's jailbait."

Chris shrugged. "Never asked, but I doubt it. She was ordering drinks from the bar and Brewskers is big on carding newcomers. Besides, it's been more than three months. How can you expect me to—"

"Where'd you do the deed?"

"Second and third time at my place, which is why she knew where to find me the day of the fire."

"Well, at least this letter gives us her full name. That should make it easier to get some background on her," Fletcher mumbled.

"What do you think you'll find?" Chris leaned forward, hoping Bambi was married, that he wasn't the father who would end up paying child support for the rest of his life, although if it *was* his kid, he'd step up at least that much. But marry her? No way! Wasn't that what Bambi was aiming for, what she'd hinted at in the letter?

"Why do you think she wrote me—instead of sending me a text or just coming over to my place and telling me in person?"

"If she had trouble talking to you before, maybe she felt it would be easier this way. I suspect she wanted to create a physical record, something more permanent than a text, which could easily be retrieved, even if she doesn't know that. She didn't mention she's had legal advice, although some of the language she used sounds like she might have consulted someone." Fletcher looked up from the book he'd pulled off his shelf. "I gather you didn't exchange information about family members? Marital status? What her friends do for a living? Jesus, Chris. You need to be more discriminating when you pick a bed partner. At the very least, confirm her age. Better check the age of those condoms, too."

"I'll do that." But the last thing he wanted right now was another hook-up. In spite of the many-weeks-long sexual drought he was in. Last woman he'd had sex with was Bambi, and given the mess he was in now, there wouldn't be another. At least not until he was out from under the trouble she represented. Definitely time to take a break from the dating sweepstakes.

He sucked in a breath. "What can you do to get me off the hook?"

"Best way to eliminate you from any responsibility you have toward a baby"— Fletcher halted at Chris's barely audible curse—"is to find out if she's really pregnant. She might be lying. But since she claims she's seen a doctor, we'll assume that she *is* pregnant. Paternal status has to wait until the baby is born and a DNA test confirms that you are, or are *not*, the source of half of the baby's chromosomes."

"I'm stuck until then? Have to see her, pay her doctor bills, that sort of thing?"

"You could push the issue, but I say, leave it alone. The best way to find out while she's pregnant is another test, chorionic villus sampling. Trouble is, there's a risk of miscarriage with that test, and she might not agree to that. Jacqui used it, even though it scared both of us. The possibility of losing the pregnancy …"

Fletcher glanced up at Chris. "She didn't mention money. At least not yet. Probably wants to see how you react to her news. Let me see what I can find out—her credit history, criminal history, if any, where she's been living other than this address she gave you, whatever I can dig up."

Fletcher finished jotting notes, then met Chris's worried gaze as he leaned back in his chair and rested one shoe on the edge of his desk. "Just so we're clear, what are your feelings for this woman?"

"None! Especially not after *that!*" He pointed to the envelope holding that coiled snake of a letter. More calmly, he added, "Although sex the first time was pretty good." But he recalled how empty he'd felt after their third night together.

Bambi had left before dawn, confirming that she was no more inclined than he to continue whatever they'd done hours earlier. He'd wakened when she was gathering up her clothes and preparing to leave. Although she'd glanced his way, she hadn't spoken when she saw that his eyes were open. Instead, she finished dressing, slipped into her *do-me* stilettos, and walked out the door.

Fletcher's gaze seemed to soften when he said, "You seem … I don't know … kind of lost, maybe?" He huffed out a breath. "Whatever it is you're looking for in all those women you date isn't likely to be found in bed." He loosened his tie. "And just because you look like him, you don't need to act like Dad, always taking off whenever he's tired of kowtowing to Mom's demands. That's what you're doing, isn't it? Keeping those so-called dates to one-offs? Instead of finding a woman, getting married and then hiding out in your shop when her demands get to be too much, you're jumping in bed with who knows how many women, then deserting them before they can get close to hinting that they might want more than sex."

Chris wanted to object, but the mental picture his older brother had painted felt painfully close to reality. "Logan's the one who looks the most like Dad. He says so all the time."

"Well, I've never seen it, probably because Logan's hair is so blond. Not like the rest of us."

"What about Ivory? She's blond, too."

"Hale says she gets it from his mom."

"You're saying Logan may also have skipped a generation? Takes after one of the grandparents, the ones who were dead before he was born, who already had white hair when we knew them?"

"Could be. Back to you and the Bambi problem. You're twenty-seven. Plenty old enough to get real about what you want to do with the rest of your life." Fletcher held up a hand, mimicking a stop sign. "Let me finish. You've got a good handle on your construction business. And the furniture-making, although you took a nasty hit with the fire. A minor setback, one you'll probably look back on as something easily forgettable."

He looked over his shoulder at the credenza where that letter lay. "As for your behavior with women, maybe you should talk to someone—about why you don't seem to want to, or can't, establish, lasting relationships."

Chris's heart took a leap, as if over a steeplechase jump and his lungs squeezed together, pushing out a whoosh of air. Was Fletch right? Was he somehow lacking in the man-woman department?

"I have friends, bro. Lots of them."

"Oh, yeah? You're always working. You run a construction crew, male. They work for you and most of them have been with you for years. Shows you know how to build a good working team. But women friends? Not counting Eden, Deb and Elaine, and now Lexi, what other women are in your life—ones you *don't* sleep with?"

Chris drew a blank and he felt frozen in his seat as his mind scanned through a list of the women he knew. "Does my banker count?" He glanced back at his older brother and allowed a grin to slowly form.

"That's one, but again, a professional relationship, not someone you'd have dinner with. Right?"

Chris frowned, then grinned, feeling triumphant. "What about Teddy? *She's* a woman. Part of my crew. We're friends. Been pals for years. Since kindergarten! Doesn't she count?"

Fletcher seemed to relax his intense gaze. "Right. Forgot about her." He shifted in his seat. "But I'm guessing you don't think of her as a woman, the kind you'd date. She's always been just one of the guys, not a male guy, but same category. I'll bet you've never once looked at her and seen a woman, and I don't mean for one of those *wham-bam-thank-you-ma'am* sessions. Someone you could go out to dinner with, enjoy good conversation with, and not hop into bed with afterwards. Know any women like that, bro?"

Chris had to admit he couldn't think of one. What kept swirling in his mind was his last view of Bambi as she'd headed out the door of his shop. Maybe Fletch was right. What he wanted couldn't be found in sex play. *What's the matter with me?* Was he simply trying to banish loneliness by scratching a mutual sexual itch?

The emptiness on her side of his bed after Bambi left had mirrored the hollowness in his heart, his sense that something was missing. Even before she left, Chris's sense of disquiet had returned. But he'd refused to dwell on it by heading for the shower and getting ready for work. And when he returned home that evening, he'd laundered the bed clothes and her scent on the pillow had disappeared down the drain, mirroring how he'd erased her from his mind after she disappeared into the predawn darkness.

Until she'd shown up at his shop, and now, in the guise of that letter, was accusing him of fathering a child. He didn't even know if she wanted the baby, or what she would do after it was born. Nor did he dare ask.

What if Bambi showed up at his jobsite? Would any of the crew remember her from their night at Brewskers?

"Chris?" A more brotherly tone sounded from behind Fletcher's desk.

He looked up, realizing he'd spaced out for a minute. "Yeah?"

"Don't go looking for Bambi, don't text or call her. I'll get back to you about what I find. If you happen to run into her — at your house or the building site— tell her you can't talk to her. If she argues the point, tell her you're acting on your lawyer's advice." Fletcher stood up. "Got it? No contact. Of any kind. Particularly physical, and I don't mean shaking hands."

Chris nodded. "Got it. Never figured I'd have to talk to you about ... you know." He raised a hand then let it drop to his side.

"Life sucks sometimes, little brother. Go home. Think about how to keep your nose clean. Turn down dates, even if the women you always seem to attract come on to you and don't want to take no for an answer. Tell them you're getting married—"

"Jesus, Fletch!"

His brother laughed. "That kind of news usually works. And the women unlikely to be put off by it aren't the ones you should get mixed up with in the first place."

Fletcher pointed to Chris's right shoulder. "I see you're out of the sling. Means you can concentrate on all those build-outs."

"I'm still icing it at night. As long as I don't try to lift anything heavier than a regular hammer, I'm okay."

"Good to know." Fletcher walked Chris out to the elevator and hit the down button. "You've got a lot to think about. Now, let me get to work. Time is money, you know, and pro bono family work means you're costing me plenty."

He motioned for Chris to enter the elevator.

"Thanks, Fletch. Appreciate it."

As he walked across the main floor lobby of Fletcher's building behind a pair of suits— more lawyer types, he suspected —Chris was reminded of his older brother's words the day he got married. One of these days, the rules Chris had established about no more than two dates with the same woman weren't going to be enough. He was going to want more.

Six

Teddy returned home from her meetings with Yancy's teachers, relieved. She'd worried that their previous comments about him not working to his potential would be repeated. But the homework assignments he'd completed after the fire seemed to have satisfied them.

She beamed when Yancy wandered into the kitchen. "You didn't eat this last piece of pizza?"

"Saved it for you. You should have eaten before you went to meet my teachers."

"I was too nervous."

"Why were *you* nervous? It was *my* bad grades you were going to see, and how many times I've skipped school."

"Your counselor already filled me in on that." She waved Yancy closer and gave him a one-armed hug. "You made me proud."

"Oh, yeah?" He gave her a quirky grin.

"All but one of your teachers said you're all caught up with your homework. I told your English teacher I'd make sure you turn in those last two book reports that are still missing."

"I did one tonight."

"Good. Your Chemistry teacher surprised me. Why didn't you tell me about that special project that explained how yeast makes bread rise?"

He shrugged. "It was no big deal." But he seemed to stand a little taller. She wondered when his skinny form might begin to bulk up with muscle. Like Chris and the other guys working construction.

The doorbell rang.

"Will you get that?" She took a seat and leaned over to take off the silver-toned heels she'd worn for her visit with the teachers.

Yancy opened the door to Chris.

She felt his gaze as it slid upward from her bare feet, past her knees, past the neckline of her black sheath and onto her face before sliding back down again. Chris's stare seemed caught on the extra-long silver scarf that she'd wound around her neck and tied so that its ends fluttered just past her breasts. She wiggled her toes and stood up.

"What?" she asked. "Why are you looking at me like that? Did I get tomato sauce on my face?" She felt her cheeks blossom with heat and ran a finger around her mouth. "Or did something bad happen at the jobsite?"

He swallowed then croaked out, "Uh, no. Er, yes. That is, I came to talk to Yancy. Privately, if that's okay."

"Sure." She motioned him to enter. "Shut the door, will you? Since you don't need me, I'll just leave you to it."

She detoured around the kitchen counter and set up the coffee maker. "Yance. Get Chris a mug when it's ready."

She entered her bedroom and tossed her shoes into the closet before shimmying out of her dress and donning an old pair of jeans, a sweatshirt and a pair of fluffy socks.

When she left her bedroom, Chris was talking in earnest, quiet tones. Rather than interrupt their conversation, Teddy wandered into the living room and grabbed a magazine. She flipped the pages and tried to concentrate on an article, but her mind was captured by words she couldn't help but overhear. She looked over her shoulder at Chris.

"You want to hire Yance? It's not that we can't use the money, but he's underage."

"He'll be supervised. Val and I agree. We need someone dependable to clean up at the end of the day."

"The new guys do that."

"Yeah, well, one of them is working out fine and may be promoted to other stuff. The other one … not so much. He pulled a stupid mistake. Val had to send him home, told him not to come back until he doesn't have to wear a bandage."

"What happened?"

"Axel couldn't be bothered to use a push rod when he was cutting some wood and almost lopped off one of his fingers. Val drove him to the ER."

"It was bad?"

Chris nodded. "Could have been worse. Just a deep cut. But Axel turned so white Val thought he was gonna pass out. Seems he isn't good around blood."

"Did the other guys say much?"

"Nah. They went right back to work like nothing happened, and the other rookie —Flint, I think— he offered to finish what Axel was working on."

"And he can't take care of clean up?"

"Already is. But he's taking night classes at the community college. Asked if he could leave no later than six so he won't be late to class."

"I like Flint. He's a go-getter."

Chris nodded. "I thought Yancy here might like to help out, at least until Axel can work again, and maybe even after he comes back, assuming he shapes up and follows orders."

Yancy spoke up, sounding eager. "I'll get paid?"

Chris nodded.

"If you're working, you *should* get paid. But I thought you were going to apply at the Shrimp Sha—" Teddy started to say, surprised at Yancy's change of direction about a possible job.

Yancy's brow furrowed. "Never mind about that. They were only hiring part-time. If I work every day after school, I'll make more money with Chris."

"But how're you going to get to the jobsite? It's at least a mile from school."

"I'll walk or take the bus."

"You're sure? Don't care if your friends spot you?"

Yancy frowned. "Whatever they say doesn't count. I want to do this."

Chris rose from the table. "I'll let you two talk about it. Text me with your decision, Yancy. No later than tomorrow." He thanked Yancy for the coffee.

Teddy watched them go out the front door, their heads at the same level. *Yancy's as tall as Chris? When did that happen?*

"I don't have to discuss it," Yancy declared. "I'll do it. Can't wait to start."

Chris offered his hand. Yancy shook it and muttered something to Chris that made him laugh.

When Yancy came back inside, he greeted Teddy with a broad grin. "I'll get paid! Same as the rookies, Chris said."

"Minimum wage, I'll bet."

"So what? It's money. And it means I can pay off my doctor bill so you don't have to. Maybe even the hospital."

Teddy nodded. "Yes, but working for Chris can't interfere with your homework. You promised me—and your teachers—after you talked to Ms. Lambert. If you can't keep up at school, I'll tell Chris to let you go."

"Not gonna happen." Yancy ambled toward his bedroom. "Guess I'll get started on my new chem project."

"Something I need to know about? Sign off on? You're not going to blow up the house, are you?" and immediately regretted her words.

"No!" Yancy's door slammed, ending their conversation.

"Sorry, Yance." Teddy knocked and opened his door. "Did Chris say anything to you about the fire?"

"All he said was not to talk about it when I'm working. As if I would. He knows why I was there—to get your stuff so you could carve at home." Yancy pointed to the books on his bed. "I need to get to it, sis. So I'm not up half the night."

Teddy nodded. "What else did he say to you on the porch?"

"Nothing." But Yancy's neck and cheeks were stained beet red when he glanced over his shoulder at her.

"You're blushing, Yance. Was it about girls? Please don't tell me you were asking Chris for advice. Since you claim I can't help you with that sort of thing." She felt her own cheeks heat.

"It was sort of that," he admitted. "I have to study, sis." He sat down on the bed and grabbed his books.

"Don't you dare take after him and his one-date wonders," she muttered under her breath as she closed her brother's door.

Teddy retreated to the kitchen and cleaned up the last of the dirty dishes. She mulled over the pros and cons of Yancy receiving dating or sex advice from Chris and decided to leave it alone. He might be one of those guys who dated every woman in town—except her, of course—but she doubted he'd steer Yance in the wrong direction.

~ ~ ~

The next day, Teddy and Flint hauled drywall up the stairs and into the largest of the three rooms needing walls. She liked this particular rookie. He wasn't allergic to hard work, was respectful, asked good questions and seemed eager to learn.

As they trotted downstairs for more wallboard, Flint pointed toward the front of the house. A woman stood, framed in the front door opening, the toe of one of her killer stilettos tapping impatiently.

Under his breath, Flint asked, "A new owner? A couple of people stopped by earlier to see which houses were near to completion. You know her?"

Teddy shook her head. "Never seen her before. I'll text Val. He might know."

Val, see that lady here at Number two? Is she a buyer?

His reply came back in seconds. He must have spotted her as she'd walked past where he was working. *No idea. Maybe she's one of Chris's lady friends.* Val added a grinning emoji.

Teddy squinted in the direction of the woman. *First time one of Chris's dates has come here,* she mused. She turned toward Flint. "I'll ask if she wants to buy this place. Keep hauling up the drywall. I'd like us to finish hanging the last two sections before we stop for today."

"Sure thing."

Teddy approached the woman. "May I help you?"

The woman peered at Teddy, as if trying to decide who or what she was. In words coated with barely hidden disdain, she said, "In those clothes, you can't be a Realtor."

"No, I'm part of the construction crew."

The petite woman entered the building, stepped past Teddy and glanced around as she moved into the dining room space, its flooring strewn with discarded pieces of the framing lumber.

"Are you interested in buying this home?" Teddy asked. "I can get you a brochure if you'd like."

The woman gave no notice that she'd heard the question. She appraised Teddy, her lips a line of pink that paled to white before she spoke. "I'm looking for Christopher Lambert. And you're part of his crew?" She chuckled. "Definitely not his type."

The blonde returned to the doorway. "When will your boss be back?"

"Careful where you step," Teddy cautioned, a part of her wishing the woman, who didn't look to be more than five feet tall, would trip on the pieces of scrap lumber scattered about. "When he's done with whatever he's doing," Teddy replied, tired of being polite to the woman, whose words stung. "He keeps his own schedule."

On the other hand, she might be a buyer. *Make nice*, Teddy reminded herself. "If you want, I can tell him you stopped by. What's your name?" She reached into a side pocket just above the right knee of her work pants, and pulled out a small notebook.

The woman handed her a pen.

"No need. I got it," Teddy said, grabbing the pencil she'd slid into her braid. If it was good enough to mark drywall cuts, it was good enough to write a note to Chris.

"Ms. Crawford. Bam—er, Bailee Crawford." She turned and sashayed out the front door, providing a great view for the men whose sawing and hammering upstairs seemed to have stopped. Teddy imagined them taking in the woman's curvy figure as she approached a shiny black car parked near the entrance of the driveway with its ridges of dried mud.

"Back to work, guys," Teddy called out, and construction sounds resumed.

A wolf whistle sounded from the house under construction two lots over.

Teddy walked outside and spotted Val coming toward her. "Who was that over at Number four?" she asked.

He frowned. "My usual crew. If you mean the whistler, probably Axel, now that he's back. I told him to sweep up." He pointed to the car that turned the corner and sped off. "That the woman you texted me about?"

"She was looking for Chris."

"I was right? A girlfriend?"

"I guess." Teddy pointed to the completed home. "The custom is ready for occupancy inspection?"

He nodded. "The cleaners did a great job. I closed all the windows this morning so dust won't get back in and mess up the look of the place. Appliances are in and working. I was going to do a final check of each room, make sure nothing was forgotten. Remember last year when the plumber forgot to connect the pipes under the sink and surprised Chris when he turned on the water?"

Teddy chuckled. "Not what he expected to happen."

"Right. If everything checks out, I'll call for final inspection and occupancy sign-off even if the landscaper isn't finished with the backyard patio."

"By the end of this week?"

"Very likely." Val headed for his truck.

Teddy helped Flint carry more drywall up the stairs. When she spotted Axel heading her way, she went back downstairs and waved to get his attention.

"Yeah?" He squinted up at her.

"Could you come inside for a minute?"

"Whatever." Axel didn't bother to hide his smirk as he approached the back door leading into the kitchen area.

"You whistled at that visitor?" Teddy asked.

"What about it?" Axel slouched against the wall.

"You don't remember what Chris said about bad language and stuff like that? You don't know that woman. She could have been a buyer."

"So? She has a nice ass. I was just letting her know I liked it."

"Well, you're not supposed to do that here. Consider this a warning. If you do something like that again, I'll have to tell Chris and he'll fire you."

"Oh, yeah?" He straightened up and took a menacing step forward. "Since when are you the boss? Or do you just play tattletale?"

"I call it a report of behavior Chris doesn't tolerate." The activity previously requiring Teddy to raise her voice to be heard had stopped again. She looked around and saw that three of the men who'd been hanging drywall upstairs now lined the stairwell, watching her and Axel.

The shortest and stoutest of them, Huey, crossed his arms over his barrel chest, the tattoo of the naked woman on his bicep appearing to dance as his muscles flexed. "Need any help, Teddy?" he drawled.

She shook her head and addressed Axel. "Val sent you over to clean up Number four. Are you done?"

"Not quite."

"Then I suggest you get to it." Turning her back on him, she motioned for Flint to help her pick up the last of the drywall. "Okay, guys. Let's see if we can get the rest of these walls hung before we go home."

Huey approached. "You want me to talk to him?"

"No. I'll check Number four before I take off. How about you show Flint here how to tape the drywall you guys have already hung in that front bedroom?"

"Come on, kid. Let's get this wallboard up the stairs." Huey manhandled the last four sheets and headed up the steps in front of Flint, whose eyes widened.

"Huey's just showing off," Teddy said under her breath.

Flint grinned.

Two hours later, Teddy waved as the last of the crew headed for their vehicles. She did a final check of the work completed upstairs, noting how well Flint had swept the area. She hauled the plastic trash can downstairs to do the same on the main floor. Chris would be happy to see a clean work space when he arrived tomorrow.

She hiked past the empty lot that would soon become Number three, although the lot seemed smaller than the others. Another, even smaller lot across the street and closer to the curve of the road into the cul de sac, would make a great pocket park, graded for grass under the three trees growing there.

She walked up the ramp into the front of Number four. The upstairs area, its framing complete and ready for drywall, was clean enough. She dragged the trash can downstairs, along with the broom left lying on the floor nearby. Axel must have taken off soon after being reprimanded. The downstairs flooring looked untouched by the broom, and numerous scraps of lumber were scattered around, primed to trip up an unwary worker. Teddy grabbed the broom and began sweeping. After cleaning up, she hauled the trash can outside and tipped its contents into the dumpster.

As she returned to Number two, she saw Chris. "You're still here?" he asked. "I figured everyone would have left close to an hour ago. Everything's good?"

"Pretty much. Axel swept the top floor, but the main floor in Number four needed clean-up. I kept the guys at Number two a couple minutes longer than usual so we could finish the drywall upstairs. I hope you don't mind, but I asked Huey to show Flint how to tape. He said he wants to continue with that tomorrow."

"Good. I like how eager he is to learn. Anything else I need to know?"

"A woman stopped by and asked for you. I thought she might be a buyer."

Chris's previous half grin thinned into a frown. "What'd she look like?"

"A little over five feet tall, big blond hair, and nice shoes. Black, shiny, four-inch heels, I'm guessing. Gave me her name." Teddy pulled out the paper she'd shoved in her pants pocket and handed it to him. "Bailee Crawford. Val's betting she's your latest girlfriend."

Even in the fading light, Teddy noted how Chris's tanned cheeks seemed to lose color in contrast to the skin hidden by his late-afternoon beard shadow.

"What'd she say?" he rasped then cleared his throat.

"Nothing much. When you weren't here, I offered to take a message, but all she said was to let you know she stopped by."

Chris's head bobbed. "Thanks for telling me."

"Val says he's calling for occupancy inspection on the custom. Probably no later than Friday, which means we're done there a few days earlier than you estimated. Even though you couldn't do much the last couple of weeks except order us to work faster." Teddy hoped her light-hearted statement would return a smile to Chris's face. He seemed uncharacteristically solemn, maybe even worried about something.

"Good to know," he replied, staring at the paper with the woman's name on it.

"Are you mad that I kept the guys a little later than usual?"

Chris ran his hands along the edge of the nearby table saw. "Uh, no. You and Val and all the guys did good. Better than good. If taping is already half-done upstairs, we're at least a day ahead of schedule here, too."

She pulled her keys from the left chest pocket of her flannel work shirt. "I really like that rookie, Flint."

But Chris didn't reply.

Teddy headed for her car, surprised that he didn't want to know why. *Wonder what's bugging him?*

Seven

Chris entered his mother's front door.

"Glad to see you made it, Chris," Nathan Lambert said. "It's been a while."

"Yeah, Dad. Been busy."

"Other than that fire at your place? I would imagine you'll rebuild as soon as the insurance money comes through," his father pressed.

"That, too." Chris slid into the empty chair next to his mother.

"Debra says you've been building houses in that neighborhood not far from her house. A custom one, too, from what Fletcher said."

Iona Lambert slipped a hand onto her husband's shoulder as she smiled at Chris. "You really shouldn't allow your work to prevent you from joining us for Sunday dinner, dear. Makes me wonder if you don't like my cooking."

More like your prying, Mom. "Like I said, I've been busy. Weekend's the only time I have to work on furniture." *Even though I'm not building anything right now.*

"Nathan, please tell everyone to come to the table. Chris, you can start the cheesy potatoes around." She handed him a bowl as other family members trooped upstairs and into the formal dining room.

General conversation swirled around the big table for the better part of the meal and Chris slowly relaxed, hoping he could get with Fletcher to ask if he'd uncovered anything about Bambi.

As plates emptied and the coffee pot was passed around a second time, Fletcher spoke up.

"So, Chris. You back to making furniture yet?"

"Still working on the forms the insurance guy sent over. What we lost made a bigger list than I thought. My stuff and Teddy's."

"You're combining her claim with yours?" Eden asked.

"Teddy?" Iona asked.

"TJ, Mom. Theodora Jameson. You remember. Chris's best bud since kindergarten—after she bopped him on the nose," Elaine explained. "How is Teddy? Haven't seen her in ages. Didn't she leave town to go to art school?"

"She's back. After her mom died." Chris took a last bite of the roast beef on his plate, disappointed that the focus of the conversation had turned to him and the fire. And Teddy.

"If you saw her, you'd remember her, Mom," Elaine added. "Long red braids, big blue eyes. I love her coloring. As tall as you, isn't she, Chris? I remember her on the girls' basketball team in high school." His twin chuckled. "And that time at the park? How old were we then, twelve? I know it was before you started shooting up. Teddy was already taller than me. That's when she said, 'I see you're still short.' So funny. You pushed her into the pool. Dad made you go sit on the blanket."

Chance giggled. "You shoved a girl, Uncle Chris?"

Kenyon glanced at his mother and chortled. "We'd never do that, would we, Chance? 'Cause of what our moms would do. Or dads."

"Nope," Chance agreed. "We'd be nice."

"Mom, big ears here," Fletcher cautioned. "Boys, if you're done, why don't you go downstairs with Grandpa? You, too, Ivory. We'll call you when dessert is ready."

Chris watched as his father herded the two boys and his granddaughter away from the dining room table.

Iona grimaced. "You're working with *that* Teddy Jameson?" She frowned. "Red hair? Lots of freckles? Kind of gangly? Lived a block off the warehouse district? That's the girl you mean? Christopher, you really shouldn't be associating with such people," his mother declared. "Her mother was into drugs, wasn't she? Cocaine or heroin or something terrible like that." Iona grimaced as she reached for the coffee carafe but then pulled a trembling hand away.

Chris stared at her frowning countenance. "Teddy's never done drugs. And she's one of my best people. Even helped me set up my website, which is bringing in business. Not just construction jobs. Furniture reclamation, and orders for new pieces, too. I owe her, big-time."

Debra spoke up. "I saw her work on that fireplace surround. Eden, you should see it. Beautiful work. Todd and I may hire her to do something similar at our place, now that Chris has finished our kitchen remodel. Which I love, by the way. Teddy does stained-glass windows, too."

Chris nodded, hoping Debra's comments would deflect his mother's attention away from Teddy's family.

"I never understood why she never uses her regular name, which is old-fashioned but reminds me of someone with character. Class. Not at all the same as Teddy or TJ, although using her initials or a boy's name probably fits her better." Iona snif-fed. "I seem to remember that she was stick-thin. Not someone who would ever grow into a beauty. And such a tomboy. Playing so rough. Even boys' games."

"So was I, Mom," Deb interposed. "A tomboy."

"But you grew out of it, dear. You don't suppose Teddy prefers ... She's not a lesbian, is she?" Her tone turned disgusted.

Chris glanced around the table at his sisters. Even Logan looked embarrassed at their mother's words.

"I seriously doubt it." Chris rose and pushed his chair in. The dressed-up Teddy he'd seen when he'd stopped over to talk to Yancy had momentarily stopped him cold. If he hadn't sworn off the opposite sex because of Bambi and her secret baby, he might take Fletcher's hint and ask Teddy out. At the very least, she could hold a decent conversation. About work, sports, even the news.

"Fletch, can we talk later? Maybe in an hour? I've gotta go. Call me when you get home." He stalked out the front door without waiting for a reply, and made for his truck, angry at his mother's derogatory assumptions about Teddy.

~ ~ ~

Later that evening, Chris paced as Fletcher slouched on the couch, one leg resting on the coffee table, the other bent at the knee as he reviewed, with some eye-rolling, what he'd learned about Bailee, aka Bambi.

"That's all you've got? That she used to be married, she lied about being pregnant three years ago and that's why her first ex dumped her?"

"It's a pattern, bro. She convinced the guy to marry her because he thought she was having his kid and when it was obvious she wasn't … well, he severed ties. Two months later, she and the new guy got hitched, but it didn't last a year. I suspect she was after his money. Maybe that's what's she after with you, too." Fletcher's brow furrowed. "Although she'd have a better chance had she made her claim before the fire. When will you rebuild?"

Chris resumed his pacing. "Last time I asked my insurance guy, all he said was 'these things take time.'"

Fletcher nodded. "I can tell you're frustrated."

"At least my crew is on their toes. I doled out bonuses on Friday, for finishing the custom house early."

"That's good news."

"Yeah, and the three other homes going up look to be right on schedule or close enough. I hired Yancy as my clean-up man. He starts on Monday, assuming the doctor clears him for pushing a broom without damaging his shoulder."

"I thought your rookies do clean-up duty."

"True, but one of them is already doing drywall and taping work. I let him take off early a couple days a week to attend his college classes. The other guy?" Chris sat down and faced his older brother. "I'm getting vibes that he's not worth having around."

"What do you mean?"

"The other day, Teddy had to finish sweeping for him. And what he'd cleaned, he did a piss-poor job of. I'd rather pay Yancy and know he'll do a good job."

"Because Teddy will make sure he does?"

Chris grinned. "Because Yancy is eager to get paid and I like his enthusiasm." He reached for his coffee mug and drained it. "Back to the important stuff. What do I do about Bambi? She showed up at my jobsite two days ago. Lucky for me, I wasn't there."

"What did she want?"

"According to Teddy, all she did was ask for me. Teddy seemed to like her shoes. What is it with women and shoes?"

Fletcher laughed. "I can see Bambi wearing really high heels, but I doubt Teddy even owns a pair."

"You're probably right." But the image of Teddy in that black dress shimmered in his mind's eye. And hadn't she been holding a pair of heels?

"Did Bambi say anything else when she talked to Teddy?"

"Not that I'm aware. One of the guys overheard her say something about Teddy not being my type." He felt his neck heat. "Imagine that, me and Teddy."

Fletcher grinned. "Actually, I could." His left brow rose in a question. "You're both in construction, both creative. You making furniture, her carving and that stained-glass art she does. And, Teddy doesn't take any crap from you." Fletcher's eyes twinkled.

Chris looked away, his heart thumping at his brother's words. "Bambi was pretty insistent about talking to me. Can't you do something about that, Fletch? I don't want her around the construction. What if she falls or bumps into something? Heels like she wears can be treacherous at a work site."

"I'll mention it when I reply to her letter, which I'm not quite ready to send. I haven't finished looking into whether she has money problems. In the meantime, if she shows up again, tell Val or Teddy to hand her a hard hat. She strikes me as the kind of woman unlikely to want to mess up her hair. If she comes to your house, don't ask her in. I know you said if the kid is yours that you'd step up and pay child support. But for now, don't offer her anything—like paying for her prenatal care. Just listen to what she has to say. After she leaves, write down exactly what she said. Every word. Then email me."

"You want a record?"

"Got it in one, bro."

~ ~ ~

After Fletcher left, Chris took his brother's place on the couch and munched on a potato chip. He reached for the remote, clicked it on to a basketball game in progress, watched for a few minutes, and turned it off. He'd always enjoyed sports. But what he couldn't get out of his head was that image of Teddy in a dress.

Probably because whenever she was in his shop, she look-ed like a guy. Her work pants were baggy, the pockets often bulging with tools. She seemed to favor shapeless flannel shirts in winter, cotton ones in summer. The chest pockets usually were half torn away, preventing her from using them to hold her ever-present cell phone. And at the worksite, the only time he saw her arms was when the warmth of the day forced her to push the sleeves above her elbows.

She wore her hair tight against her head in a coiled braid most of the time. She'd said once that it kept her neck cool, that it was safer. No way did she want her braid to brush against a newly painted wall. He'd rarely seen her with her long red curls down. And he didn't recall her wearing heels. Doing so would have made her even taller than she already was, taller than almost all the guys on his crew, including him.

He'd been surprised at how long her hair was that night he'd talked to Yancy. Almost to her waist. Like Rapunzel. He smiled, remembering reading the story to Eden's daughter on a babysitting night for his older sister and her husband. Little Ivory had tossed her shoulder-length hair back, looking adorable. After he'd finished the story, she beamed at him, her bright blue eyes sparkling. "See my hair, Uncle Chris? I'm going to grow it as long as Rapunzel, so I can let it down when I'm in Kenny's tree house. But if Chance tries to grab it, I'll pull it up so he can't climb up, like in the story." She'd giggled at the thought of teasing her cousin.

Teddy wasn't like the girls Chris dated. She'd always been his BFF, someone he could tease, who teased him right back. He'd hired her because the references she'd provided had sung her praises, claimed she was good at what she did. The rest of his crew respected her for her skills, liked her. And she'd taken Flint under her wing. Probably why that rookie was doing so well, wanted to learn more, had asked if Teddy would show him how to tile, too. Flint was a good addition to Chris's crew. But would he stick longer than a season? *I'll have to ask what he's studying.*

Chris dipped a chip into the bowl of guacamole. Which turned his thoughts to Yancy, and his eagerness to work for Chris. The kid had walked out on the porch with him, and surprised him.

"You can't look at my sister that way," he'd declared.

Chris had glanced back at him, his heart thumping. "What're you talking about?"

"I saw you checking her out." Yancy's cheeks had bloomed red. "I know all about you. Don't think you can date my sister once and then toss her away like you do those other girls."

"Hey, hold up there, Yance. Teddy's on my crew, one of the guys. I would never—"

"Yeah, well, you better not."

"Don't worry." He'd tried to explain, unsure how to reassure Teddy's kid brother. "Look, I was just surprised to see her in a dress. Not exactly what she wears on the job."

"Well, she *is* a girl." Yancy's voice dropped into a lower register. "And since our dad's gone, it's up to me to look out for her. Even if she's older'n me."

"No worries, Yance. She's safe with me—with all of us."

He'd headed for his truck, startled that Teddy's brother felt he had to take on a protective role for Teddy. She was her brother's guardian, officially. But maybe it was right that they looked out for each other.

Chris closed the bag of chips and picked up the guacamole bowl. He washed up his dishes and headed for bed. Tomorrow would roll around early. After his last chat with Val, he wanted to be on scene when Axel and Flint showed up. The better to check out how each was working with the rest of his crew.

~ ~ ~

Ten days later, his hand and shoulder fully mended, Chris's anxiety about Bambi had subsided. There'd been no sign of her, no calls, no texts and no more letters. Even better, the owners of the custom home were thrilled that their place was completed. The second moving truck had just moved into place and four men were hauling furniture through the front door. Chris sent Teddy over to assist Mrs. Poindexter in directing the moving men into the correct rooms. More specifically, Teddy was there to make sure that no walls were scraped up and that the floors sustained no gouges.

Chris glanced up as Val approached. "How's Flint doing? And Axel?"

Val grinned. "Flint earned every bit of that early raise you gave him. I know you usually wait six months, but I'm glad you included him. He fits right in. We all like him. Trust him, too."

"What about Axel?"

Val shook his head. "He does his job, what I ask him to do, but I caught him taking an extra break the other day when he was supposed to be helping Teddy. He doesn't like taking orders from her. A couple times I heard him baiting her, trying to get her to react. She didn't. But you know how Huey is, kind of old-fashioned when it comes to women? He totally respects Teddy, doesn't like Axel, and doesn't care that he knows it. Huey was on him the other day about cleaning up his language when he started dropping F-bombs again."

"What about the other guys working on the Teddy's team?"

"Old hands. Totally happy following her lead. They've all worked with her, knows she pulls her own weight. If I were you, I'd let Axel go. We've got plenty of work, and we could use him if he'd do the job, but maybe we're better off without him and his big mouth, trying to pick fights and show he's better'n a woman. Maybe Yancy could step up, do more than clean-up."

Chris slid a hammer into the loop on the left leg of his work pants. "I doubt he'd be interested. Last time I talked to him, he said he wants to become a chef."

He turned, a smile firmly in place when Mrs. Poindexter approached. "You're all moved in?"

"I wouldn't say that, but the furniture is. Thank you for sending Teddy over to make sure those movers didn't mess up what a beautiful job you all did. We're planning a housewarming, and we want you to come. So we can brag on you to our friends. Especially after they see all the extras that make our new home so special."

"When is your party?"

"A week from Saturday. In nine days. Jacob will be manning the grill on the patio. He told me he'd put your name on one of those steaks. Please come, Chris. We're so pleased with your work."

Chris watched her thank other members of his crew before he disappeared into the house.

"You heard what she said?" he asked Val, who nodded. "I'll talk to Teddy about Axel. Could you check Number four? Ask the head roofer when he expects to be done there and when they can start on the next one."

Chris followed Val down the sidewalk before detouring into Number two's driveway, aware of the newly sodded lawn in the Poindexter's front yard. He waved Teddy over to the truck parked in a mud-encrusted driveway.

Wasting no time, he said, "Tell me what you think of Axel."

"He does his job." She nibbled her lower lip, then added, "Not always happily, not always well."

Chris clenched his jaw. "Val said he mouths off at you."

"Words don't bother me. I ignore him. As long as he gets his work done, I don't care what he calls me, what he says." She stared back at him, their eyes level, her hair a braided crown except for a few strands that had escaped and floated near her ears in the light spring breeze.

"You know I don't like that kind of thing. No F-bombs on my jobsite, which I hear he's dropped."

"I know." She glanced across the street and watched as the big moving truck slowly backed out of the Poindexters' driveway.

She smiled. "Mrs. Poindexter asked me to come to their big do now that their house is done. She wants me to meet two friends who might have some stained-glass work for me. I'll have to tell them it's all on hold until I can find a new place to work."

"You should still talk to them. Line up those jobs. I'll keep you in the loop about my rebuilding plans."

Teddy caught his eye with a concerned gaze. "Are you going to fire Axel? He'll think I complained."

"Can't help what he thinks. I'll make sure he knows I'm the one firing him. Not because you said anything. He mouthed off to Yancy, too."

Teddy's brow furrowed. "I didn't know that."

"When he was sweeping up in Number two, according to Huey. I hope Yancy didn't take it personally."

She shook her head. "He likes working here, doesn't mind the grunt work. And he's getting his homework done. So I wouldn't have to ask you to fire him." Her lips curved upward.

"Yancy's a good kid, Teddy. I'm totally happy with his work." He gave her shoulder a playful punch. "I guess he didn't tell you he wrote up a contract and insisted on me signing it. Just between him and me."

"Really? Can I see it?"

Chris chuckled. "No, you can't see it. Didn't I say it's between him and me?"

Teddy laughed. "That little twerp. I'll keep your secret— as long as he doesn't slough off."

"He won't. He wants you to be proud of him."

"Is it okay if I leave early today? I want to check out a place that might work as a temporary studio."

"Of course." He reached up and tucked a strand of hair behind her ear. "You're turning into a workaholic, Teddy. Not a good sign."

"You should talk, boss." She turned and strolled in the direction of her car, the subtle sway of her hips catching Chris's attention.

Eight

Chris approached the open door of the Poindexter home after parking nearly two blocks away. Even though theirs was the only home in the neighborhood to be completed, he hoped that would change quickly. The house no longer carried the smell of newly sawn wood or drywall mud. Instead, a flowery scent wafted his way, along with a classic jazz tune. He tensed at the sound of a crackling fire, but these flames were contained behind a hearth guard.

Standing next to the fireplace was the judge's wife, and nearby, with her back to the door, a woman who towered over tiny Ms. Poindexter. The stranger's long red curls almost touched her waist and she wore a pale green top and forest green pants that looked like silk. They reminded Chris of the harem pants his twin sister had worn at his parents' New Year's party. Or maybe it was the strappy black sandals with four-inch heels that caught his attention.

Then she turned, and Chris gaped.

Teddy spotted him and grinned. "Oh, hi, Chris. I was just telling Ms. Poindexter how I came up with the design for the carving." She touched her fingers to the side of the hearth, just above the wing of the hawk that seemed ready to soar from one side of the huge fireplace to the other, where its mate rested on a nest high in an evergreen tree just below the mantel.

"It's even more beautiful than when I first saw it," the homeowner gushed.

"That's because it wasn't sealed that day."

Teddy thanked her and moved deeper into the house toward the arm-waving judge.

Chris watched her, belatedly aware that he had yet to say a word to the judge's wife. His mother would chide him if she knew he was standing there like a doofus, gob smacked at a Teddy he'd never really seen before. A woman. Not just TJ, his best friend in middle school, or Teddy, who'd joined his construction crew. She'd somehow morphed into Theodora Jameson, an offbeat beauty his mother might even approve of. *Ms.* Theodora Jameson. In any other setting, a woman Chris would date in a New York minute.

Chris glanced around the room. Several of the men had noticed Teddy, too. Her statuesque beauty, the slight sway of her red curls that moved in counterpoint as she strolled toward the men surrounding the judge, her slim ankles peeking out of those dressy pants, teasing Chris with his imaginings of mile-long legs. Nor did the men seem to care that Teddy was taller than most of them in those killer heels, probably would be taller even barefooted.

One particular man seemed especially taken with her. He stood next to the judge, looking so much like the older man that Chris concluded he had be related. Mr. Junior Judge's gaze angled upward as if to capture Teddy's attention. When that didn't work, he grasped Teddy's hand, slid his other hand around her waist and stepped closer to her, pulling her away from the three men clustered near the judge.

Chris's blood pressure climbed. *Whoa! Too close. Back off, dude.* What gave the judge's son the right to touch Teddy like that, to look like he wanted to kiss her? He imagined Yancy yelling, *Get your hands off her!*

But why was *he* reacting like that? He knew Teddy could hold her own against any guy.

After a too-long pause during which Chris held his breath, Teddy slipped out of the man's grasp —*Good for you, Teddy. Tell him to keep his distance*— but then she patted his arm and laughed at something Mr. Junior Judge said before walking into the kitchen toward some women admiring the tile backsplash behind the six-burner stove.

Chris turned around to retreat outside, to cool down, get a handle on his unexpected reaction to this new, dressed-to-the-nines Teddy, er, Theodora. Second time he'd seen her in clothes that proved she was a girl, er, woman, and not just one of his crew. This time, the effect was even more electric.

"Christopher!" Judge Poindexter called out to him. "Come on over here! I want my friends to meet you. Teddy just bowled them over with her carving and the tile work. How did you manage to convince her to work for you?"

Chris forced himself to smile, hoping it didn't look plastered on, and shook the judge's hand. "Nice party you have here, Judge."

"My wife's doing. We wanted to show off this house you built for us. Not that you aren't already working the entire neighborhood, but you didn't hesitate when we asked you to make those custom changes we asked for."

For the next several minutes, Chris exchanged pleasantries with two more judges and one of the defense attorneys, whose name he recognized. Fletcher must have mentioned him. Or maybe Todd.

He glanced past the shoulders of the men with whom he was chatting. Where was Teddy? And the Junior Judge? He relaxed when he saw her come downstairs and angle past the kitchen, tricked out as if for a chef with that huge walk-in pantry that had taken the place of what was supposed to be a small office. That made him think of Yancy, who wanted to be a chef. Would probably make a good one if the sandwiches Teddy usually ate for lunch were an example of the kid's work.

When Chris had made the Poindexters' changes, he'd agreed that it would set their home apart from the other homes. But he'd also shown the house designer his changes, in case someone else might like a bigger kitchen, a more spacious pantry. Someone who didn't need an office on the main floor.

"Steak's are done!" someone called out.

Chris turned to see that Mr. Junior Judge had donned a chef's hat. Although Teddy was nearby on the patio, Chris saw his chance and approached her.

"Nice outfit, Teddy. Not exactly what you wear on the job." He couldn't stop checking out the v-neck of the blouse and the flared sleeves that ended just below her elbows. If only she hadn't been wearing that beaded necklace with six strands of different-size baubles he could have copped a glimpse of her décolleté.

The color in her cheeks deepened at his words. "Yes, well, I wouldn't want to get sawdust on it."

"Right." He gulped. "Sawdust. Pick up any new clients today? I saw you talking with the junior judge." He angled his head in the direction of the griller holding forth with two other men.

"You mean Lawson?" She chuckled. "He isn't in the market for carvings or stained glass."

No, what he wants is you*!* Hoping he sounded casual, he replied, "Too bad."

"But Mrs. Poindexter introduced me to two of her friends. One of them wants something like what I made for the mayor. I guess he's been showing off his eagles, now that they're in his office."

"Carving you can do at home."

"Right. As if I have time. One of Yancy's teachers roped me into doing a job-fair talk—about women in the trades. I told her I'd do it, but only if I could also talk about being an artist, and I don't mean painting houses." She giggled.

"She agreed?"

"Yes, but it means I'll have to come back a second time." She brushed a curl off her shoulder. "That class meets in the morning, so I'll have to clock in late. After she tells me when I'm scheduled. You don't mind?"

"You always do more than your share. Take whatever time you need."

"Thanks." She angled in the direction of the door.

"Leaving so soon?"

"I promised Yance I'd pick him up from his friend's house." She waved and trotted down the steps. But she must have forgotten something, for she turned on her heel and headed for the patio where the grilling was continuing.

Chris watched her say something to a man standing next to Lawson, who then spoke to Teddy before leaning forward to buss her cheek with a quick kiss.

Teddy was smiling as she departed.

Chris debated telling Lawson to keep his hands off Teddy and wipe that superior smirk off his face, when his phone buzzed in his pocket. *Fletcher.*

"Chris! Could you pick up Chance at his soccer game and drop him off at home?"

"Sure. Where are you?"

"The office. I'm tied up here. May take another hour and I don't want him to have to call Lexi. She wasn't feeling well this morning."

"Think she'll let me sample whatever goodies she brought home from the bakery?"

Fletcher laughed. "I'm sure she will. I'll text her that you'll bring Chance home."

~ ~ ~

Chris waved at the boy when the Chance's team came off the field. To the coach, he said, "I'm Chance Lambert's uncle here to pick him up. You okay with that?"

The man, probably a parent of one of the other second-graders, waved at the boy. "You know this man?"

"Sure! My uncle Chris. He builds houses." He grinned up at Chris.

"Okay. He can go with you. Fletcher had a change of plans?"

Chris nodded and placed a hand on Chance's shoulder. "Let's go, buddy."

"Why didn't Dad come?"

"Some kind of problem at work."

Chance clambered into the passenger seat and buckled up.

"How was your game?" Chris asked.

"Good. Even though we lost. By one point."

"You like being goalie?"

"Yeah, even though the other team's ball got past me."

"I'm sure the next game will work out better. Isn't Kenny on your team?"

"Yeah, but he hurt his ankle at school, so he didn't play today." Chance sighed. "I hope I do better next time. Me and Dad have been practicing in the backyard."

"I'm sure you will. Think your mom will feed us a great dessert when we get home?"

"Maybe. She went back to bed after we had breakfast. Told Dad she didn't feel good."

"A bad cold?"

"Maybe. She said her stomach hurt."

"Hmm. Maybe she ate something that didn't agree with her." He swung into the driveway. "Here we are. Let's go in quietly, in case your mom is resting."

"Okay." Chance led the way through the doorway off the renovated kitchen. "I'll go see if she's awake," he stage-whispered, and galloped up the stairs to the second floor.

As if she's not going to hear him. Chris recalled his mother always complaining about the herd-of-elephant sounds her boys made going up or down stairs.

Chance called out. "Uncle Chris? Could you come up here? Mom wants you."

Chris stopped on the landing when he saw the boy's concerned expression. "What's going on?"

"She says she's hurting. Real bad."

Chris pushed open the master bedroom door.

Lexi's face was almost as pale as the pillows against which she was resting. A moan escaped her lips.

Chris leaned down over the bed. "Bad stomachache, Lexi?"

"Could you help me up?" She slid one pajama-clad leg out from under the covers, clutching her abdomen.

Chris slid an arm across her back and helped his sister-in-law into an upright position.

She cried out then looked down.

His gaze followed. A rivulet of blood dripped onto the carpet.

"Chance. Get me a towel, will you? Quick!" Chris pushed Lexi back onto the bed. "What's going on?"

"I—I think I'm losing the baby," she managed to gasp out before Chance returned.

Chris handed the towel to Lexi.

He turned to Chance. "Go downstairs and call your dad. Tell him I'm taking your mom to the Emergency Room at Pacific Knoll Hospital. Tell him to meet us there—as soon as he can."

Chance's eyes resembled oversized blue marbles, but he nodded and ran downstairs.

"I didn't even know you were pregnant."

"Not quite three months. We wanted to wait until next week to tell everyone. In case—" Her tears halted the rest of her explanation.

He nodded. "Let's get you downstairs. Think you can walk? Want to change clothes first?"

She shook her head. "Just help me up again." She leaned against Chris's arm and stood up, clinging to him. "Keys are on the hook near the back door."

Together, they moved slowly out of the room and down the stairs, arriving in time to hear Chance saying, tearfully, "You better hurry, Dad. Here she comes. 'Bye."

"Chance, honey. It's okay. Come walk with me." Lexi held out her free arm and Chance hung up the phone and rushed to her.

She gave him a hug. "Can you run ahead and open the car door? I'll lie down in the back."

Chance did as she asked.

Chris helped her into the backseat of her SUV.

Chance climbed into the front passenger seat, turned and looked back at her. "We'll get you help, Mom. Don't you worry."

Chris shot a look at the little boy's worried face. "Buckle up, bud," he said, patting Chance's thigh. After carefully backing the SUV around his truck, he hit the accelerator, honking repeatedly to encourage other drivers to move aside.

"Almost there, Lexi," he called out as he swung into the curving drive that led to the emergency entrance of the hospital. "Chance, you stay here until I get your mom inside. I'm come back for you. Lock the doors."

"Okay."

Chris yelled at a nurse walking out the door. "I need a wheelchair!"

The man in green scrubs disappeared for a moment and returned, pushing a chair. "What's the problem?"

"Possible miscarriage," Lexi panted, clutching her abdomen.

"Your wife?" the nurse asked, as they approached the admitting desk.

"Sister-in-law," Chris replied.

"Okay. Why don't you wait over there?" The man pointed in the direction of the waiting room.

Chris nodded, then retraced his steps to retrieve Chance, whose tears streaked his face.

"Is my mom gonna die?"

"No. Of course not. We'll wait inside for your dad."

Chance nodded. "I wish he was here," he hiccupped and rubbed a hand across his face.

"Me, too, buddy." Chris put an arm around Chance, then pulled out his phone and texted Fletcher. *On your way? We're at the ER.*

Less than a minute later, the door into the waiting room flew open hard enough to bang into the wall. Fletcher charged in.

Chance looked up and raced to him, his soft sniffs morphing into full-fledged sobs when Fletcher lifted the boy into his arms.

"Hey, now, calm down. I'm here." He nodded at Chris and took a seat next to his brother. "Chance? Listen to me. Uncle Chris and I—we'll make sure your mom is taken care of." He leaned toward Chris. "Where is she? What have they told you?"

Chris pointed to the closed double doors. "In there. We just got here. Haven't heard anything yet."

Fletcher took a deep breath, as if to calm and steady himself. He looked at Chance. "You're getting almost too big to carry, son. Let me put you down for a minute. Take my hand. We'll find out how Mom's doing."

Fletcher and Chance approached the nurse's station. "My wife was just brought in. Can someone take me to her? Or tell me what's going on?"

"Sure. Follow me. But it might be a bit much for your little guy."

Fletcher nodded and leaned down to Chance. "You go sit next to Uncle Chris. I'll check on Mom."

Chris motioned for Chance to join him. Reluctantly, the boy did so after watching his father disappear past the swinging doors.

"Need a hug?"

Chance scrambled into Chris's arms. He held the boy, aware of his rapidly beating heart, the heat of his small body against his chest. His heart swelled. Was this what it felt like to be a dad, to want to protect a kid against all hurts? Which brought to mind Bambi and her declaration that he was her child's father.

After minutes that seemed more like hours, Fletcher returned to the waiting room. "They're taking her up to a room to keep her overnight. Make sure things stabilize. We can see her there."

"Good news?" Chris asked.

"She's on a drip to try to save the baby." Fletcher grasped Chance's hand. "Chris knows our secret?"

He nodded. "Mom told."

"Because Uncle Chris needed to know."

Fletcher motioned for Chris to follow as he and Chance headed for the elevators. They emerged on the third floor into an area much quieter than the ER. Fletcher asked the nurse for Lexi's room number and pushed open the door. She was in bed, looking pale, though not as ghost-like as before. She held out her arms to Chance, who climbed onto the bed and pressed his face into her neck.

"I'm okay, honey. Really. But I'm afraid—we might—lose the baby." Tears slid down her cheeks. She glanced up at Fletcher. "I'm so sorry."

He kissed her forehead and brushed her blond hair off her cheeks. "Not your fault. It happens. And if it's not to be, we'll try again," his voice breaking.

"Are you crying, Dad?" Chance asked.

"He's sad, honey," Lexi explained. "Just like me. But I'm very proud of you for how you helped Uncle Chris get me out to the car so fast."

"Why didn't you call me?" Fletcher asked.

"I kept hoping the cramping would stop. It did for a while. It only got bad right before Chance showed up with Chris."

"I think I should take off," Chris said, feeling like an intruder. "I'll bring your car back to your place and pick up my truck."

He approached the bed and grasped Lexi's hand. "I'll think good thoughts, Lexi." *As if that will help.* "It might be nice to have another niece."

"But I want a baby *brother*," Chance asserted.

"A nephew would be fine, too. Right, buddy?" He ruffled the boy's hair.

Fletcher followed Chris into the hallway.

"Thanks for helping."

"Hey, brothers stick together. You going to keep this quiet until Lexi's ready to share?"

"For now. Especially if she's right and we lose the baby. She won't rest if everyone comes over. Listen, I've gotta go back in there. Depending on what happens in the next couple hours, the doctor might keep her until tomorrow. If that happens, could you come for Chance, get him some dinner, maybe put him to bed?"

"Of course. He can sleep over at my place if that'll be easier."

"He'll probably do better in his own bed. Depends on … things. I'll let you know."

"This doesn't mean she can't have another baby, does it?"

"No. The doctor said about twenty-five percent of pregnancies don't … make it. I trust you to keep your mouth shut. Let us be the ones to tell everyone, even if it's bad news."

Chris demonstrated sealed lips, gave Fletcher a brotherly hug and grinned. "Not that you owe me anything for picking up Chance and running red lights to get Lexi here in under five minutes—but one of Lexi's lemon cakes would be a nice token of gratitude."

"Whoa! You ran red lights with my boy in the car?"

"No, but I leaned on the horn and was lucky—no cops in sight. I think I even surprised Chance when we took that last turn. His eyes were huge."

"My brother, the race car driver. If Chance says he wants to be like you, I'll tell him what you did was illegal, that you're going to need a good lawyer to get you out of trouble."

Chris chuckled. "Go back in there and take care of Lexi. And tell her I love her. Chance, too."

"You got it. Listen, one thing that kept me at the office today was Bambi. After Lexi's home, I'll give you a call."

"Take all the time you need." Chris left the hospital, returned Lexi's SUV to its place in the driveway and drove his truck home, staying within the speed limit.

So Fletch and Lexi had been making a new baby. Chris hoped they were successful. If not this time, next time. Chance was a great kid, deserved a baby brother.

All of which prompted Chris to wonder what it would it be like to *want* to have a child. With a woman Chris wanted to be with, someone he loved. Would he enjoy, as much as Fletcher seemed to, having a son of his own, someone like Chance, so bright and full of energy? But a son would require a mother, and that thought prompted a hitch in his breath. Chris never would have chosen Bambi as the mother of his kid. He shook off the quick thought that someone like Teddy would be more suitable. She had stepped up when Yancy needed a parent figure. She was responsible, worked hard, was intent on building a future for herself and her kid brother. Was trying to point him along the right path, not at all like their mother, who'd blown the Jameson house to kingdom come. Herself, too.

~ ~ ~

After changing out of the clothes he'd worn to the Poindexter open house, Chris fixed himself a quick dinner and waited for Fletcher to call. *Good news,* he hoped. But when Fletcher called, he told him Lexi had lost the baby, and Eden had taken Chance to her place for a sleepover with Kenny.

After Chris's promise not to share what had happened to Lexi, he was stuck for an idea about how to let Lexi know that he cared about her, and acknowledged her loss. He needed a woman's take. He was down to too few people he could talk to without spilling the news. Val was married, but Chris didn't know Paula all that well.

He scanned his contact lists, realizing that several no-strings-attached friends of the female species were still saved in his phone. He deleted them. Which left only one person who might be willing to give him some ideas.

Teddy. She was artistic, creative, the best possible person to help him out. She wasn't exactly a mom, but she was Yancy's guardian. Sort of a sister qua mom. He picked up his phone.

"What do you want, Chris? A little late to be calling me on one of your date nights, isn't it?"

Taken aback at her snippiness, he asked, "What put you in such a bad mood?"

"I'm antsy, is all. The lumberyard where I usually find great pieces of wood had nothing worth considering."

"The Poindexters are in no rush. Why don't you chill about the wood? And just to be clear, my date tonight was with Chance, my nephew." He huffed out a breath and mentally crossed his fingers that she wouldn't hang up on him.

"Listen, I have a question. Since you're a girl ..."

"Oh. One of *those* questions?"

"Sort of. But you have to promise this is just between us."

"I'm good at keeping secrets. Talk."

"If you were going to visit someone who was pregnant, but she might have lost the baby, what would you bring her? You know, a gift to make her feel better, or at least to let her know that you cared about her."

"Hmm. Depends on how close you are to her. If she's not a relative, I'd probably go with flowers and a card. Not really personal, but nice."

"I could do the card, but flowers? Not a good idea. I think she has allergies."

"Hmm. Well—" Teddy gasped. "Oh my gosh! You're talking about your girlfriend, aren't you? The one who was looking for you."

He opened his mouth to answer, but she rushed on, nearly choking over the words.

"Never thought you'd be that careless, Chris. Why weren't you with her at the hospital? Geez, what's wrong with you?"

Each question sounded more accusatory than the previous one. *Christ! She guessed that?*

"No! Teddy! Not a girlfriend. She's more like a relative. By marriage, I mean." Chris hoped his denial came through loud and clear, even as his pulse galloped.

What would he do if Bambi lost the baby she claimed was his? That would let him off the hook. But guilt washed over him that the child he had inadvertently helped create might never draw a breath.

He forced himself to think of Lexi. He knew without Fletch telling him that Lexi would be devastated after losing the baby. From the look on Fletcher's face in the hospital, he probably was, too.

Lowering his voice, hoping he sounded concerned and caring, Chris repeated, "No, Teddy. It's not like that. She's someone I like, even love, like a sister."

"Oh." After a lengthy pause, Teddy replied, "Well, in that case, why don't you make her something? Something special that she'd know only you would give her." She hummed a non-tune for several seconds, as if mulling over her own suggestion. "How about something small, that she could hold in her hand? Something she could keep in a pocket. If you made it, that would make it special. A gift like that and a card might work. But don't say something stupid like, 'you'll have another baby.' I read somewhere that's really hurtful. And when you see her, focus on *her*, how *she* feels."

Chris cleared his throat and blinked his eyes. "No stupid comments, concentrate on her. I can do that. Thanks."

"You sound kind of weird. Are you okay?"

"I'm fine." He hung up before she heard him start to cry. Chris hauled himself off the couch and trotted outside to the pile of lumber left over from his last trip to the dump. By the light of a flashlight, he rummaged for a piece of wood untouched by the flames that had destroyed his shop, or at least not so singed that he couldn't sand off the burned spots.

He picked up a small piece that looked like maple and brought it into the house. He'd have to cut it in half and then in half again, but in doing so, he'd lose the charred parts. He retrieved a small saw and some sandpaper from the toolbox in his truck and returned to the house.

Within two hours, he'd created what Teddy had suggested, a small stone-like piece with carefully rounded edges that fit easily in the palm of his hand. Small enough that Lexi could hide it in her palm, too. The wooden stone needed only a coat of lacquer for the grain of the wood to be permanently revealed. Pleased with how it looked, he placed it on the kitchen counter and headed for the shower. Tomorrow, he'd look for just the right card and hope that Lexi liked what he'd created.

~ ~ ~

Two nights later, Chris was sprawled on his couch, having fallen asleep in the middle of a Mariners game. His phone buzzed on his chest, still perched where he'd placed it in case Fletcher called.

"Hey, bro. How's Lexi?" The pause that followed his question told Chris that the news might not be good.

"Getting there. I can't seem to convince her it wasn't her fault. She's still claims that working extra-long hours at the bakery all last week was what caused her to start bleeding."

"That's crazy. Didn't the doctor talk to her?"

"He said time would help. Chance brought her a handful of daffodils from the garden and she started crying all over again.

Both of them ended up in tears. I finally called Eden to take Chance to the park with Kenny and Ivy. Lexi's taking a nap, so I thought I'd give you a call. Before I make dinner."

"I'm really sorry, bro." Another loss for Fletcher, this time for Lexi, too. "I have something for Lexi. Do you think it'd be okay if I came over, or should I wait until the weekend?"

"Weekend might be better. I'm hoping she'll feel better by then. Enough to talk about going back to work, anyway. When she does that, I know she'll be more herself."

"How'd Eden take the news?"

"Surprised and sad. Elaine and Deb, too, but I told them I'd never speak to them again if they breathed a word to Mom. She'll insist on bombarding Lexi with questions she shouldn't have to answer right now."

"Is this call about what you mentioned at the hospital? You know, Bambi?"

"Right. I told her she wasn't to go to your jobsite again, and that all future communications should come to my office."

"How'd she take that?"

"Better than I thought. At least she listened, and I followed it up with a letter, making it official. I have a feeling she'll show it to an attorney, in case she decides to demand some kind of restitution from you."

"You didn't offer to have me pay for anything?"

"Not unless she asks. And even then, we may not need to."

"Why's that?"

"She went back to keeping house with husband number two. But not recently, which could mean he's soon to be an official ex. It seems she kicked him out about the time she probably got pregnant, assuming what she told me is true, which means it could be his baby. But she denies having been with anyone but you."

"Know who he is, the ex?"

"Yes, but I don't want you getting in his face. I'm trying to pin down whether she was still sleeping with him when she also slept with you. Which means *she* may not know who the father is."

"We were only together three times."

Fletcher scoffed. "And it only takes one time. Just your bad luck if your swimmers beat the other guy's to the motherlode. So to speak." He sighed into the phone. "This kind of scare should set you straight about flitting from one woman to the next. Dating's fine, but sleeping with them? Not great. Even when you use protection—with condoms that aren't past expiration. I hope you're practicing abstinence for the time being, even if it isn't exactly your style."

"What I'm doing. Not that I like it." Chris stretched and eased into a sitting position. "You think Bambi'll actually stay away from my work site?"

"I hope so. It's sure to be obvious that something's up if she keeps trying to see you there. Only girl who's ever there is Teddy. Right?"

"Yeah." Fletcher's mention turned Chris's mind to that image of her at the open house. "Ever see Teddy when she wasn't working, Fletch?"

"Not that I recall. Why?"

"Nothing." But he couldn't seem to get out of his mind how she'd looked. How Mr. Junior Judge had given her the old up-and-down-appraisal, then touched her, even kissed her cheek.

"Something bothering you?" Fletcher asked.

Chris set his empty mug on the table. "I knew you guys wanted another kid, but not this soon."

"We've been married almost two years, bro." Fletcher chuckled. "And you expected us to announce it ahead of time? Come on."

Chris felt his neck and cheeks warm. "But you two never said you ... you know, so soon after she became partners with Monet at the bakery."

"Yes, well, we both want another child. A brother or sister for Chance. Maybe more than one."

"Then you'd better get to it. Chance wants a baby brother."

Drily, Fletcher chuckled. "I'll expect you to help him see the positives of whatever he gets."

Nine

Teddy measured the front doors a second time and repeated the numbers to herself as she trotted over to her car for her notebook. Lawson Poindexter had asked her to create new doors for his parents' home. And he wanted it to be a surprise. She'd decided the door had to be western red cedar.

She'd warned him the cost might be more than he wanted to spend, but he'd given her a reassuring wink. "Doesn't matter. Maybe we could discuss it over dinner. I trust you to pick the right stuff."

He chuckled. "Because you're the right stuff, too. Got it?"

Teddy concluded that his comment bordered on weird, but if he wanted to treat her to dinner while they talked price, she was okay with that.

The sound of a car stopping across the street in front of a home under construction caught her attention. She glanced up as a woman alighted. The same shiny black car she'd seen weeks earlier, the same woman who'd been overdressed for a work site. This time the woman wasn't mincing around the mud holes. Today, the ground outside the homes was bare of lumber leftovers and other detritus. Yancy's work. *I'll have to tell him he's doing a good job.*

Teddy straightened out of her crouch and approached the woman. "If you're looking for Chris, he doesn't usually work on Sundays." The woman's cold stare sent a slight shiver down Teddy's spine. "If he doesn't work on Sunday, why are you here?"

"I work on my own stuff."

The woman sniffed. "Well, I have no intention of talking to anyone but him, especially not his snooty lawyer brother. You can tell him that." She spat out her words as if they tasted sour.

"Why don't you call him then?" Teddy replied, not interested in becoming a go-between for the unpleasant visitor. "You have his number?"

"He never got back to me."

"Oh." *I wouldn't either, if you talked to me like that.* Teddy chose to stare down the woman, whose jeans emphasized her slightly rounded belly. Her shirt strained to stay buttoned over ample breasts. But her beige booties with a zipper up the side were cute.

When Teddy looked up again, she saw Chris's truck pull up behind her vehicle. She started toward it. "You're in luck. He just pulled up." She reached her car, slid behind the wheel, then watched Chris approach the woman.

It's none of my business.

But Chris's stiff posture as the woman stalked toward him suggested a confrontation. Curiosity begged Teddy to stay, but she forced down that thought and started her car. She was about to leave when the sound of a loud slap forced her to glance at Chris and the woman.

"*Why'd* you tell your brother? That news was only for you. Soon everyone will know."

Chris rubbed his cheek. "Fletcher's a lawyer, *my* lawyer. He keeps stuff like that confidential. And who knows if I'm the father! You'll only find out after a DNA test, after the kid is born. Which I insist on. What about that other guy you were banging? Is he giving up *his* DNA? Or does he already know it's his?"

Teddy raised a hand to her mouth to stifle her gasp. The woman was pregnant with Chris's baby?

In spite of the warmth of the day, she rolled up her window. But she took her foot off the gas and stared at Chris, for the first time seeing him as other women did. Too handsome for words, even in high school. She knew he'd dated all the cheerleaders, pretty much everyone in the senior class. *Everyone but me.*

From what she'd heard, he was always looking for fun, happy to share with any female similarly inclined. But a player? No. Chris was too nice for that.

Even though Chris came from a big family, she couldn't see him settling down and raising one of his own. Maybe because he was so involved with his brothers and sisters and their kids. He'd brought two little boys with him to the jobsite one day. Cute kids, full of questions, minding Chris about staying out of the workers' way, not touching the tools or running up and down the stairs in the unfinished houses.

That he intended to stay single was his business. It shouldn't matter to her. Except, somehow, it did. She glanced again at the woman, who was slashing the air with both arms. Even with her car windows closed, Teddy could hear her screamed accusations. The late afternoon sunlight bounced off Chris's dark hair, turning the lighter strands golden as he stood, arms crossed over his chest, listening to the woman rant.

The woman raised her hand as if to strike him again. But Chris halted the forward motion of her arm and pulled it down to her side. When she slipped to her knees, Chris hauled her upright and she fell against him, but he didn't pull her closer, didn't kiss her. Instead, he pushed her away.

Whatever Chris said must have convinced her to leave. The woman stalked to her car, executed a tight turn and gunned the engine as she pulled out of the construction site.

Chris, still frowning, strode over to Teddy's car.

She rolled down her window. "You don't need to say it, Chris. I won't say anything."

"Never figured you would, and wasn't planning to pledge you to secrecy. I'm sorry you saw that. Bambi—" he ran a hand through his hair — "she just doesn't know when to keep her mouth shut."

He shot her a glance that seemed to include both embarrassment and pleading that she understand. "I don't want you to think—"

Teddy shook her head. "What I think isn't important."

"Yeah, it is. We're friends. You probably—" He pulled open her door and reached for her hand. "Could you step out for a minute? I want to explain—"

"I don't need to hear the details of your sex—your *social* life." Teddy's cheeks felt aflame at the thought. "But if that woman is pregnant with your baby, you're going to be a family man whether you want to or not."

Teddy could easily imagine another woman's attraction to Chris. She recalled how good he had looked that day at the housewarming. In business casual. His shirt and slacks hinted at the muscles she'd seen when Chris was working, usually in a shirt with the sleeves rolled up, or on hot summer days when he'd tossed it into his truck, gaining the tan he seemed to maintain year-round. She could see why that woman might have wanted Chris to make love to her, to feel him, to revel in his closeness. A sudden flush of heat raced through her body.

Desperate to change the subject, Teddy asked, "How'd that other woman like the gift we talked about?"

"It was for Lexi, my sister-in-law."

"What'd you give her?"

"A piece of wood, small and round, about the size of what I thought her baby might have been. She loves it. Told me she'll keep it. Always."

She nodded. "I'm glad. Gotta go, Chris, so could you—" She pushed his fingers off her arm.

He looked toward the road that led out of the neighborhood and waved when the Poindexters' pulled into their driveway. "Is that why you were here? To talk to them?"

"No. I came to measure the doors so I could get started on a new ones as soon as I find the right piece of lumber, which is where I'm headed now. Lawson ordered it. But please don't say anything. It's a surprise."

"You and the junior judge are on a first-name basis now?"

"Why do you care if I know his name? He's a client, not a date." She pushed his arm off the edge of her car window and backed out of the driveway. If only she could stop imagining Chris in bed with that woman who'd accused him of getting her pregnant. Not the kind of distracting image she needed right now. She had enough to deal with, like how much money she needed so Yancy could go to cooking school. And getting back to Lawson Poindexter, who'd asked her to carve the doors for his folks. He'd offered to pay her more than she'd previously agreed to if she could get it done quickly. For their anniversary, he'd said, which was coming up next month. Money from that job would be the start of Yancy's cooking school fund.

So what if Lawson was kind of creepy when he'd sought her out at his parents' party, insisting on talking with her in one of the bedrooms? She'd kept one hand on the door handle, refusing to move closer when he'd perched on the edge of the bed, all made up with white satin pillow coverings that stood out against the pale blue duvet that matched the newly hung window coverings. She firmly shut that disturbing image out of her mind.

Minutes later, Teddy pulled up at the lumber store and walked in to where the wood was stored. When a yellow-aproned helper approached, she asked, "Where are your long planks? Something I could turn into a door or doors? I'm looking for western red cedar if you have any."

"Follow me. We got in some nice pieces last week."

Under the lights that swayed slightly in the gusts of wind that blew through the storage area, she spotted likely candidates and pulled out her measuring tape. The big plank she liked best was slightly smaller than the current double entry doors at the Poindexter house, but that was okay. Creating a single door meant her carving could be larger than what she'd first described to Lawson.

Teddy ran her fingers along the face of the wood, eager to explore the hint of grain that would become more obvious after she sanded it. The distinctive smell of the wood called to her as she imagined a woodland scene.

Teddy turned to the lumber store clerk. "Any chance you could haul this out for me?"

The young man nodded and lifted the wood away from its fellows.

"Let me help."

Teddy's heart leapt at Chris's voice. What was he doing here? When she glanced at him, he refused to meet her eyes.

Chris grabbed one end of the wood as he and the clerk carried the door to the cash register.

Teddy handed over her credit card, and the clerk rang up the purchase. "May I have two copies of the receipt?"

After the clerk handed her the two receipts, she turned to face Chris, her hands on her hips. "Why'd you follow me?" She looked around. "Where'd that clerk go?"

"You don't need him. I've got this," Chris replied as he grabbed a pallet and eased the wood onto it. "Good-looking cedar. For the judge's place?"

"For Lawson, who hired me." She lifted her chin, and mentally dared Chris to contradict her.

"Ah. Mr. Junior Judge." Chris's jaw muscle clenched, and a furrow appeared between his brows.

"Why don't you like him? Are you jealous that he's in law school and plans to make big bucks? He's my client, which means he deserves your respect."

"Not when he—never mind." Chris pressed a hand on his nape and rubbed. As if trying to dislodge an ache that had settled there.

He pulled out his wallet. "If this is for the custom, I should have covered the cost."

"No! Lawson hired *me*. You're done with the house. This is something I'm paying for. It's *my* work to complete. Besides, you have oth—"

"Other things to worry about? Is that what you were going to say?" Chris's voice dropped a register.

"You never answered me. Why'd you follow me?" Teddy demanded again, as she pushed the pallet holding her purchase away from the cashier's desk.

"I wanted to explain. What you overheard."

"I'm not your mother. No explanation needed."

Chris reared back as if Teddy had slapped him. He stared at her for several moments then followed her out of the store with her purchase. With one hand he pushed the pallet she was guiding toward her car.

"No way is this going to fit in your car, Teddy. Let me help you get it home."

"Oh, yeah? Watch me," she dared. "I've carried large pieces before." She opened the trunk, hit a lever, opened a passenger door and pulled the second seat forward until it rested next to the back side of the front seat. From the trunk, she lean-ed forward and shoved the back rest of the second seat flat and then the back rest of the front passenger seat, too.

"Hmm. Didn't know you could do that," Chris mumbled, as he helped shove the wood into Teddy's car. "But, how are you going to drive? It'll crowd you."

"Shove it sideways a bit, then all the way up so that it touches the windshield."

"But it's more than ten feet long." The end of the wood extended well past the end of Teddy's trunk. "See?" He backed the wood out of Teddy's car. "I'll put it in my long bed. You want it at your place?"

Teddy nodded, reluctantly realizing he was right. A cop would be sure to stop her with that much wood sticking out of the back of her car.

"Where are you going to store it when you're not working on it? Living room floor?"

"No. Can't have Yancy stepping on it. I'll slide it under my bed where it's out of the way. Mostly." She felt herself blush as she spoke, and dared not glance up at Chris to see if he'd noticed.

"Whatever." He grunted as he slid the door into the bed of his truck and tied it down, then turned toward her. "About Bambi being pregnant. That kind of news doesn't stay secret."

"What about you being the daddy? The way you date a different girl every week … maybe every day?" Why she felt like goading him, she couldn't say, even as guilt coated her thoughts.

"That's not what I'm doing now." He glanced at her, his neck reddened. "If it's mine, I'll step up. Problem is, I won't know for months." He opened the door of his truck. "Let's get this to your house before it starts raining."

Teddy nodded, for the first time noticing droplets on her windshield. All the way home, she felt Chris's gaze on her back as he followed her in his truck.

When they arrived at her house, Chris pulled the wood out of his truck bed. "Where's Yancy? He can help me get this inside."

"He's at Peyton's, working on a chemistry project." Teddy propped open the front door, then grabbed the nearest end. "We can do this without him."

They angled the wood slab into the house and leaned it against the living room wall. Teddy wiped her hands on her jeans. "Thanks. If you hadn't shown up, I'm not sure I could have got it home by myself."

"You'd have found a way. Maybe that kid at the store would have agreed to deliver it."

"Not without an extra fee."

"About the Jun—Lawson," Chris said, giving her a sidelong glance. "Watch out for him. He's—"

"I can take care of myself, Chris."

"Not saying you can't. But he's got at least fifty pounds on you, maybe more." He shuffled his feet and looked past her shoulder before his gaze settled on her face. "And I've heard things."

Teddy thought Chris's cheeks seemed redder than when they'd manhandled the door into the house. "Yeah? Like what?"

"Just … things. Nothing specific."

"Well, whatever you've heard isn't going to happen. Not with me, anyway. I don't date customers." *Or anyone else.* She mentally started at the unbidden thought of how, in high school, she'd waited for Chris to ask her out. But he never had. Was that why she'd never dated in high school, and only rarely in college, chalking up her lack of experience to her intention to concentrate on developing her art? She wasn't pretty like the other girls, and rarely bothered with make-up other than the occasional lip gloss and mascara on her too-pale lashes that were more blond than red.

"Which shows you're smart, Teddy. But if he tries—"

"He won't." She crossed her arms over her chest, thinking about her agreement to share a dinner— strictly business — with Lawson to go over the cost of the wood. Money she should ask for right away, so she could pay off her credit card bill.

Chris backed toward the front door. "Not that you probably care, but I'm glad you're going to carve new doors. Let me know when you're ready to hang them." He stared at the wood leaning against her wall. "This piece looks different from what we framed in."

"I'm thinking of making it a single door, with a plain sidelight." She allowed herself a half smile at the thought. "We can always use the double doors on another custom."

Chris coughed out a short laugh. "That'll work, since it was never carved." He tromped down the steps to his truck.

~ ~ ~

Teddy walked into the restaurant. A slow glance at the occupied tables told her Lawson hadn't arrived yet. *Good.* She'd decided she should study his actions after what Chris had said, or not said. What was it about guys that they tended to mistrust other men's motives when it came to women?

She followed the hostess to a corner booth and glanced toward the door before allowing laughter at the bar to capture her attention. A group of women were having what looked like a party. One looked familiar. *Elaine Lambert?* Teddy stared at Chris's twin. She looked as though she'd been crying. Teddy hoped they were happy tears. Wasn't Elaine engaged? She recalled Chris saying something about that shortly after Teddy set up her stained-glass corner in his workshop. Maybe her friends were celebrating Elaine's upcoming wedding.

Teddy approached the group at the bar, three more of whom she recognized. Not that they'd been best buds in high school, but at least they weren't part of the crowd that Teddy had always avoided.

"Hey, Elaine. I heard you were engaged. You're celebrating?"

Unexpected tears flooded down Elaine's cheeks as she shook her head.

"Engagement's off, over, done," a woman announced.

Teddy backed up. "Oh. And you're all here to boost her spirits?"

"You could say that." Elaine pointed to a stuffed doll, the name "Norm" pasted across its chest and held in place by three stick pins. "Wanna add another pin?"

"I'll pass." Teddy patted Elaine's hand, certain her embarrassment showed on her heated cheeks. "Sorry if I misunderstood. I hope you feel better real soon."

Teddy returned to her booth and settled into it, mentally tabulating the number of women from high school who weren't already married or engaged. Like the one who'd spoken, who was wearing what Teddy estimated to be a three-carat rock on her left hand, along with a wide gold band studded with tiny diamonds. A few others were not officially matched with a man, and some others already had children. Still others had moved away. And Elaine was no longer among the first group, the supposed-to-be-happy group.

Nearly a half hour passed as Teddy waited for Lawson, sipping her second glass of water and staring down at her phone. Just as she concluded that he wasn't going to show, that she should text him and ask when they might reschedule, his voice jolted her.

"There you are. Am I late? Wasn't expecting to see you here already." He slid into the booth.

Yeah, you're late. "I was early." She reached into her over-size purse and pulled out the sheets of paper on which she'd sketched three different designs.

"What do you want to drink?" Lawson waved an arm to gain the attention of their server.

"Water for me." At the look of surprise on Lawson's face, Teddy explained, "I never drink when I'm talking business." Was she imagining it or did the man look disappointed?

He ordered two beers. "In case you change your mind," he explained. "After all, dinner's social. Right, Teddy? Or should I call you Theodora?" He seemed to drape sexual innuendo around her name when he drawled it.

"Nobody calls me that, Lawson. It's Teddy, if you don't mind. Or TJ." But she tucked the designs back in her purse. "Okay. Dinner first. Then business."

Lawson immediately launched into disparaging comments about the noise at the bar. Through the dinner service, he blathered on about how much he enjoyed law school and what he planned to do after he passed the bar. "I'm thinking I'll join my dad's old firm and then run for office after I make some bucks, become better known around town," he stated, as if his expectation was a foregone conclusion. "You agree that's a good plan, right? What about you?"

"I'll keep doing what I'm doing now."

One speculative brow rose above Lawson's pale blue eyes. "You don't want more for yourself than working on a construction crew?" He ran a hand through his blond-streaked light brown hair. "I figured you'd want to maybe even become a bigtime artist—you know, with those carvings of yours."

"Maybe. If I'm lucky," she replied. *Gotta get Yancy through cooking school first.*

Lawson shoved his plate to the side, emptied his beer glass and leaned forward. He grasped Teddy's hand. "Stick with me, hot stuff, and you'll get there faster. I'll tell my friends about your work, so you can get more woodworking gigs. You know, the connected ones, the people with money to burn. With my help, you'll get so much business, you'll be able to hire helpers." He smirked, as if already proud of having helped her build a career. "Then I can tell *my* people to get in touch with *your* people. You can thank me later." He winked and chuckled, his gaze seeming to burn as it scanned her upper body. He squeezed her fingers. "If you don't want that beer, mind if I have it?"

"Go ahead." She pulled her hand away, sensing by Lawson's glances repeatedly gliding from her face to the cowl neckline of her wrap dress, that he was less interested in her carving than he'd initially implied. *I shouldn't have worn this dress,* she thought, suddenly feeling unpleasantly warm. At least Lawson didn't know that the dress ended at her knees, that one pull on the bow at her hip would allow the dress to slide open, or that she was wearing four-inch heels. Could she run away from him if she had to?

Yancy had said her date might not like that her shoes would make Lawson feel small. He couldn't be more than five feet ten. She wondered if Yancy was right that Lawson might feel intimidated. If so, would he try to establish dominance by refusing to accept the design she favored, the one she hoped he would select? He kept insisting that this was a dinner date, as if trying to make a point. Even though she'd corrected him, twice, calling it a business meeting.

Yancy had also questioned why she'd dressed up. "If it's not a date, why are you going to a restaurant? Wearing that dress and those sexy shoes? Chris always has *his* meetings at the jobsite."

"He doesn't wear a dress, either," she'd replied stiffly. "This is different. This meeting is to convince my customer that I can make that door for his parents. It's more like a preliminary meeting—like me applying for the job, and getting the advance payment so I can cover the cost of the wood I bought."

"But you said you already have the job; that's why you bought the wood."

"I still need to convince him to pay me the advance."

"Ri-i-ight. Over dinner." Her brother remained unconvinced. Teddy hoped he wasn't right that Lawson might refuse to pay her the advance she planned to ask for. He'd expressed surprise when Teddy insisted on meeting him at the restaurant rather than allowing him to pick her up. Now that she was certain he had more than her designs in mind, she was glad she'd driven herself.

Teddy waited until the server removed the dishes. She pulled out the designs and spread the sheets of paper in the center of the table. "Here's what I came up with, although the one in the center is more likely than the others to show off the grain of the wood. But it's your choice. Tell me which of these designs you like best, which one you think your folks would be happy with."

She watched as Lawson glanced at each of the sheets of paper. Too briefly. He took another sip from the beer that should have been hers, leaving a damp finger mark on the corner of the center sheet.

"They all look fine to me. You decide. You're the expert." He pushed the pages together so that only the center design, the one Teddy liked best, remained in view. At the burst of laughter from the bar area, he looked over his shoulder.

"We should find a quieter place to discuss your, um, carvings."

Teddy's pulse started to climb. Lawson looked downright predatory when he stared back at her, slowly rose from his seat and held out his hand. "Come on. I know a place where we won't have to shout to be heard."

Teddy reached for her designs. She took her time rolling them and then slid them into her purse. "You know, Lawson. Since you told me to choose, I'll work on the most complicated one—what I think your mother would like. If you'll pay me my advance, I'll get started right away so that the door can be hung in time for your parents' anniversary."

Lawson pulled out his wallet and tossed some bills on the table. "I agreed to that? You're sure? I was under the impression that payment is made *after* I approve the finished work. Like what my dad did with the house."

Damn! Yancy called it. "No. He paid in advance for the materials. Final payment only covered the rest of the cost of the build-out." Teddy shifted in her seat, unwilling to leave the table until Lawson gave her the advance. But if he refused, how could she force him to pay? He had yet to sign the contract she'd forgotten to bring in her rush to leave the house.

After a moment's hesitation, Lawson sat back down. "You *have* to have that advance?"

She nodded.

He sighed and asked her how much she needed.

She told him, and he wrote her a check, sliding it across the table at her.

"Thank you." She tucked it in her purse, then handed him a receipt for the wood and another for the advance, glad she'd written it out ahead of time. "I'll get started first thing tomorrow." She stood up, eager to leave.

"Whoa!" he exclaimed, stepping away from the table and tipping his head back, the better to look her in the eye. "You really rock in that dress."

"What's that got to do with anything?" Chris asked, startling Teddy and Lawson, who bumped into Chris when he stepped closer. "She's right, Lawson. You pay in advance for the supplies. In your case, that slab of wood she'll carve for your folks' door."

Lawson's neck reddened and the color deepened as it reached his cheeks. "Got it." After staring hard at Chris for a long minute, Lawson moved away from the table. "Stay in touch, Teddy."

"As soon as the door is finished." Teddy watched Lawson stalk out of the restaurant. Relieved that she'd received what she'd come for, she slid back into the booth, aware that her knees were wobbly.

"He stalled about paying, didn't he?" Chris frowned. "Unless you—"

"Don't say another word, Chris. I handled it. I didn't intend to leave without that advance." She looked past him toward the bar. "You're here to take Elaine home?"

He nodded. "One of her buddies texted me. She's in no shape to drive. Call it karma that you were here, too."

"How much did you hear of my conversation with Lawson?"

"Enough to know that Junior wasn't all that interested in your work or paying you."

She nodded. "I forgot to bring the contract. A dumb move."

"Yeah, well. If you don't get his signature, you may not get him to pay up at the end. Why don't you send it to him right away, with a quick deadline?"

"And tell him no payment means we won't hang the new door?"

"If he gives you any trouble, I'll have Fletcher give him a call."

Teddy shook her head. "I'm sure that won't be necessary." She glanced up and caught Chris appraising her. "I'm sorry about Elaine, that her engagement is off."

"Yeah. Well, we all wondered why it kept going on and on." He rose from his seat. "Looks like her pals are getting ready to leave. My cue, too."

Chris spoke briefly with the bartender before grabbing Elaine's hand and leading her out of the restaurant.

Teddy took a final sip of her water and clutched her purse. She walked purposefully toward her car.

Out on the street, Elaine was arguing with Chris.

None of my business, that. Teddy slid the key into the ignition and drove slowly out of the parking lot, passing Chris as he hefted Elaine into the passenger seat of his truck. He gave her a quick wave as he trotted around to the driver's side.

Chris had been right about Lawson. Yancy, too. And she, Theodora Jameson, aka Teddy, aka TJ, should have remembered the contract. A mistake she didn't intend to repeat.

Ten

Chris helped Elaine into her townhome and ignored her slurred complaints that he should leave her alone, that she was fine. She didn't look it.

"Okay, I'm leaving. But if you don't call me tomorrow and tell me you're up and at 'em, I'm calling Deb *and* Eden and maybe even Mom," he threatened.

"Please don't," Elaine pleaded, right before a sob softened her words into mush. Red-eyed, she poked her head out of her bedroom. "I'll don't want Mom telling me she knew all along that Norm wasn't right for me. Especially since she was always crowing how the family *needed* a professional musician. That it gave us *class*." She grimaced.

"You still love him? Even after what you found out?" Chris hid one fist behind his back. "I should break his arm, the one that holds his bow, or smash that damn violin over his head."

She opened the door the rest of the way and leaned against the jamb. "No, Chris. Leave him alone. Me, too." She paused in midsob. "Concentrate on your own love life. Did you see Teddy tonight? When she dresses up, she's really something, don't you think? She thought my pity party was for my wedding, for ha—ha—happiness," she hiccupped. "I should have danced with that guy who kept buying us shots." She giggled and burped. "Or, maybe not."

"You need help?" He shifted his weight, prepared to catch her when she shook her head, and the movement threatened to send her sliding away from the door frame.

Elaine righted herself. "No. Remember when we were going into seventh grade? Most of the boys that year were shorter than the girls, but Teddy? She was miles taller than everybody, even the ninth graders."

Chris's heart thumped and thumped again. "Why do you keep mentioning Teddy?"

But Elaine was clearly on a roll. "I'll bet if the boys' basketball coach could have recruited her, he would have. You guys were *so* bad! Never won a single game."

"We did, too. One or two, anyway. Stop talking and hit the shower, then go to bed. Sleep off all that booze and forget about Norm. You were too good for him."

Elaine's crooked grin disappeared in a look so sad Chris wanted to hug his twin, but she stumbled back into her bedroom and began to pull her blouse over her head.

"I'm leaving," he announced. "Lock up behind me, sis."

"Yeah, yeah," she muttered.

Chris drove home, his thoughts swirling around what Elaine had said about Teddy. In those killer shoes, Teddy had towered over that douche bag Lawson. *Even I had to look up.* And the dress she was wearing, its brown tone reminded him of milk chocolate, setting off the brightness of her red curls as they rested on her shoulders or slid down past the soft folds of her neckline beyond her breasts. Elaine was right. Teddy definitely was a looker in that outfit.

Not at all like at the jobsite, when she was showing one of the rookie painters how to operate a sprayer or Flint how to reload a nail gun. In her bib overalls and flannel shirts, she had always been just one of the guys. All the more so, with her red curls stuck up under a baseball cap.

If I hadn't sworn off women ... Chris shook his head as if to banish the outrageous thought. Why was he going there? He imagined what the other men in his crew would think if they suspected he wanted to date Teddy. Not that he hadn't known she was a woman before now. He just hadn't let his mind drift in that direction. Maybe because his crew never did, either.

Except for Axel. He'd refused to accept Teddy's leadership when Chris was laid up with a bad shoulder and Val made crew assignments. *I need to get back to Val, find out if Axel's minding his manners, leaving Teddy alone.*

But the image of Teddy in that dress clung to him, and probably had stayed with Junior, too. Those curves he, Christopher James Lambert, had been oblivious to, continued to tease in a way he didn't want to be teased. At least not until after he'd settled whatever his responsibilities were toward Bambi and that baby of hers. His. Or someone's.

~ ~ ~

Chris's call to his insurance adjuster two days later yielded another frustrating delay. He was tired of holding off rebuilding his shop, especially after he'd received three new inquiries about furniture jobs.

He pulled out a blank piece of paper and began to scribble numbers. The totals he came up with would set him back at least six months' worth of construction profits. He leaned back in his chair for a minute, then reached into his center desk drawer and pulled out the bank book recording the monies in his trust. *I wouldn't have to wait if I use what's left of Grandpop's trust.*

He'd applied a portion of that money to buy his work truck and some of the equipment and tools he needed for his furniture business. But what remained of the trust fund wasn't going to cover a complete rebuild. Sure, he could replace most of the tools he'd lost, like his lathe. And his miter saw, sabre saw, router, doweling jigs, planes, sanders, bevel gauge and chisels and the myriad other tools he'd added a little at a time, whose replacement cost he'd never really paid much attention to. Not so now, when he no longer had them. The last time he'd wandered around the debris pile before he began the first of num-erous hauls to the dump, he'd picked up a melted plastic handle of what he guessed had been a screwdriver. He was keeping the odd-shaped remnant as a memento of the fire, a reminder of what he hoped never occurred again.

He added a table saw to the list of necessary tools. His grandfather's old work bench was about the only thing that had survived, though it, too, sported burn scars. He hated the thought of replacing it. He'd plane away the damaged portions of the legs of his grandfather's bench and where it had been scorched from falling timber. Then he'd continue using it, a tribute to the old man who had willed him the table and encouraged Chris when he'd shown an interest in woodworking.

He glanced at his buzzing phone and answered, "Yeah, Fletch, what do you want?"

"Why are you in such a downer mood?"

"Still waiting for the insurance money. I need it to replace my tools and rebuild the shop."

"What about the rest of your trust fund?"

"I just checked, but it won't cover more than half; maybe less, depending on the tools I replace."

"It's what Grandpop would want you to use it for. If you don't go that route, what about a loan?"

"I doubt the bank will lend me more than what I already owe. I toyed with getting a mortgage on my truck, but its value doesn't support it. If only the insurance company would get off dead-center …"

"What about the family? I could—"

"Don't go there, Fletch. You know how I feel about asking for money from Mom and Dad, or you. You have your own family to take care of. You and Lexi just bought that house and with her recent medical bills—"

"Our insurance is covering what happened to Lexi."

"Yeah, well. I'm not going that get-a-loan-from-the-family route. I need to do this on my own."

"You mean so Dad doesn't beat up on you again for not getting a college education?"

"He would, too." Chris huffed.

"How's the build-out of that neighborhood going?"

"On schedule. If I could figure out how to get my crew to work a little faster without cutting corners, we could start maybe two more houses by the end of the month instead of next month. The sooner we get them finished and sold, the more profit I'll have. As soon as I can see my way clear to a stronger bottom line, I'll talk to Paige at the bank and see what I can arrange."

Fletcher scoffed. "Having a former girlfriend as your banker has to come in handy."

"That's not why I went to her. Besides, she's married and handling lots of commercial lending since old man Collins retired."

"My apologies for inferring there was another reason you'd see her." Fletcher laughed, then said, "Man, you're touchy these days. Because of Bailee, I'm guessing."

"She showed up again, at my jobsite. Ran into Teddy and gave her an earful. I figure it won't be long before everyone knows she's in the family way. Why can't you *do* something about that?" Chris's gut churned, imagining Teddy's disappointment, maybe even scorn. He suspected he'd lost the respect of his best female friend.

"What did she say? Ms. Crawford, I mean," Fletcher clarified.

"Demanded to know why I told *you* about her … condition."

"Guess that means she received my letter."

"God, Fletch. Could my life be any more in the toilet? First the fire and losing most of the furniture I was getting ready to deliver, then Bambi barging in, and the insurance people *still* not handing over the money I need to rebuild?" He ran a hand through his hair. When he encountered a snarl, he jerked his fingers free, resulting in yanking out a tuft of hair just above his left ear. Which made his scalp burn.

"Hey, look on the bright side. Nobody was badly hurt, and you've still got your construction work. Speaking of, maybe if you hired a few more people, you could build those homes faster."

"Easier said than done. Good people aren't exactly walking around begging to be hired. Of the last two rookies on my crew, only one of them is worth keeping. Flint's good and he wants to learn more, but I just hired Yancy to do clean-up. The other guy is practically worthless. I've only kept him on because I need what he *can* do, even if it isn't all that much."

After Fletcher rang off, Chris slid his phone into his pocket and reached for his coffee mug, its contents cold. While he rinsed it out, he ran through his contacts list until he found Flint's name, and left him a text. That done, he called Val and said they needed to meet to revise their plan for completing the neighborhood build-out. After which he talked to the developer, and asked him to light a fire under the realtor so they could line up more buyers who might want to customize and bring in more money for Chris and his crew. With one custom house finished and its owners in residence, two homes moving along but as yet unfinished and unsold, there remained another eleven lots to fill with homes.

~ ~ ~

After their lunch meeting on Monday, Val and Chris returned to the site in time to hear Teddy yell, "You heard me! No! You're fired! Now get off the property before I call the cops!"

"What the hell?" Chris said.

Val shook his head. "Axel must've crossed the line again. We should have canned him weeks ago."

As if Val's words had conjured up the worker in question, Axel slouched out the door of Number four, followed by the rest of the crew. The noise had also attracted the attention of the men working in Number three, some of whom hung out the upstairs windows, taking in the scene below.

Axel turned and raised his fists as he confronted Teddy on the porch. "You can't tell me what to do, bitch."

"I can, I did, and you're gone! As of now. You're a lousy worker, Axel. A ten-year-old could do better." Teddy's braid uncoiled and swung over her shoulder as she spun on the man. "Chris never should've hired you. You've messed up for the last time."

Even as Chris broke into a run, Axel grabbed her braid and yanked, pulling Teddy off balance and kicking her knee, sending her sprawling to the ground.

Huey ran out of the doorway at Number three, looking like he intended to tackle Axel.

"No, Huey! Leave 'em alone," Chris said, blocking his progress. "Teddy will take care of this."

"But, boss—"

Lowering his voice, Chris warned. "Listen to me. She'll cut you a new one if you interfere. Axel was part of her crew. If she says he's fired, let her handle it."

While Huey stood on the porch, grumbling under his breath, Teddy launched herself off the ground. Her head plowed into Axel's crotch. He expelled his breath with a pained *Ooomph*. She wrapped her arms around the man's legs, propelling him backward and into a puddle that splashed mud in all directions.

Laughter rose up from the men around the construction site.

Before Axel could scramble to his feet, Teddy grabbed his right arm, twisted it behind him and rolled him onto his face. She shoved his head into the mud once, twice, three times, stopping only when he coughed out a choked yell that he couldn't breathe.

Hauling him to his feet, she shoved him in the direction of his beater truck. "Chris will *mail* your check so nobody has to look at your sorry face again. Now, get out of my sight!"

She stepped back and wiped her arm across her forehead, adding another smear of mud across her cheek.

Applause from the windows of Number four and the front door of Number two caused her to look over her shoulder, her face turning all shades of crimson as Axel drove off the work site.

"Show's over, guys," Chris called out, wanting to spare Teddy more embarrassment.

He handed her the oversized handkerchief he'd stuffed in his chest pocket that morning.

She wiped her face again before handing it back to him. "Sorry I couldn't get him to go quieter, but he deserved his face in the mud."

"No argument from me. You can tell me what he did after we're finished for the day."

Teddy nodded. "But now we're down one man. Not that he was doing a full day's work. Even so …"

"Don't worry about it. It was your call. I'd rather be down one man with his poor work ethic than have to worry about you taking him down again."

The corners of her mouth quirked upward even as she wiped her hands down the front of her overalls.

~ ~ ~

The next day, Chris tossed his notebook into the cab of his truck. Two men had called in sick and another had asked to come in late because his girlfriend was in labor. Which probably meant he wouldn't be showing up at all that day, maybe not even the next. Chris looked around, aware of the sounds of the rest of his crew already hard at work. Being this short-handed was a worry, even if the people he had left were experienced and trustworthy.

If only he could keep his mind on the job. The image of Teddy in that dress at the restaurant days earlier continued to distract him. He wondered if she wore lacy undies under that flannel shirt and those baggy work pants with the multiple pockets that bulged with small tools. A pair of hammers dangled from the belt hugging her waist.

"How close are we to staying on schedule?" she'd asked that morning.

"Not as good as last week. We're three more men down right now, so I had Flint work with me today. Windows will arrive tomorrow. He's set them in place before, so I'll have him take that on. Is Yancy coming over after school today?"

She nodded.

"Good. The Realtor sold Number three over the weekend, which means we'll have to fast-track it, even short-handed. I'll ask Val to super that job. I want you to take two of the men and start framing up Number seven, now that the foundation's in."

"We need more lumber."

"Another load's already scheduled. Watch for the truck, tell them where to park. Half near Number seven, the rest across the street next to the Poindexters' place, but *not* on their lawn or we'll hear about it from the missus."

Teddy gave him a thumbs-up.

"You're working nights on their new door?"

"Yes, but I'd rather not talk about it. So no one spills the beans." As if anticipating his next question, she added, "I swore Yance to secrecy, since he tends to yammer at the guys when he's here. Especially after he said Val was going to show him how to work a nail gun."

"You worried about that?"

"Not if he learns from Val or you."

"Yeah, well, I told Yancy we'd only teach him more skills if he asked. He claims if he can do what you do, you can get back to your carving and stained-glass work."

"Oh, yeah? My kid brother's looking out for me." She grinned. "Nice." Teddy shifted her belt on her hips and headed toward the house two doors down.

~ ~ ~

Late that afternoon, Yancy leaned the broom against the wall and grinned at Chris and Val as they walked in where he'd been sweeping.

"All done, boss. Before you head out, will Val show me how to use a nail gun, like he promised?"

Chris chuckled. "You cleaned up that other house? And the presale across the street?"

"Yep. I waited till all the men were gone so I wouldn't have to go back again. Only people here are you two and me. And Teddy." Yancy glanced out the window. "She's still at Number three. Said she wanted to do a final check on the paint job."

Chris walked outside and pointed to a piece of plywood propped against the exterior wall. He handed over his nail gun. "It's all yours, Val."

Val palmed the equipment. "Okay, Yancy." He motioned for the boy to stand closer. "You see how this plywood was placed, the nails in a straight line centered on the upright?" He pointed to the nearest wall not yet completed.

Yancy nodded.

"Okay. What you need to remember is that the gun does the work. All you do is place it where you want the nail to go. Hold it perpendicular to the stud so the nail goes in straight, not at an angle. Watch me." Val demonstrated by placing three nails in quick succession into the plywood. "I'll do three more. Then you can set the next piece."

Chris watched as Val eyed the plywood, squeezed the trigger on the nail gun, the sound telling both men that the nail went in true. "See? Easy." With the second nail, Val pulled the trigger but immediately yelled, "Aghh!" He grabbed his hand. The nail gun fell and hit the ground, barely missing the toe of his boot.

Chris jerked and straightened. *Oh, shit.* A nail protruded from the fleshy part of Val's hand, between his thumb and first finger, the wound oozing blood.

"Criminy! What happened?" Yancy yelled, his face turning a pasty white.

"Shit, shit, shit." Val, white-faced, spit out the words, looking like he was fighting not to pass out.

"What do we do?" Yancy asked. "Want me to get Teddy?"

Chris heard running steps from the nearby house.

Teddy's head appeared from around the corner of the structure. "Holy moley, Val."

"Let's get him to Urgent Care," Chris said.

Teddy stepped closer and bent over the injured man. "Can you walk, Val? Yancy, help him up. Other side," Teddy order-ed. "Try not to jostle his arm." She reached down to assist Val into a standing position.

"That sound when the nail hit. It wasn't like the others," Yancy said.

"Probably hit a knot in the two-by-four," Chris explained as Teddy and Yancy hauled Val to his feet. "I'll drive."

They walked Val around the corner of the house.

~ ~ ~

Minutes later, Val was ushered into a room at the clinic, where a doctor applied a local anesthetic, irrigated the wound, removed the protruding nail, and bandaged his hand.

Sometime later, determined to show everyone that he could manage under his own power, Val walked into the waiting room and waved at Chris, Yancy and Teddy, who were huddled together in the waiting area. "Let's go."

Chris pushed the door open. Yancy and Teddy followed Val outside.

"How long do you think he's going to be out of commission?" Teddy asked.

"At least a week. Maybe more. If it's like when I did something similar, he's probably going to have to come back for the doc to check him in forty-eight hours."

"For infection?"

"Probably."

"That nail didn't hit a bone?"

"Not from the way it looked, or how Val acted."

Yancy's eyes widened. "I never guessed you might nail your own hand. That thing's more dangerous than it looks. Does it happen a lot?"

Chris coughed. "Not an everyday thing. Just goes to show that you can get hurt on the job. You still want to handle a nail gun?"

"Did Val do something wrong?"

"No. Like I said, he probably hit a knot in the stud, which is why the nail ricocheted back into his hand."

Yancy glanced in Teddy's direction. "I still want to learn how to do it. Maybe on another house?"

His sister laughed softly. "Why don't you stick to sweeping up, Yance? After Val is back, he'll teach you. Or you can help the painting crew, along with sweeping up. No wood knots to worry about with a paint sprayer or a brush."

"That ever happened to you, sis?"

Teddy shook her head. "Like Chris said, an occupational hazard. First time it's happened this year."

Chris closed his eyes at the setback Val's injury represented. The way he figured it, Val would lose a week when he could do nothing more than supervise. How was he going to get that presale done on time without taking men off the other two houses that were half-done? And if he did that, how much would that change of plans set him back? This year was turning out to be a real nightmare.

Eleven

Chris stood in the doorway of Number five, pleased with what had been accomplished, even though he was short of manpower. Reviewing the work after his crew had left gave him an opportunity to create a checklist for next week's goals. But then he saw that he wasn't alone. Teddy walked out of Number seven, heading for her car. She had her head down, like she was thinking hard about something. He was about to call her name when Bambi walked around the corner and approached Teddy.

Oh, shit. Not again.

Teddy glanced up and spied Chris. She edged away from Bambi and pointed toward him, sending Bambi in his direction.

Time to set her straight, hopefully for the last time. Chris approached Bambi. "Didn't Fletcher tell you not to come here again? If you have something to say to me, you go through my lawyer."

She pouted then raised her voice, her hands on her hips. "I don't care what he said, what he wrote. It's not fair that you won't talk to me." As if contemplating her next words, she paused, then added, "You'd have a lot more money for me and what I've been going through if you didn't have to pay a lawyer, Chris."

I should have guessed it would come down to money. "We don't even know if that baby is mine yet. And—" *Can't tell her that. TMI.* "You need to lower your voice if you don't want anyone to know about" —he motioned to her abdomen— "you know, especially around here." Was her belly more prominent than the last time she'd shown up, or was he imagining things? "My crew isn't that great at keeping secrets. If they see you, it's gonna be all over town by dinner."

"Why do you think I came here so late in the day? You think I'm stupid, Chris?" her voice rose higher, her erratically waving hands reflecting her agitation. "Who's here besides us and that girl? She's the only one who's *ever* here when you're not. Even when you *are* here, supposedly by yourself." Bambi grimaced. "I'll bet she's your girlfriend, isn't she?" Her voice rose. "And you're sleeping with her! Were you sleeping with her even before you dumped me?" Bambi screamed the question.

Chris stepped toward Bambi and placed a hand on her arm, determined to get her to shut up, to leave the jobsite. "You need to leave. Now. And stop insinuating things that aren't true."

He glanced at Teddy, who had climbed into her car. She appeared to be watching him and Bambi. Had she heard the woman's accusations? Chris's gut clutched.

Bambi shouted as they passed Teddy's car. "Don't expect him to stick with you. That's not his style, Mr. Bigshot Lambert."

"Shut up, Bambi! Where'd you park?"

"I ran out of gas. Had to walk the last two blocks." She started to sniffle. "Out of money, too."

Chris waited for Teddy to back out of the muddy driveway and turn onto the main street. She gave him a searching look as she passed.

What does she think of me now? Probably nothing good, if she believes Bambi.

"Come on, then. I'll drive you home. I have a spare gas tank. I'll fill it and put some gas in your car. That'll at least get you three gallons."

"Don't bother," she pouted, jerking her arm from his grasp. "I'd rather walk."

"But you live all the way across town."

"Since when do you care?" Tears created muddy streaks down her cheeks. "Maybe if I walk, I can get rid of this stomachache. I must have eaten something I shouldn't have. While I was waiting to talk to you." She pressed a hand against her belly before picking up her pace and darting into the intersection.

Chris paused at the corner, debating whether to follow Bambi, before guilt forced him to conclude he should drive her home. He turned to go back for his truck, but a flash of green caught his eye.

He glanced to the right. One of the oversized city buses was lumbering toward the corner. With a green light giving the big vehicle the right-of-way, it didn't look like it was going to stop for the woman now more than halfway across the street.

"Bambi, watch out!" Chris raced after her and shoved her toward the curb as the bus bore down on him, its brakes screaming. *Not going to make it,* he thought as he tried to leap out of the way.

His body slammed into the front of the bus, and a scalding pain shot up Chris's left leg. His head collided with the windshield, stunning him. Next thing he knew, Chris was floating through the air, away from the sound of screeching brakes. But it was only when the back of his head smashed into something that he spiraled into a black hole.

~ ~ ~

Wooziness surrounded Chris in a cocoon of cotton before pain that felt like shards of glass in his gut, his head, and his left leg took over. Especially his leg. He groaned and tried to shift his body, tried to raise an arm, but he couldn't seem to move. *Am I paralyzed?* That thought, accompanied by a quick sucking in of air, was interrupted by a bright light that seemed intent on boring through his lids. And people were talking. *Where am I?*

"His name is Christopher Lambert," a woman, whose voice sounded familiar, said somewhere near his right side.

Who is she? Who's she talking to? Chris moaned as he recalled the bus hurtling at him at nine hundred miles an hour. Had it passed through him? Since he couldn't move, did that mean he was dead? But that couldn't be right. He hurt all over. If he was dead, he wouldn't feel anything, would he?

"Sounds like he's coming around."

A man's voice, not one he recognized.

"Mr. Lambert? Open your eyes. How are you feeling? What day is it?"

Hammers pounded Chris's temples as light bored into his skull again. Had he stopped the bus with his head?

"Huh? Saturday? Friday? Who cares? Jesus. My leg's killing me."

"You had a fight with a bus. It won." Someone nearby chuckled.

You wouldn't think it was so funny if it was you. Chris tried to raise his arms, but as hard as he flexed, nothing happened. "Why can't I move?"

"You're strapped down, Chris. So we can attend to you. Try to relax." That woman again.

A man asked, "What's the name of the woman you shoved out of the way?"

He'd been with a woman? He struggled to remember. Hadn't he gone to the jobsite? Teddy? He'd shoved Teddy? But why? Wouldn't she have shoved him back? Was that why he hurt so much? Like when they were in fifth grade, fighting over the teeter-totter in the park.

"She's here?" If only the lights weren't so bright. He squeezed his lids against that awful light.

"Her name, Mr. Lambert," the man ordered.

"Teddy? I shoved her? But she's my best friend."

"That's oh for two, Doc." Another man? "EMTs said he wasn't making any sense when they were bringing him in."

"One more try," the man said.

He's a doctor? I'm in the hospital?

"Who's the President of the United States, Mr. Lambert?"

"I pushed him, too? That no-good SOB? What's he doing here?"

Male voice again, chuckling. "Seems he's back. Mr. Lambert, open your eyes."

"You're in the ER, Chris." Woman's voice.

Why can't I remember who she is?

Chris dared to squint with one eye and a flash of light seared his brain. He groaned. "You trying to kill me?"

"Just checking your pupils. That's better. Equal and reactive."

"My leg hurts like hell."

"Which one?"

"Both, but especially my left one. Can't you do something about that?"

"You broke it. Hang on."

Chris floated away into darkness.

~ ~ ~

Pale light filtered into the room from a window that didn't belong on that wall. Chris turned his head away from the light and groaned.

"Finally. Wake up, bro." Fletcher leaned over the bed and stared into Chris's face. "You look like hell. Probably feel like it, too. Since when do you try to stop a bus with your body? Next time, wave it down and if it doesn't stop, get out of the way."

"I did that? No wonder I hurt."

"Know where you are?"

"What's my leg doing in the air?" Chris pointed to the contraption dangling from the ceiling that held his left leg above his head.

"You broke it. Badly. Both bones in your lower leg."

Chris raised a hand then let it drop back onto the bed. "You're the only one here, Fletch?"

"After surgery, you were in ICU for a while. We sent Mom and Dad home. Deb and Todd saw you when you first came up here, but they reported you weren't making a lot of sense. Eden should be back soon with Elaine. She said Mom wouldn't stop crying. Logan's holding down the fort with Hale, watching the little kids. Probably not happily."

"What do you know?"

"According to the doctor, you've got three cracked ribs, a concussion and you broke your tibia and fibula. Looks like you're out of commission for a while."

Chris grimaced. "No way. I've got too much to do not to work. I'm already down three men."

"Too bad about that, but you're not going to be building houses until you're off crutches and a cast or boot or whatever it is they use these days for broken legs. I called Val. He said he and Teddy will take care of things while you recover. The orthopedist put your leg back together with screws and a rod. Which could mean you might set off alarms at the airport, the courthouse, wherever there's security. Depends on the kind of metal they used."

"Crap. Did he say how long before I can walk again?"

"Didn't think to ask. But I have other news." Fletcher relaxed into his chair. "About Bambi, according to Paula, your favorite ER nurse. Remember her from high school? Never mind about that. She remembers you. Said you mentioned things when you were floating in and out of consciousness." He unsuccessfully stifled a chuckle.

"Paula! If she was in the ER, *that's* who I couldn't remember." Chris groaned. "Bambi's here, too?"

"Not likely by now. Before Deb went home, she talked to Paula. It seems you pushed Bambi out of the way of the bus, and she's banged up some. Has a scraped up back and she's not pregnant. But not from when you shoved her out of the way. Paula said she might have been planning to tell you when she showed up at your construction site."

"Huh?"

Fletcher leaned back in the chair near Chris's bed. "Seems she likely wasn't ever really pregnant, or maybe that she wanted to think she was because she hadn't had a period in a few months. Paula said stress will do that. Bambi didn't say you were off the pregnancy hook?"

"No."

"One of the witnesses to your heroics said the two of you were arguing pretty fiercely right before Bambi headed across the street."

Chris slid a hand to the back of his head and flinched when he touched a lump. "That I remember. In between giving me what-for, she complained that her belly hurt, said she ate something that disagreed with her. Maybe she was getting ready to."

"Paula said she was probably cramping when she was brought in. While she was here, she started bleeding. They checked her out. But it was the usual. You know, woman stuff." Fletcher stared at Chris.

Silence reigned as Chris absorbed that unexpected news. "But didn't she say a doctor confirmed her pregnancy?"

"A doctor I couldn't find. She might have made that up."

Chris felt Fletcher's glance on his face.

"You look kind of sad, bro. I'd have figured you'd be relieved."

"I am. It's just that I was getting used to the idea of maybe having a kid, even if it wasn't how I wanted to have one. You know, with her."

Fletcher patted Chris's right leg. "You have a big heart, bro. Too bad everyone seems to think you're a player."

"You know that's not true."

"Yeah. You just like women and they like you." Fletcher rose from his seat. "Remember what the docs asked you in the ER? To see if your brain was functioning?"

"No."

"You mentioned Teddy."

"I did?"

Fletcher grinned. "Paula said you made some funny responses to the docs' questions."

Chris nodded. "Must have been outta my head. When can I leave here?"

"No idea. One of the docs said three or four days. Probably depends on how well you can manage the crutches. The nurse said they're going to get you up pretty soon. Don't know if that's later today or tomorrow. You'll have to ask."

"But my leg's in a sling." Chris pointed toward the contraption keeping his leg elevated.

"Hey, talk to your nurse. She told Mom you're going to need help at home—getting out of bed, taking a piss, eating, that sort of thing."

Chris grimaced. "Mom said she'd take care of it?"

Fletcher grinned. "Got it in one. You're going to put a crimp in Dad's golf game if he has to stay home to help her out. Mom isn't strong enough to get you out of bed by herself, which means she'll probably insist on hiring a nurse to help when you come home. Looks like you'll be using crutches for a while. Mom'll probably put you in Logan's room since you won't be able to climb stairs."

"How'm I going to even get in their house? This boot thing is up above my knee, and they've got stairs. Even into the kitchen."

"Good point. Your place is better, only one story. Maybe you should mention that to the doc when he comes in."

"If I can go back to my place, maybe the sisters will bring me food?" Chris asked, hopeful he wouldn't have to be helped by Iona. "No way do I want Mom moving in and babying me."

"Hale has a bet going—he says you'll be stuck here for a week, because of that big bump on your head. Eden thinks the doctors will kick you out sooner. They don't keep people here all that long anymore. We'll know you're ready to leave when you stop flirting with the nurses."

Chris's stomach growled. "What time is it? I'm hungry."

The door opened. "Good morning, Mr. Lambert." A forty-something nurse with salt-and-pepper hair sounded way too cheery. She held a tray that Chris hoped held food. "It's time for your breakfast and other activities after that."

Fletcher grinned. "I'll leave you to it, bro. We plugged in your cell, so it should be fully charged. In there." He pointed to the drawer in a table next to the bed. "Val said he'll stop by later today. Or maybe Teddy. To talk business."

Chris nodded, then flinched when the nurse pulled him more upright, adjusted his pillow and the head of his bed.

"See that button?" She pointed to the object attached to the edge of his pillow. "If you need pain relief, punch it once. It'll make you feel better."

At the stabs of pain in his chest, he said, "How about if I give it two or three hits? So I don't feel what I'm feeling now?"

"You only get so much pain relief, no matter how many times you try within a certain time period." She grinned. "You're probably feeling those cracked ribs. Here's a hint. Punch the button and after you feel better, practice taking deep breaths."

"Easy for you to say."

The nurse removed the covers from the plates holding his breakfast. "The doctor should be in shortly. We'll be helping you move from the bed to the chair after you have breakfast, and you're cleaned up."

He glanced again at the sling holding up his leg. "You've got to be kidding."

"I don't kid, Mr. Lambert," she replied, her expression implying that she brooked no nonsense from her patients.

Chris chose not to argue the point. He concluded there'd be no flirting with that particular nurse. He'd concentrate on convincing the doctor to spring him. Three bites of what had looked and smelled inviting no longer appealed. He pushed aside his breakfast tray. Even after a punch of his drug button, his chest continued to ache and his elevated leg throbbed. Rather than use the call button for the nurse, he leaned his head against the pillow and tried to ignore the pounding in his head, made worse if he turned his head quickly. Chris closed his eyes and started counting backwards from one hundred, hoping he wouldn't get past fifty before the pain meds kicked in.

Twelve

Teddy loosened her braid and rubbed her neck. The last couple of days had been crazy. Chris was in the hospital. She'd chosen to stay away, not wanting to run into the elder Mrs. Lambert.

But Val stayed in touch with the family and then Elaine called to tell her that Chris would be available for nonfamily visitors now that he was in a regular room.

The sounds of the shower confirmed that Yancy must have finished his homework and was getting ready for bed. Teddy glanced at the clock. *An hour later than he usually crashes.*

"You going to bed, Yance?"

"Yeah. What's gonna happen now that Chris can't work?"

"The rest of us will pick up the slack. Job's still there, waiting to be done."

"But you guys are short of men. Can I do more than clean?"

"I thought you were already part of the painting crew. Didn't Huey show you how to tape off the windows?"

"Yeah."

"Well, keep doing that. If Val's happy you're part of Huey's crew, Chris will be happy, too. Night, Yance." Teddy freed her hair from its thick braid, fluffing the strands until her hair lay down her back.

She picked up her phone. "Val? I hope it's not too late to talk."

"No. Is this about Chris and the job?"

"More about what we're going to do. Him being hurt puts us that much lower in manpower."

"I was hoping you'd go see him at the hospital tomorrow so I can go straight to the jobsite, make sure everyone is pitching in."

"Yancy says he'll stay on the painting crew. Not just doing clean-up."

Val chuckled. "He's turned into a good worker. Reliable."

"What about your hand?"

"It's still sore, but I can use it more than I could last week. By Monday, I should be back to regular work. You and I need to put our heads together, figure out how to keep to the completion schedule."

"Monet's bakery opens at seven. Let's meet there for coffee and a sweet. Planning's easier over cinnamon rolls."

Teddy pulled out a sheet of paper and wrote down the names of Chris's employees. She ran a line through the names of the two guys out sick and Benny. And a hatched line through Val's name. He could supervise and direct traffic, make sure there was space for the trucks delivering lumber and other supplies. But he wouldn't be doing much hammering or sawing or using the nail gun for another week.

House Number two was the closest to being finished, but it didn't yet have a buyer. Maybe they could take the crew off it while the electricians were in there, and the plumbers.

In House Number four, the upstairs was ready be hung with drywall and taped off. With Flint on that crew, other guys could work downstairs, hanging the upper cabinets in the kitchen along with the pantry shelves.

That left the Lot three presale. Chris had said he wanted it completed as soon as possible, even though it hadn't been started at the same time as Number two. Was it ready for carpet? She'd have to check. Ditto regarding the plumbing work. Had all the shower doors and mirrors been hung? *I'm good with detail work. I'll make sure the drywall is good and make any touch-ups after the painting crew finishes up.* She'd give Val the check-off list she'd created. He didn't need two hands to make sure everything was done in the presale.

Teddy tossed her clothes into the hamper, turned out the light, and stared at the ceiling after climbing into bed. Not that she could see anything in the dark, but she couldn't seem to relax. First the muscles in her back tensed, then those in her arms and shoulders and then her toes and legs. She rolled over, first onto her right side then her left. Finally, she tossed the blankets off. Maybe she'd do some push-ups, pull-ups. Anything to deliberately tighten and then relax her muscles.

She kept seeing the pain reflected in the flex of Val's jaw after the nail had penetrated his hand, the intensity of his gaze when he'd glanced her way. He had to be really hurting if the paleness of his forehead and how stiffly he held himself as they drove to the urgent care center was any indication. And then how carefully he'd supported his wrist when Yancy opened the car door.

Then there was Chris. From what she'd heard from Fletcher, he wasn't going to have a quick recovery. Cracked ribs? A badly broken leg? Concussion? He wasn't one to sit on the sidelines. He'd probably be anxious to get back to work, but how could he? It was up to her and Val to keep things moving. If only they could with such a small crew.

~ ~ ~

Teddy stared back at Val before reaching for the coffee mug he'd placed in front of her, along with one of Monet's locally famous cinnamon rolls.

"Do you know what happened?" Teddy asked.

"I heard he was trying to protect a woman. They were brought in about the same time. It'd be just like Chris to step into the street to try to stop a bus."

Teddy's heart sped up. "Is she all right? If it was his girlfriend, I was on the job when they left. Maybe if I'd stayed longer, I could have helped."

Val shrugged. "Paula heard the woman wasn't watching where she was going. And they were arguing pretty hot and heavy." He sipped his coffee. "But we didn't come here to talk about how Chris got hurt." He pointed to the paper Teddy had placed on the table. "What've you got there?"

"Some notes I jotted down. I was thinking we'd divvy up the work this way for a few days. Think Chris'll try to come back once he's on crutches?"

Val chuckled. "I'm bettin' he's going to come back as soon as he can, even if he shouldn't." He drained his coffee mug. "You know the family, right?"

"Mostly him and his twin sister. We graduated from high school together. Not that Elaine and I are close." *Not like I am with Chris.* "Why do you ask?"

"Since he probably won't come clean if you ask him, maybe you could ask his sister to keep us informed. Like, when he leaves the hospital, is given the go-ahead to come back to work. That sort of thing. Can't remember if Paula said which leg he broke, but if it's his right, he'll have trouble driving his big work rig."

Val set his mug to one side. "As good as our crew is, what we really need is more bodies."

Teddy nodded. "Maybe we should ask Flint if he knows anybody in his classes at the community college. I know he's going for an engineering degree, but he likes working with us. Could be some of his classmates might be interested in getting on-the-job training, like him."

Val poured Teddy a refill from the carafe Monet left at their table. "Good idea. Why don't you check the tech school? Students there might like to gain practical experience, too."

Teddy leaned back in her chair. "Okay."

Val grinned. "Don't know why we didn't think of this earlier. I'll get with Flint before I check on Number two. And I'll have Huey head up the work on the presale. If you stick with Number four, since it's not quite as far along, that should keep things moving. Will you see about scheduling the landscaper, maybe by the end of the week?"

"Don't we need the go-ahead from the developer?"

"Not necessary," Val replied. "Chris talked to him a couple days ago. He already arranged with the Realtor to hold open houses every weekend, now that Number four is practically done."

Teddy grinned. "Then let's hire more guys. Chris'll be pleased that we aren't letting things slow down. By early summer, he should be on his feet again. Even if he has to do stuff sitting down for a while." She finished her cinnamon roll and wiped her fingers.

"Now that that's decided, let's see who we can come up with. When are you going to see Chris?"

"Tonight. After we hire more people. I'd like to be able to tell him we're on top of things."

Teddy spent the next two hours talking to the instructors at the tech school, pleased that both pointed out five different students who were interested in signing up for on-the-job learning. She returned to the jobsite. When she reported her success, Val grinned and recounted that Flint had talked to four guys, all of whom had asked him where he was working, and seemed interested in gaining similar experience.

"That's great. With my recruits from the tech school, maybe as many as four or five, we should be able to bring them up to speed quickly. We'll know more come Saturday. I told their instructors we've scheduled a here's-what-we-do session for that day. Hope you don't mind that I did that without checking with you first."

"That was smart." Val beamed. "I'll ask Huey to come, too. He likes helping rookies. Flint, too. I'll tell him to let his friends know."

Things are looking up, Teddy thought. She rewound her braid into a coil on the top of her head. "If we can retain at least half of these people, we should be able to stay on track. Could you look over the foundation work at Number five while I check on the guys at Number three?"

"You got it."

Teddy couldn't stop grinning when she arrived home to grab a quick dinner before going to the hospital.

~ ~ ~

Elaine opened Chris's hospital room door. "Oh. Hi, Teddy. Come on in."

"Am I interrupting? I can come back later."

"No, I was just leaving."

"What smells so good?"

"Food I brought. Mom is convinced that hospital food makes a person sicker." Elaine laughed. "See you later, little brother."

"Little brother?" Teddy asked.

"I'm two minutes younger than her. She likes to rub it in."

Teddy placed a bouquet of blue-toned flowers on the tray next to the food basket.

Chris waved her into the seat vacated by Elaine. "You didn't have to bring me flowers."

"Isn't that what a person does when visiting someone in the hospital? Val's wife told us what you did. You know, trying to stop the bus. Saving Bambi from being hit. The guys said to tell you to get well fast."

When Chris's intense brown eyes settled on Teddy's face, she felt her cheeks warm.

"I hope you don't think bad of me. About Bambi, I mean. Turns out she never was pregnant."

"How do you feel about that? Relieved?"

"A little guilty, too." He ran his hand through his chocolate hair, his fingers calling attention to the blond sun-bleached streaks. "You and me, we've been friends forever. I don't want that to change. Don't want you to think I'm a prick, that I date every woman in town. The single ones, I mean. No married ones. Gawd! I'm making it seem worse, aren't I?"

Teddy swallowed, wishing her throat hadn't turned dry at the image of Chris in bed with buxom Bambi. "Of course not. I would never dream you'd date a married woman. Only the single ones." She forced a quick smile. *Even though you've never dated me, and I'm single.* She reached for his hand and squeezed his fingers.

"Hey, I'm kidding." But she felt her cheeks flame and hoped he hadn't noticed. "You're a guy. Guys date girls. And have sex. I never figured you for a virgin. After I heard what Bambi said, I chalked it up to bad luck that you were going to be a father, even though you weren't exactly aiming to start a family."

She offered him a glass of water and poured one for herself from the quart bottle on his side table. "Anyway, I came to tell you what Val and I did, so you won't worry."

Chris grimaced, shifted in the bed and punched a button near his right hand.

"Are you in a lot of pain?"

"My whole chest is one giant bruise."

She pointed to his elevated leg. "I guess Paula was right that it was a bad break. A hero's break."

"I'm no hero. Just stupid—for thinking I could outrun the bus, get out of the way in time." He turned his palm upward to grasp Teddy's hand. "Bambi and I weren't exactly talking nice to each other—which I guess you saw before you drove off. She was still arguing when she ran across the street." Chris reached around to punch the pillow behind his neck.

"Let me." Teddy adjusted the pillow.

"Thanks." Chris leaned his head back. "I'm starting to feel kind of woozy. Can you reach that button that lowers the head of the bed?"

"Sure. Tell me how much." Teddy released Chris's hand and adjusted the bed. "Any idea how long you're going to be here?"

"That depends on how well he follows orders," Fletcher answered.

Teddy whirled around, her heart thumping against her chest. "Oh. Hi, Fletcher."

"I'm guessing you're here to cheer him up. So he's not the grouch he was this morning."

Teddy felt her cheeks heat again. "It's what friends do, I guess."

"How are you?" Before she could reply, Fletcher leaned closer and stage-whispered. "Keep talking, Teddy. First time I've seen a smile on his face since he started taking up this expensive bed space."

She glanced at Chris. "I was going to tell him what's happening on the job."

Chris shifted his hips and sucked in a breath, then winced. "How far behind are we?"

"Not at all. Val and I hired some new workers. They may not all stick, but we're hoping most of them will. So you don't have to worry about a thing. Everything's under control."

Fletcher waved. "I'll leave you to it. Later, Chris." He walked out of the room.

Chris chewed on the ham sandwich his mother had made. "Keep talking."

Teddy mentally reviewed what she wanted him to know, hoping her enthusiasm was reassuring. "Val said the realtor may have another sale contract signed before the end of the week. Probably the place next to the Poindexters'. They'll be happy about that. Less dust on that side of their place. Do you know when you're going home? Able to come see how we're doing?"

Chris's glance in her direction shifted. At first, he'd seemed to be really seeing her, but then it was like he'd drifted away. Was it because he'd punched that button?

"Hey, you here?" She waved a hand in front of Chris's face.

He blinked and focused again on her. "Sorry. I was thinking about ..." His cheeks turned pink under his dark scruff.

"Do you know when you're going home?"

"The doctor says maybe tomorrow or the next day. Depends on how well I'm walking."

"You're up already?"

Chris coughed and groaned. "They've had me up since the first day I got to this room. Not pleasant, but it wasn't as bad yesterday. Even walked down the hall with Fletcher on one side and Lexi on the other. Not that she would have been much help if I'd tipped over in her direction."

The nurse entered the room.

"Time for my torture session?" Chris asked.

The nurse chuckled. "You said it."

Teddy rose from her chair. "Don't worry about a thing, Chris. Val and I, the whole crew, we want you back soon. Even if all you can do is order us around." She grinned, leaned closer and gave him a quick peck on the cheek.

"What's that for?" he asked, placing a hand where her lips had touched his skin.

"From a friend. Since you're not exactly dating right now." She felt her own cheeks flush. "So you'll get better fast." She edged toward the door.

"Right." He waited until the nurse lowered his elevated leg onto the bed, then slid both limbs slowly toward the floor.

Teddy left, imagining him in her own bed after what she'd glimpsed before Chris awkwardly adjusted his hospital gown.

Thirteen

Chris was grateful that he was home, even if the words of the home health care nurse still rankled. *At least she isn't Mom,* although her actions implied she'd be just as intrusive.

He glanced her way when the woman—whose bulk conjured up a Marine drill sergeant—stuck her head past the half-open door of his bedroom.

"I'm fine. Don't need your help," he anticipated her question.

"I'll get you up for lunch in an hour. In the meantime, if you need anything, ring that bell." She pointed to the side table next to his bed and shut the door. Firmly. A metaphor for how she intended to rule his life, Chris sensed.

"Like you said before," he muttered, resentful that he'd been reduced to having to ring a bell for help. Not that he planned to follow orders. But the woman had propped his crutches next to the door. Deliberately out of reach, he fumed. So he'd *have* to ring that damn bell.

He was determined to hold off as long as possible. Maybe he'd try hopping to the door. The doctor had insisted that Chris avoid putting weight on his broken leg.

He closed his eyes and wondered if Teddy would stop by. The brief visits she or Val had been paying represented the best part of his days following his collision with the bus. Without exception, they'd reported how well construction was proceeding. Too bad Val wasn't around when Chris needed to get out of bed.

He recalled that friend-type peck Teddy had given him. Her lips were petal-soft. He wondered how they might feel melded to his lips, and realized with a mental jab that he'd never kissed her. *Why not?* She had womanly curves, even if they were hidden under her work clothes. He imagined what she might feel like if he held her close, maybe while she was wearing a dress like the one that had Junior Judge drooling.

Why hadn't he ever taken Teddy out? They had similar tastes. At least they used to. He recalled their arguing about their favorite characters from one of the Star Wars movies. She'd insisted Ewan McGregor was the better actor when paired against Hayden Christensen in the third episode of the long-running saga. Chris had said he didn't care, that the action was the real star of the movie. But they'd agreed that the franchise was worth seeing on the big screen at the local cineplex.

He sat up. *Time for a test.* He slid both legs toward the floor and stood up, bearing his weight on his right leg. His ribs ached and when he tried to straighten up on one leg, he wobbled. No way could he hop into the bathroom. He sat down on the bed, causing the springs to squeak.

The door opened and the woman he'd dubbed the dragon lady peered at him. "You need to go to the head?"

Right. Former marine or army. Didn't that just figure?

"No. Just trying to stand up."

She held out his crutches. "Use these. No weight-bearing, remember?"

He leaned back against his pillows. "Changed my mind." No way was he going to let her think she was in charge.

As if she'd read his mind, one corner of her thin lips quirked upward. "Uh-huh." She leaned the crutches next to the door and left.

Damn. I should have told her to stick them closer. But Dragon Lady probably knew he didn't want her help.

Teddy would help him, if he asked. And she wouldn't hold it over him. She'd be casual, like at the jobsite when she seemed to know ahead of time what he wanted her to do. She was good at anticipating things, kept the men working without getting bored. Changed up the teams so that even the rookies got a chance to try their hand at different jobs. Chris suspected that she and Val were doing that with the new guys. The girls, too.

Two more girls. On his crew. Were either of them curvier than Teddy, who was as tall as he was? Did they dress like her, making it hard to tell them from the guys in their work shirts and bib overalls or work pants? He'd considered it a good thing that his crew paid so little attention to Teddy, that she wasn't a distraction. Not like some of the women the realtor had paraded past when prospective buyers had insisted on stopping by while his crew was still working.

Only Axel had been obnoxious, making wolf whistles and comments loud enough for everyone to hear, including the women. But Teddy had shown him the door. Which must have really frosted that asshole, Chris concluded.

His cell phone buzzed and Teddy's name appeared. His heart thumped. He felt heat climb and then descend.

"Teddy. What's up?"

"We just got another presale. Val moved three guys over to Number six to speed it along a little faster."

"Good to know. You coming over, now that I'm home?"

"I think it's Val's turn."

A wave of disappointment settled in his gut.

"How hot is it out there?"

"Hot enough. I laid in more water. We don't want anyone passing out." He imagined her down to a sport bra. Not that she'd ever doffed her shirt like the guys did.

"Good idea." He paused. "Teddy?"

"Yeah?"

He let out the breath he'd been holding, daring himself to ask. "Never mind."

"Go ahead. Ask your question."

"Slipped my mind."

"Well, if you remember what it was, text me. Gotta go. Plumbers just showed up."

Chris watched as his cell phone darkened. *Now I'm a coward? Since when am I afraid to ask a woman out?* He wasn't going anywhere fast. Not on crutches. Using them might generate sympathetic stares that would only make him feel like a wuss. Teddy would probably tell him to ignore the people who stared. Because Teddy had his back. Always had. The big question was, would she go out with him? His heart thumped against his ribs at the thought that she might turn him down.

He reached for the bell.

"Yes, Mr. Lambert?"

"Any chance you could help me into the kitchen?"

The health care nurse smiled in a way that reminded Chris of a cat having spied an injured bird. "Certainly." She handed him his crutches. "Show me what you can do."

After he reached the table without incident, he called his physical therapist. "How soon can you work me in? I know it hasn't been a month yet, but I want to get going with those exercises you mentioned."

Maybe physical therapy torture would occupy his mind enough to keep him from thinking about Teddy and the bodily reactions he'd never before associated with her. He wanted to think it was related to his too-long sexual dry spell. But what if that wasn't the only reason?

~ ~ ~

Ten weeks later, Chris stood up. "You about done? I can take care of my own dirty dishes."

Lexi hit the button on the dishwasher, walked around the kitchen table and took a seat next to her brother-in-law. "Of course you can, but consider it my thank you for that gift you made me months ago." She reached in her pocket and pulled out the tiny piece of carefully shaped wood that anyone else would think was a little river stone. In Chris's mind, it was the tiny fetus Lexi had lost.

"Hey, you deserved it." At her heightened cheek color, and what looked like an attempt not to cry, Chris changed the subject. "Fletcher says you've been to The Bluff. You liked the food there, the view?"

"What's not to like? Why do you ask?"

"I'm having dinner there. I'm going to treat Val and his wife, and Teddy, to dinner. To celebrate what they accomplished while I was laid up." He chuckled when Lexi's brows arched. "They deserve a meal at the nicest restaurant in town."

"Most expensive one, too."

He nodded. "But they really stepped up, getting so much done. Adding more guys to my crew. We still have six of them, all excellent workers, Val says. Four guys and two women."

"I'll bet the women are just like Teddy. Serious about what they do, and better than the men at getting things done."

Chris nodded. "I may hire more of them. They're some of my best workers. Don't have to worry about their language, either."

Lexi grabbed her sweater. "I'm glad you're an equal opportunity employer." She grinned. "Now that your kitchen is spiffy again and it sounds like the dryer is done, too, all you have to do is fold the clean clothes. How does your leg feel now that you're out of that boot?"

"Can't believe it took almost ten weeks. It's still weak, even with those exercises the PT has me doing. But I'm going to hit the gym every day now that the boot's off."

Lexi giggled. "As long as you don't overdo. Have a nice dinner with your buddies."

Chris closed his eyes, imagining what Val and Teddy would say after his big announcement. They'd pulled his butt out of the fire after his losing fight with the bus. And the senior developer, Mr. Unruh, was singing the praises of Chris's team.

He'd received inquiries from three people wanting to discuss building custom houses, and another call had come in from a company interested in putting up a four-story office building just outside the downtown core of Pacific Knoll. That area had seen an influx of small businesses and wasn't far from some new residential areas. Chris wanted to make that part of town his own.

The insurance guy had finally come through with a check large enough for him to begin rebuilding his shop. He looked forward to having more time to build furniture, especially if his new partnership worked out. First on the agenda would be telling his previous furniture customers that he'd soon be available to replace what they'd already contracted him to build—as-suming they were still interested. Yep, life was definitely looking up.

He pushed himself upright. Time to get dressed for dinner. Val had said he and Paula would pick up Teddy and meet him at the restaurant. He'd decided to arrive early, to make sure they were seated in one of the private alcoves that overlooked the water. As he washed up, he hummed tunelessly to himself, trying out different ways to signal his intentions.

~ ~ ~

"There you are." Val arrived at Chris's table. "You must have tipped big to get these seats."

"Worth it, don't you think?" He pointed to the view of a ferry gliding across the dark waters toward the Olympic peninsula. "Hi, Paula. How are you?" His gaze took in Val's pretty wife in a burgundy dress that hugged her curves, a contrast to her ER scrubs. "I guess you didn't have to work tonight."

"I did," Val's wife replied. "But I was able to switch with someone. When Val said your invitation included me, no way I was going to miss this."

Chris looked past Val. "Where's Teddy? Didn't you pick her up?"

"Some guy stopped her as we were coming inside. She should be here any minute."

Chris scanned the restaurant and spotted Teddy, his breath leaving his lungs at how she looked in a black blouse with a high neck and see-through sleeves that seemed to float off her tanned arms, the blouse's color contrasting dramatically with her red hair. Her charcoal gray ankle-length skirt was patterned by swirly silvery threads that sparkled in the candlelight from the tables. The sandals on her feet seemed to consist of a pair of thin straps that mostly left her feet and rose-tinted toes bare.

Spoiling his view of her, however, was Lawson Collins, whose fingers surrounded her wrist, preventing Teddy from leaving his table. *That tool! Is he flirting with her? In front of the woman he's with?* The other person at Lawson's table was a statuesque blonde whose dress accentuated her large breasts, reminding Chris of Bambi. Her scowl implied she wasn't happy, perhaps because Lawson was talking with Teddy.

Chris debated approaching the other table and was about to do so when Teddy left Lawson's side and headed in his direction.

"What did he want?" Chris couldn't help asking.

Teddy's eyebrows rose. "He was just checking on when I'd be done with the door for his parents. With all the work Val and I had at the jobsite, I couldn't meet his original deadline, which Lawson didn't like. But I've been working on it almost every night for the last couple of weeks. Since his folks aren't around right now, he asked if I could hang the new door before they return. He said he'd bring me a key to the current doors."

"To your house?"

She shook her head. "I told him to bring it to our jobsite. That he could give it to Val if he doesn't see me."

"Or me." Chris glanced over his shoulder at Lawson, who had returned his focused gaze to his date's décolleté.

Teddy looked around. "This is a pretty nice place, Chris." She took her seat and reached for the napkin, folded to look like a crown on the plate in front of her.

Chris's mouth dried and his brain seemed to short out as he took in Teddy's subtle curves.

"Uh—" He coughed to clear the rasp that emerged. "Only the best for the best people on my team." He motioned for the nearby sommelier to approach. "Time for a toast."

The sommelier filled four flutes with champagne.

"This is really something," Val said. "Sure beats my usual beer at Brewskers after work. What exactly are we toasting?"

"Everything you and Teddy accomplished when I wasn't around. Old Man Unruh is singing our praises. He wants us to see about finishing off the neighborhood ASAP, even if it means we have to order in the foundations on the remaining lots earlier than planned. He said if we can get the roofs on, to take our time with interior work. He wants us to back off on the completion schedule. To make it only two, maybe three, houses at a time. Something about keeping the competition high between buyers. I said we could easily make those adjustments."

"Yeah, that's doable," Val confirmed.

In between sips and casual conversation, Chris encouraged his guests to order. As they ate their dinner, his gaze kept sliding over Teddy. Who knew she was such a knockout? Was it how she wore her hair, three tiny braids on either side that seemed to meet near the crown of her head, the rest of her long red curls sliding down her back except when she leaned forward and strands of her glossy hair slid over her shoulders? Or was it the cluster of thin silver bracelets she wore on one wrist?

Paula grinned at Teddy. "I see you took my suggestion to heart. When we talked about what to wear."

Teddy blushed. "I knew my usual jeans and shirts wouldn't work," she replied with a light laugh.

"You look lovely. So dramatic in black with your red hair. Me and my mousy brown mop could never pull that off."

Teddy's cheeks took on a ruddier tone at Paula's praise. "Thanks," she mumbled.

After sharing a decadent chocolate dessert, Chris held up his champagne flute a second time, his heart starting to thump as he reviewed again what he planned to say, first to Val, then to Teddy. And his declaration to Teddy that required privacy.

"I have an announcement to make. But first, another toast."

Everyone at the table held up their glasses.

"I've made a decision I never thought would happen. Or this soon. But it's time." He paused for effect, as his eyes roamed over the first man he'd hired when he began his construction company. "With how big the business has become, I need to share the responsibility. Officially."

"You mean because of the new crew members?" Teddy asked.

"Actually, I'm thinking in terms of a partnership. Teddy and you, Val. I want both of you to become my partners. For real, not just in how you stepped up as leaders of my crew, dividing up the supervision, making sure everything got done on time, even ahead of some deadlines."

Paula grasped her husband's hand. "Oh, honey. Did you hear that?"

Val stared at Chris. "You mean it? What do I have to do? Sign away our firstborn?"

Paula laughed and took another sip. "You know that's not going to happen, though on his fussy days, I'd say go for it."

Chris glanced at Teddy, whose sea-blue eyes had widened, her mouth slightly agape, her lips seeming to beckon.

He turned his gaze toward Val. "So, you're on board?"

"Absolutely. Totally." Val beamed.

"What about you, Teddy?"

Her gaze bounced from Val and back to Chris. "Are you sure you need two partners?"

He nodded. "You know I want to make more furniture. That won't happen if I have to be at the construction site every day. We can work out the details later. I just need to know if both of you are willing. All you have to do right now is say yes. If you are, the three of us will meet to hash out the details on how to divvy up the work. Then we'll meet with my brother, the lawyer, to draw up a partnership agreement. He'll make it all official."

Val reached for Chris's hand and shook it vigorously. "You know I'm in." He laughed. "It's something I was hoping we'd get to. Eventually. Just never thought it would happen this soon."

Teddy reached across the table for Val's hand. "Congratulations. Well-deserved. You'll make a perfect partner, Val."

Chris turned to Teddy. "You haven't said you're in, too."

"I don't have a firstborn." She glanced at Val and Paula. "And, if it means I have to front money, my answer is no, since I don't have it. But that doesn't mean I'm not honored that you asked."

"Did I say anything about you having to buy in? You guys *earned* it by bringing in more people, training them and upping our completion rate over the past three months. What you did was worth more than money." Chris stared at Teddy, determined to get her to say yes. "I need your expertise on the website, Teddy, and the artistic touches you have encouraged some of the owners to add. All of which means more money for you, and for the company. Plus, you always manage to keep the guys working, and bringing the new people along. You deserve to be a partner, Ted. Just like Val."

Her eyes seemed extra-shiny before her gaze shifted from her lap and back to Chris's face. Almost shyly, she replied, "In that case, I accept. I'm honored." She rose from the table. "If you'll excuse me for a minute, I need to freshen up."

"I'll go with you." Paula stood and sent a searching glance her husband's way.

When the women left the table, Val said, "What is it about women always having to troop off to the Ladies together?"

Chris coughed out a short laugh. "Who knows? I'm just glad you both agreed. With three brains, we can tackle more projects. More complicated ones. Don't you agree?"

Val nodded and the two men spent several minutes reviewing how to speed up the build-out of the remaining houses.

"Have you mentioned this new partnership to any of the people you've been talking to about hiring us?"

"Only Fletcher. He said we should come up with a plan we can all agree on. After that he wants to meet with us." Chris looked up. "Speak of the devil. What are you doing here, bro?"

"Same as you. Having a nice dinner." He nodded in Val's direction.

Fletcher grinned as the women returned.

"Why are you looking at Teddy like that?" Chris asked under his breath.

"She sure cleans up nice." Fletcher clapped a hand on Chris's nearest shoulder. "Being friends first is always a great foundation for … stronger … feelings." He stepped away from the table and his voice rose. "I'll tell Lexi you said hello." He headed for the other side of the restaurant.

Chris stared at Teddy. Fletcher was right. But how could his brother know what else he wanted to ask Teddy?

Val spoke up. "Paula and I are going to head home. We have a babysitter waiting."

"Can you stay a couple more minutes? This shouldn't take long," Chris objected. "I wanted to get your take on the new name for the business."

"You're changing it from Lambert Construction?" Teddy asked.

Val shrugged. "It's your company. Whatever you decide is fine with me."

Teddy rummaged in her purse and pulled out her phone. "Keep talking, you two. I'm listening."

After thumbing her phone rapidly, she showed the screen to Paula, then Chris and Val. "What about this as a logo?" Three letters, all capitals, were linked. The fanciful L was at the top, from which an A was connected to the short horizontal portion of the L, while a J dangled from the crosspiece of the A. "You could call it Lambert and Partners. That would give you flexibility if we don't work out or you want to add someone else. Then all you'd have to change is the logo and no one will see it except on the website, since your truck is already decorated with Lambert Construction. It would be a simple matter to add 'and Partners' to that."

Chris stared at the logo and the name Teddy had suggested. He glanced at Val, who nodded.

Paula spoke up. "You did that so fast, Teddy. Very clever, too. I can see where your art background is a major plus for the company."

Chris twirled his empty champagne flute. He stared at the three-letter logo. "I like it."

Val checked his watch and glanced at Paula. "Then I'll see you two at work on Monday."

Teddy folded her napkin. "I'll call a cab so you two can go straight home."

Chris placed a hand on her arm. "No need. I'll drive you." He rose and shook Val's hand. "Glad you said yes. Probably should have done this sooner." He leaned forward and bussed Paula's cheek, then resumed his seat after Val and Paula left.

"There's something else I wanted to talk to you about." Chris's chest felt tight, his heart thumping in his chest. "Something I've been wanting to say for a while."

"You changed your mind about me becoming a partner?"

"No. I need you both. Your construction skills *and* your artwork." He glanced up at the darkness outside. "Let's take this to your place. Or is Yancy home?"

She nodded. "He's supposed to be finishing up a senior English paper."

"Then we'll go to my place."

Silence prevailed during their short drive back to his place. Chris pondered whether Teddy suspected what he was going to say. *Only one way to find out,* he concluded, but he felt like a contestant at the starting line of a championship race he didn't dare lose.

Fourteen

Chris parked his truck in front of his garage and pointed toward the ground where his old workshop had stood.

"Come on. I want to show you something." He trotted around to Teddy's side of the truck and helped her out.

With the flashlight on his cell phone, Chris led her around the cement blocks that formed the corners of his not-yet-rebuilt shop. As they walked, he described something larger than what he'd lost, more complex, more than a simple pole building. He mentioned steel girders, more windows and a metal roof.

"See here?" He pointed to an area on the back side near Teddy's portion of the old shop, where she had worked on her stained-glass projects. "I'm expanding this area so that you have more space. Not just a corner like before. Now you can work on large projects. Did you read in the paper last week about that church that shut its doors? I made a bid on ten of their stained-glass windows. Not the ones that show the Virgin Mary or the baby Jesus. Only the ones that include different colors of glass. I figured you could use the pieces."

"That's so nice of you. How much do I owe you?"

"Not a penny. Consider it part of the insurance money that covered what you lost." He brushed an errant curl off her cheek. "I was thinking if you concentrate on your carving and sculptures, and stained-glass projects, we could make what you do another one of our company's offerings. Like I'm doing with my furniture business. It'll be an offshoot of the construction work. With more space, you can spend more time here, unless you're doing the kind of carving that the Poindexters' paid for. The other day, two different buyers asked me about their fireplace—after seeing pictures of it and their new door you haven't hung yet. You know the ones, with 'Coming Soon' in the banner above the pictures." He grinned.

"Why didn't you tell me? I could have talked to them."

"Must have slipped my mind, what with concentrating on making you and Val partners." He halted his steps when Teddy pursed her lips. "You don't like the idea? I thought you'd jump at the chance to do more artwork."

"I'm not sure I want to make it part of your company."

"But it's *our* company now. Yours and mine and Val's. And you'd be in full control of any contracts you write with customers. You could run any expenses through the company books and repay them with what you make plus a portion of the profits, but the rest would be yours."

"That's what you're going to do with your furniture business?" She began to nibble her lower lip, a sign she might not be happy with his plan. "Let me think about it."

Had he made a mistake raising the issue? "Come on. Let's go back to the house."

He led her past the truck and up the steps. "I could use some coffee. Want a cup?"

"Sure." She watched him prepare the coffee. "Is that why you wanted to talk to me—your plans for *my* part of your workshop, something Val wouldn't be interested in? And how I would use the space?"

He nodded. "But not the most important part." His heart thudded in his chest and he turned away from her to fill the coffee mugs. He felt like he was fifteen again, asking a girl to a movie. His first date. Sweaty palms and all.

"After my accident, remember when I said I didn't want you to think badly of me because of what happened with Bambi?"

She nodded her head.

Chris motioned toward the living room, a filled coffee mug in each hand. "Let's sit on the couch, where it's more comfortable."

Teddy settled herself on the brown leather couch.

Chris placed her mug on the coffee table. Steam curled upward, its lazy curving path disappearing before reaching the ceiling.

"I made lots of decisions when I was stuck here, trying not to fall off my crutches. Even during those hellish sessions the PT put me through, when I was still in that blasted boot, and after."

"But they helped, didn't they? You hardly limp now."

He ran a hand down his leg. "Yeah. My leg's getting stronger. I'd like to think by fall that I won't hurt at all, or have to ice it at night." He sipped from his mug then set it down.

"About my wanting you to make your stained-glass business and the carving, the sculpting, part of what Lambert and Partners offers. It will make our company unique. Not just good at construction, but artistic, too. Which is why my custom furniture will be part of the business. I want the company to help us do what you and I really want to spend our time on—not just building houses, even though that part pays most of the bills. At least right now."

"You think Val will agree to us doing other stuff?"

"Val loves building houses. It's what he gets off on. Just like you and me—only we want to do other things. It's not that you aren't good at construction. But your heart beats faster when you're carving or creating those intricate designs in glass. You trained for it, it's what you have a passion for. And I want to spend my time making sure a piece of furniture is turned into something that will last for years and years, something its owner will pass down to future generations. Why I like the refurbishing work, too. Bringing an old piece of furniture back to life."

He reached for her hand. "I … um, this year has been hard. You know, with the fire and losing my shop—yours, too—and then that thing with Bambi, and my getting hurt right after Val ran a nail through his hand." He smiled crookedly. "The only good thing about all this was how Yancy decided he'd join the painting crew and keep cleaning up, too. Last time I stopped by the jobsite, he was also using the nail gun. And doing a great job." He ran a hand down the outside of his left leg, aware of the scars he'd always carry.

He gulped. "Actually, that wasn't the only good thing about this year." He gripped his mug and took another swig of coffee. "Been thinking a lot about how I've behaved. You know, with women. Since high school. Dating as many as I could, never for very long." He dared a glance in her direction.

Teddy's gaze had settled somewhere between the picture window and the front door. Her right foot bounced against the floor, first to the left, then to the right. A sure sign she was nervous. But why? Had she guessed what he was going to say? Wanted him to get on with it?

Chris set down his mug, and sandwiched Teddy's nearest hand between his palms. "I'm not doing that anymore. There's no future in it. I want to date like a normal person."

Teddy huffed out a breath, her expression skeptical. "You? Like normal people? Like who?"

"Well, like Val, and Fletcher and Todd, my brother-in-law. And Hale, my other brother-in-law. They all dated a girl, a woman, got to know her really well, and married her."

"Oh." Teddy's voice reminded Chris of a small child's, slightly tentative but encouraging, before it trailed off into a quiet breath.

"Fletcher said something that rang true. Probably something our dad told him, even if I can't remember him talking to me about it."

Lexi's glance slid across his face, sending heat down his body. "At the restaurant?"

He nodded. "He and Lexi still have date nights. Even though they're married. You know, without their little boy."

Chris hoped his smile would relax Teddy. She'd shifted in her seat, looked stiff, tense, not what he'd been hoping for when he'd opted for the couch. He was desperate for another sip of coffee to moisten his mouth, but he didn't want her to move, and she seemed wary, as if trying to discern where he was going with their conversation.

"Anyway, Fletcher said that friendship was a good foundation. For something serious, something permanent." He decided to just say what he'd finally acknowledged, something he'd always equated with only one woman. Teddy. "We've been pals forever, Teddy, and I'm really glad about that, but I want more than friendship. From you. With you."

Her eyebrows rose, and her eyes widened.

His mouth had gone totally dry. He'd have to wing it if he tried to say another word. No way was he getting up if it meant letting go of Teddy's hand. What if she bolted out of her seat and ran for the door?

He brought his other hand up to her cheek, brushed a strand of hair off her shoulder and leaned close enough to feel her breath as it floated past his ear on her quiet exhalation. Her lips seemed to beckon and he pressed into them for a tentative first kiss that tasted slightly of coffee and mint. They were as soft as he'd imagined.

When Teddy didn't move, Chris leaned closer, determined to show her that he cared about her, not just as a friend, but as a date, the serious kind, and that they might sometime in the future be even more serious, as lovers, the committed kind.

The tiny sound she emitted gave him the confidence to conclude that she wanted what he was offering and he brought his arms around her, pulling her closer.

But Teddy slid her hands onto his chest and pushed him away. "Chris, no. Stop."

Her cheeks were flushed, the pupils of her eyes darkened with what he hoped was desire, but her words didn't match what he thought he'd seen.

She studied him, her furrowed brow and serious gaze reminding him of a scientist studying a bug wiggling on a pin.

"You're right, we are friends, have been anyway, and now you want us to be business partners."

She ran her tongue along her lower lip, reminding Chris how much he wanted to kiss her, coax her into opening her mouth for a deeper kiss.

She scooted away from him.

Damn. Misread her. Shot down. Although he wanted to slide closer, he didn't dare.

"I'm not sure we should mess that up with … you know, another kind of relationship." Her rosy cheeks darkened to a nearly purple hue.

He didn't want to agree, not when he'd said what he wanted, that theirs wouldn't be a one-off, like with other women. Didn't she understand that?

"You think our being friends and business partners is enough? But it isn't. Not for me, not now."

She shook her head. "Val will make you a great partner. I know he will."

"And you will, too, Teddy. Otherwise, I wouldn't have asked you." Chris reached for her nearest hand, but she placed it out of reach in her lap. He leaned forward and grasped it anyway, hoping his touch would soften her resolve.

Wondering if he'd focused too much on the business, he asked, "Did I put too much on the table tonight?" He hoped his quirky smile would relax Teddy, whose expression suggested she was disinclined to agree to anything now. Even his partnership offer. Never mind the other stuff.

Teddy chewed her lower lip.

Fearful of her answer, but determined to know where they stood, he asked, "Are you having second thoughts?"

A tear dropped from between Teddy's thick brush-like lashes and onto her skirt, darkening the fabric with a stain that resembled a question mark. Her voice almost at whisper-level, she said, "Now I get it. You want me as a business partner, but only if I tie my carving and other stuff to your company. And you thought telling me you wanted to date me would make me agree?"

She's crying? What the fuck?

"No, Teddy. Why would you think that? I still want you. As a partner in the company. It's just that…" *I want more. You. That's who I want.* "And, I want to date you, too. Seriously. More than once or twice. Not like with those other women. Don't you see—"

He slid across the couch close enough that he could wrap an arm across her back and around her shoulder, even though she leaned away.

"But, Chris, I—"

"Look, we're already partners. Will be sharing shop space like we did before the fire. I knew you needed more space than what you had before—like for carving doors and other big pieces. I'll give you all the space you need in the new shop. No strings attached. And if you don't want your work to be part of the company, it doesn't have to be. I just thought—"

She shook her head and stood up. "I have to leave now." She walked over to where she'd dropped her purse and plunged a hand inside. "You don't need to drive me home. I'll call an Uber."

"No, Teddy. Please. That's not necessary."

She backed away from him. "I need to think about all this. About partnering with you and Val. Maybe on Monday, we could talk again."

"But there's so much more I wanted to say."

"You've already said more than enough." She strode out his front door.

He followed her, flummoxed at how badly he'd misjudged how to approach her. "About us dating? But I want to, Teddy. You're the kind of woman I *want* to spend time with. Not just on the jobsite. Don't you get it?" To his own ears, Chris sounded desperate, but that was how he felt, realizing he'd laid too much on her too soon and now Teddy was backing out of ev-erything, maybe even their friendship.

Chris retreated to the kitchen, his left leg aching. He leaned against the counter and counted to twenty slowly, then turned to follow Teddy, hoping she was standing on his porch, waiting for him. He grabbed his keys from the hook near the door and stepped outside just as headlights from an Uber car swung into the driveway.

The driver stopped, jumped out and helped Teddy into the car.

Chris trotted into the front yard, aware of the ache in his left leg as he limped over to the car and opened Teddy's door.

"Wait. I'll drive you home. I'm begging you, Teddy."

Her eyebrows rose in startled surprise. "You? Begging? Since when?"

"I've groveled before. When I had to." He grabbed her hand, pulled her out of the little car, and waved the Uber driver away. Chris then walked Teddy over to his truck and held the door for her.

When he'd pulled himself into the driver seat, he stared back at her, surprised she hadn't tried to escape. "You don't think I've never groveled before?"

"Not to me," she sniffed. "Besides, it sounded rhetorical." She sucked in her breath and whooshed it out again. "Okay, maybe it wasn't, but women come on to you all the time, Chris. I've watched you, for years and years. And I can't imagine you *ever* begging a woman for *anything*."

"Then I guess my groveling tonight puts you in a better class of womanhood than them." He turned the key in the ignition and backed slowly out of the driveway before glancing her way.

Teddy frowned. With her hands fisted in her lap, she looked like she was gearing up to give him a bloody nose.

Chris pulled over into the first parking space he came to. Sensing that touching her now might give her an excuse to do just that, but needing to talk, he turned to face her, one arm draped on the steering wheel, the other along the top of the seat. "Teddy. I—" he gulped, relieved that he'd parked where an outside light illuminated her face and upper body, the better to reveal her reaction to what he had to say, hoping his words, this time, would change things for the better.

"You're one of the best guys on my crew. The best *woman* on my crew. But I don't want you on my crew anymore."

She gasped. "You're firing me?"

He shook his head. "I said that wrong. Hear me out, please. It's not what you think. I have to stop calling you Teddy. You're not a guy. I've been wanting to take you out for months. Maybe even years. Don't know why I never did. For some reason, I overlooked you. And I shouldn't have. Call me stupid, blind." He squeezed his nape, as if that would help him concentrate, find the right words to convince her.

"That's supposed to make me feel better?" Tears welled in her eyes, seeming to magnify them in the light from the streetlamp.

"I want you as a business *partner*, not just on the crew." He paused and tentatively reached for her nearest hand, its fingers tightly clenched. Heedless of the danger her fist represented, Chris plunged ahead.

"But that's not all. I want us to see each other every day *after* work. Not just to talk about how the job's going, who on the crew needs to be fired or taught another skill. I want us to be a couple. Dating. You know, watching movies together. Exploring different restaurants. And I want to take you home. And kiss you good-night. Maybe even go dancing," though he wasn't sure she danced or would want to with him. He felt his neck heat, his body wanting more than kissing, but he knew better than to go there. Not yet, anyway. He stopped talking, aware that Teddy's grimace had turned into a fierce glower.

"What?" he asked. "You don't want us to date? Don't want us to be a couple?"

"You don't listen! Me dating *you*? It'll never work!" She unsnapped her seat belt, opened the door and leapt out of his truck.

"Wait! Teddy!"

She stomped off down the street, one hand reaching for her cell phone. Less than a minute later, the same Uber car he'd dismissed pulled up next to her. She climbed in and when the little car swung around Chris's truck, the grinning driver flipped him the bird.

~ ~ ~

Chris tossed an envelope at Fletcher who caught it in midair and set it on the counter next to the salad bowl he was filling with sliced carrots.

"What's this?"

"Tickets to the Wheel. Maybe you could take Lexi. If you call, you might even be able to pick up an extra ticket. For Chance."

"You got these for us? Thanks."

Chris glanced away, but not before his brother saw that he wasn't smiling. Far from it. He clenched his jaw. "Let's just say I had plans that didn't work out."

"Oh, I get it. You asked a woman and she turned you down." Fletcher smirked. "That has to be a first. Who was it? Someone you met at Brewskers?"

"Teddy."

Fletcher stopped tossing the salad and motioned for Chris to take a seat at the kitchen island. "Speaking of Teddy, I take it she opted out of your partnership, too? She has yet to call me back."

Chris nodded.

"You know why?"

"Refuses to include her carving and stained-glass work."

"Why didn't you tell her she doesn't have to relinquish control over her artwork?"

"When I tried to explain, she acted insulted, like I was trying to take it away from her, even though I assured her I was-n't, wouldn't." He shook his head, as if to remove Teddy's recurring accusation from his mind. But it clung there as though attached with super glue.

Fletcher whisked the salad dressing then poured it into a jar, which he capped and placed in the refrigerator.

"So, you bought the Wheel tickets as a kind of celebration, or maybe a bribe? Hoping she'd reconsider her decision?"

"Not exactly." He slammed his hand down on the granite counter before rubbing his palm against his other hand, regretting that he'd taken out his frustration on the unyielding stone. *Damn.*

Fletcher stared at him for a long minute before a grin slowly morphed as the corners of his mouth curved upward and his chuckle cranked up into a full-throated laugh.

"Teddy turned you down—on the partnership *and* the ride on the Wheel. Probably shocked you good. How many other women have ever turned you down, Chris? I'll bet I can count them on one hand, maybe one finger."

"I've been turned down plenty of times!" But he couldn't recall when or by whom.

"I wondered how long it would take you to see Teddy for more than what she's always been, your friend. And one of your best workers. Doesn't put up with your shit, does she? And that's why she turned you down. You *assumed* she would say yes and she decided to teach you a lesson? Or did you even ask, just hand her the tickets and tell her when you would pick her up? Please don't tell me you told her to meet you there."

Fletcher's statements struck too close to home for Chris not to mentally squirm. He *had* assumed she'd want to ride the Wheel. But she'd cut him off before he had a chance to tell her about the tickets or talk about who would drive.

His brother broke off staring at Chris when Lexi entered via the kitchen door, Chance in tow.

She kissed Fletcher then detoured to Chris's side and bussed him on the cheek. "Nice to see you, Chris. You're eating with us tonight?"

Chance cheered. "Dad and I made lasagna. You'll like it and you should see my new train set. In the basement." The boy grabbed Chris's hand as if to tug him off the bar stool.

"Not right now, Chance. How about we give it a whirl after dinner?"

At Chance's look of disappointment, Chris added, "I have business to discuss with your dad first. After that, I'm all yours." He ruffled the boy's thick blond hair.

Chance glanced up at Fletcher. "Will your business take lots of time, Dad? Can you make it fast?"

Fletcher grinned at his stepson. "We're almost done. Uncle Chris is right. We'll eat first and then you can show him what we did. Maybe even have him race you on the double track we set up."

Chance nodded and followed his mother upstairs.

Fletcher turned to Chris. "Back to what you were saying. Answer me this: was this date part of your business partnership conversation with Teddy? Or did she think it was? If you mentioned it in practically the same breath, maybe she thought you were trying to butter her up with those tickets so she'd change her mind and say yes to the partnership, with or without her artwork in the mix."

Chris felt a strange buzzing sensation. *Oh, shit! Is that why she turned me down? On all counts?* He stared back at Fletch.

"You could be right about that. Never thought of it that way."

"How *exactly* did you ask her?"

Chris reiterated the dinner discussion with Paula and Val that had ended so well. Then his later conversation with Teddy that had taken a wrong turn.

Fletcher turned off the warming oven, donned oven mitts and pulled out a large casserole dish. "Put this on the table, will you?" He tossed the oven mitts at Chris and waited until he resumed leaning against the kitchen island.

"Sounds like you totally blew it. If you wanted her for a business partner, why didn't you stop while you were ahead? She said yes, after Val did. Right? She seemed to be totally on board until you got all control-freaky about her artwork. And then oh-so-casually told her you also wanted to date her. Like it was an afterthought."

"I just wanted to be up-front with her from the beginning, so she'd see that I was turning over a new leaf. Not treating her like other women."

"Yeah, well, it may have been clear in your mind, but how was Teddy to know that? Seems to me you made it sound like dating her was just another way of tying her into the partnership. Sheesh, Chris. With all your experience with women, I never would have figured you'd be so obtuse. You owe Teddy a gigantic apology."

"Hey, I already begged to take her home so we could talk. You know, straighten things out," he replied, stung at Fletcher's words.

"Doesn't sound like she was all that impressed." He placed the salad bowl on the table and opened the refrigerator door. "Call Lexi and Chance down, will you? We'll continue this later. Maybe after Chance is in bed." He pulled out the salad dressing. "Are you willing to move forward with a two-person partnership? Not partnering with Teddy might open up the chance she'd change her mind and go out with you. *Assuming* you want that." Fletcher's left eyebrow rose.

"I'd rather have a threesome partnership." But he wondered if his mumbled words were lost when Chance thundered down the stairs.

Fletcher nodded. "Then let's see what we can come up with that will make Teddy feel better about things, the business at least. You're on your own about the other thing." His knowing smirk accompanied the twinkle in his eye.

~ ~ ~

Chris glanced at Lexi as she came downstairs. "Chance's down for the count?"

"He said to come over again for another race." Lexi grinned. "You are the perfect uncle for him, Chris. You take him seriously. And I love you for it." She gave him a hug. "Now, what's this about you having love life issues?"

Chris jerked his head toward Fletcher. "What did you tell her?"

"Only the bare bones, that you asked Teddy for a date and she said what you've never heard from the fairer sex. 'No.'" He air-quoted in a falsetto tone.

Lexi rolled her eyes. "Now Fletch, don't be mean."

"Can I help it if I have the wisdom to know what not to do when it comes to women?" He bowed in the direction of his wife. "Not that I don't need reminders every once in a while. Right, hon?"

"You said it." Lexi kissed his cheek.

Maybe it was time to ask for help, although Chris felt his man-card burning to ashes in his pocket. "Okay. What should I do?"

Fletcher took a seat on the couch and rested his left ankle on his right knee. He slid his arm across Lexi's shoulders when she cozied up to him. "Speaking as your lawyer, why don't you focus *first* on the partnership. Since you still want her to be a part of that. I'll send you a copy of a new contract. What we talked about, with no mention of her artistic endeavors. That could be all she needs to see that you're not out to steal her creative thunder."

"What about the shop space? I'm totally fine with her using it. Freely. No rental fee, either. Because we're friends."

"Why don't you mention that yourself—*if* she agrees to join the partnership. Or doesn't. One thing at a time, bro."

Chris ran a hand through his hair. "You'll email the new agreement to her?"

"To *you*. Print it off and sign it, you and Val. Then *mail* it to her. Maybe attach a note saying that her artwork is no longer part of the contract. But don't go seeking her out on the job. Give her some space. Tell Val not to mention it, either." Fletcher glanced at Chris. "He doesn't know about your dating faux pas, does he?"

"Not unless Teddy said something, which I doubt. She stayed away from both of us all week, except when it was required. You know, construction issues."

Lexi rose from her seat next to Fletcher. "Coffee, guys?"

"Nothing for me." Chris followed her into the kitchen he'd renovated. "Mind if I ask you a question?"

"Fire away."

"You have long hair. You always wear it up at the bakery?"

"Yes. And under a hair net. No one wants to find a hair in their bread."

"But you're wearing it down now."

Lexi shook her long blond locks. "Feels good when it's down. Makes me feel more feminine, if you must know." She grinned at him and at Fletcher, who'd followed Chris into the kitchen.

"Teddy wears her hair up, too. In braids. Usually under a Mariners cap." But Chris liked seeing her long red curls as they'd skimmed her shoulders, then slid down to breast level. "Says it's safer."

"She's probably right. Think of all the equipment she works around. Paint, too." Fletcher declared. He picked up a coffee mug, headed down the hall and entered his home office.

Lexi followed Chris to the front door. "Mind if I make a suggestion?"

With his hand still on the knob, he turned to face her. "Feel free."

"Why don't you send Teddy some hints that you're attracted to her? Boyfriend-style hints, like flowers or something you know she would like."

"I already saved some old stained-glass windows from that church being torn down. I figured she'd be able to use the glass."

"That was a wonderful gift, one I'm sure she'll appreciate. But it relates to her work, her business. What about something she'd like for herself? I was thinking of something she might wear in her hair, even if it's tucked up under a cap. A gift that would remind her of you. I'll bet if you give it some thought, you could come up with little reminders of how much you like her, something that has meaning only for Teddy. After all, you've known her forever. Fletch said you two were friends all through school."

Lexi pulled the small stone-like piece of wood from her pocket. "This little babe—it's how I think of it, our baby too small to be born—means so much to me. To Fletch, too. It's made it easier for us to talk about … our loss." Her tear-washed eyes shone brightly.

"I'm glad."

"But don't ask her out again. Let that lie for a while."

Chris nodded.

"Maybe she'll even ask you out," she murmured when she hugged him.

"I doubt that."

"You never know, Chris. I suspect she's a woman who knows her own mind. All you need to do is remind her of that."

Chris studied Lexi for a long minute. "Fletch really lucked out. To have you and Chance in his life."

"I'm the lucky one." She smiled. "And I have a feeling you'll be lucky, too, one of these days."

Chris trotted back to his car, hopeful for the first time since tossing those Wheel tickets Fletcher's way that, if he waited long enough, Teddy might change her mind.

Fifteen

Teddy called Val. Would he help her transport the new door to the Poindexters' so that it could be swapped out for the current doors?

"Be happy to. You're home?"

"Right." She glanced in the mirror and grimaced. Her eyes remained red-rimmed, almost every muscle in her back and arms ached, and she wanted to go back to bed. If only she could, but she'd promised Lawson she'd hang the door today when he confirmed his parents were still out of town.

"You have a key to get in?" Val asked.

"Yes."

"See you in a few."

Val helped Teddy remove the original doors and hang the new one. He then assigned one of the crew to install the sidelight that filled in the remaining space previously taken up by the original double doors.

Val ran his hands down the carving that included some of the same elements Teddy had created in the fireplace surround.

"They're going to love this door. Where's your phone? Let's get a picture of you standing next to it. In front of the sidelight. If you send the picture to Lawson, he'll know you did your job."

"I don't need to be in the picture," she countered. But she took several pictures including a couple of close-ups, and locked the new door. "All done." Except for getting paid.

"You going to meet me and Chris over lunch to talk over what he mentioned on Saturday?"

"Depends on if I finish the work on Number twelve. The owners asked me to install a stained-glass sidelight like the one they saw on my website. It needs final finishing. Why I'm headed back home after I check with the painting crew."

"Okay. If you can't make it, I'll let Chris know you're tied up."

"Thanks, Val."

Teddy returned home to pick up the new sidelight, spent an hour working on a sketch for another stained-glass window, and returned to the construction site, parking at the end of the cul-de-sac where the nearly completed house sat. She picked up the stained-glass window and carried it inside, nodding at two carpet layers headed up the stairs with a roll of carpet.

One of them called to her. "What've you got there?"

"A sidelight." She scored around the vinyl window casing and interior wall and slowly separated the casing from the reveal board. She taped the window glass in the sidelight to reduce the likelihood of breakage when she pulled it out of position and removed the screws that held it in place. From behind her, she heard a noise. *Please don't let it be Chris.* She glanced over her shoulder and heaved a relieved sigh. *Carpet guy.*

"You need help getting that window out?" he asked.

"No. It isn't that heavy. I can manage." She pulled the window out from where it had been seated, leaned it against the wall and used the toweling she'd wrapped the stained glass in to protect the wall. She then lifted the new sidelight into place and inspected the dry fit. *Perfect!* She pulled the new sidelight out, ran a bead of silicone along the edge of the window, slid it into place and screwed it into the jamb.

She backed up two steps and smacked into a hard body as the familiar scent of Chris's shampoo wafted her way.

She took one step forward, her heart thumping. "Sorry. Didn't know you were there." Why did her cheeks have to burn whenever he was in touching range?

"No problem." He grasped her arm, the heat of his palm seeming to mark her skin even as he held her steady. "That sidelight looks great."

"Thanks." She ducked under his arm, needing distance.

"We missed you at our meeting. Val and me." The golden flecks in Chris's brown eyes seemed to spark at her.

"Didn't he tell you I might not make it?"

"We can't make decisions without you. Need your input."

She shook her head. "No, you don't. Two against one means your side wins."

"We don't work that way, Teddy. It's consensus—what we agreed on." Chris followed her out of the house. "Does this mean you're turning down my partnership offer?"

"Still thinking about it."

Chris pointed to the house. "I guess you worked on that window at that place you rented downtown?"

"Only when I was cutting the glass. I took it home to finish it. Wanted to get it done quickly." She squinted at him, wishing he was taller so that he might block the afternoon rays doing such a good job of blinding her. "If you don't mind, I've got bills to pay, so I'm going to go pick up my checks—from Lawson and for this window."

Chris frowned. "We'll talk again when you come back." He stalked toward the next house under construction.

Teddy watched him stop on the sidewalk facing the Poindexters' new front door with its intricate carvings. She'd been pleased with how various facets of the design always seemed to turn golden when strong shafts of sunlight bathed it, even as streaks of shadow called attention to the intricate curves.

When I come back? What if I don't come back, Christopher Lambert? Since when do you know what I want? She headed out of the neighborhood, arguing with herself about what to do. Chris deserved an answer about the partnership offer, and the *other* one, too, although she thought she'd been clear about not dating him. Her surprise at his declaration had been exceeded only by that preceding kiss that had rocked her nearly off her feet, even though she'd been sitting down.

After picking up her checks and gaining written permission to feature both pieces of art on her website, Teddy texted Yancy. *Where are you working? I'll pick you up. We're doing pizza tonight. Be ready when I honk. I will* not *come looking for you.*

I'm at Number seven. He texted back and added a smiley emoji.

At least Yancy was happy, doing well in school and at work. If only she felt as good about her life as her brother did.

~ ~ ~

Teddy lay in bed, the victim of another night of insomnia. All because of Chris. As much as he appreciated her work on his construction crew, Teddy was certain there was no room for her in his heart. He probably just wanted to check her off as the last person he hadn't dated who still lived in town.

His parents certainly wouldn't approve if they knew what he'd said. Teddy sighed. She'd dreamed about Chris during her childhood and teen years. When her friends started going on group dates and then single ones, she'd wondered if he might ask her out.

But after seeing the girls he dated, she decided that he'd never think of her as more than a friend. He wasn't into gangly redheads who barely needed a bra. The girls he dated had big boobs, were blond, shorter than him and on the cheer squad. He was one of those guys all the girls wanted to date, one of the sports stars they talked about in the halls when they were discussing prom dates.

During her high school years, Teddy usually walked home alone, determined to keep secret that her mother was often sleeping off a drunk from the night before.

At least she'd made sure Yancy spent his afternoons with their grandparents. When he wasn't at their house, Teddy paid a neighbor to watch him from what she earned at her part-time job at the local grocery outlet. Her boss occasionally insisted that she take home dented cans and fresh vegetables closer to wilted than fresh status.

But she still felt guilty that she'd gone off to college. Even though her grandfather had insisted. Her mother had been doing better back then. Not drinking as much. And her grandparents were around, a safety net for Yancy.

Grandpop had loved taking her and her brother to the high school games. Chris played three sports in high school, not counting his foray into wrestling his junior year. He was a wide receiver in football, not as big as some of the guys but faster on his feet, and blessed with what Grandpop called "magic hands." He always seemed to snag the ball from the sky as he raced for the end zone. Chris also played basketball and landed almost as many three-pointers as she did. It was their own private joke—how many he made compared with what she landed during their pick-up games in his backyard or in the gym. Yancy preferred to go with Grandpop to the baseball games, too, although Teddy considered the play to be slow. But Chris played center field, because he was so good at catching those long fly balls that sent him racing to the far fence at the back of the field. Yancy claimed he wanted to be a center fielder just like Chris.

How she and Chris had remained friends all those years was a mystery. She and Yancy were from "across the tracks," according to Chris's mom, even though train tracks didn't bisect Pacific Knoll. But Teddy knew what she meant.

Was it because Chris had always picked his own friends, didn't seem to care what his parents thought? Maybe his mom didn't ask where he went after school, thought he was at the playground with his twin sister or busy with the middle and high school teams whose jerseys he wore.

Teddy tried to put Chris out of her mind when she went to college on the art scholarship everyone was surprised she'd received. Except Chris, who sided with Grandpop when she'd reluctantly applied for it. He'd said she would be a famous artist someday. And when she'd received that scholarship, her best pal, her friend since kindergarten, had slapped her on the back and told her that he would buy her paintings and hang them proudly in his house, the house he intended to build with his own hands.

That afternoon he'd stopped by the florist shop, her other part-time job, to pick up a corsage for his prom date. He'd asked her to save a dance for him, and she let him waltz out of the florist shop without correcting him. She wasn't going to the prom, wasn't dating anyone. And the following week, she gave him some excuse about why he hadn't seen her there.

She'd tried not to think about Chris after she left home. Not that a change of scene improved her social skills. But at least she didn't have to lie about why she wasn't a social butterfly like Chris and his twin sister, Elaine.

She knew he hadn't gone to college, that he was intent on learning a trade in spite of his father's insistence that he at least go to community college. Instead, he'd latched onto a furniture maker, learning skills from him and adding to them when he hired himself out to contractors who were building apartment buildings downtown and tract homes on the outskirts of Pacific Knoll close to the I-5 corridor.

How ironic was that? She'd supplemented her art scholarship by working on various construction crews, too, first as a house painter—something her college roommates kidded her about, that she'd graduated from fine art to house art. Later she'd joined a crew of workers that framed and roofed tiny houses for homeless people, even supervised the volunteers who built Habitat for Humanity homes.

Now that Chris had his own crew, his skills had helped him land contracts with developers whose homes were more upscale, including custom jobs. He was building a reputation for making creative changes that two house designers had incorporated into their house plans. Probably the reason he wanted to include both his furniture-making and her carving and stained-glass work in his company. Chris was on his way, Teddy was certain of that.

But Chris was hot. She didn't need pictures to know how well muscled he was. Her first summer home from college, he'd hired her, and she'd had numerous opportunities to check out his muscles when he manhandled drywall or helped to lift wall boards into place. On summer days when he doffed his shirt, she'd seen enough to people her dreams with plenty of images of man beauty. She could easily imagine what his sun-warmed skin would feel like, as his muscles rippled.

Her cheeks burned. It wasn't right that Chris claimed he wanted to date her, as if that, too, was part of his partnership. In her heart she knew that Chris could never *really* be her boyfriend. Which was for the better. At least they'd remain friends. The kind of friend who never noticed how she looked when she dressed up. Except ... he had noticed at the Poindexters' housewarming and that evening he'd offered the partnership to her and Val.

But if he was only pretending to want to be with her, why had Chris warned her away from the judge's son? Maybe she was imagining things, wanted him to acknowledge that she was a desirable woman, and not just a worker on his crew.

If only he'd asked her out a long time ago, before they became so involved in his construction business.

Teddy sighed and glanced at the clock. *Almost two. Why can't I go to sleep?* She walked into the bathroom and ran a wet washcloth across her cheeks. Her meeting with Chris was in less than five hours. She walked past Yancy's room and heard his soft snores. If only she could fall asleep as easily.

~ ~ ~

A week later, Teddy swiped her arm against her forehead, completed her end-of-the-day check on the painting crew she'd put to work earlier that day, and leaned down to pick up an empty paint can the new guy had forgotten to remove.

"I've got it." Chris grabbed the can. "Looks good in here." He nodded in the direction of the newly painted rooms.

"They did a nice job."

"Because you trained them." He looked around. "You're the last to leave? Again?"

"You need something?" Teddy glanced at Chris, aware of the hairs on his lower arms that looked almost blond in the slanting rays of the late afternoon sun.

"I came to see you, to ask how you're feeling now. About the partnership."

She gave him a sidelong glance. "Are you worried that I'm not pulling my own weight, not working fast enough at Zoya's store?"

"Not at all. She called the other day to tell me how pleased she is with what you're doing. Can hardly wait for you to tear down that wall to combine the two spaces."

Chris set the paint can down. "I've been thinking that you should take on another one of those renovations after Zoya's place is finished."

"You got a new contract?"

He nodded. "A realty office. Maybe you know the owner. Quincy McCue."

"Name doesn't ring a bell, but I'll take your word for it."

"His place is a block down and over two from Zoya's place. At the end of Cavanaugh Street. They want to expand into the space next door, and maybe even upstairs, eventually. The owner says his associates will work from home while you do the interior work. Here." He gave her a coiled floor plan. "This first page is their office as it is now. The second two pages show what they want on the main floor. Last page is the upstairs area for his place and the adjoining space."

Teddy scanned the plans. "Looks straightforward."

"It is. I'm guessing it's an easy two- or maybe three-week job, especially if he decides not to finish off the upstairs immediately. Why don't you and Flint take a look at the place? I'll call the owner and tell him you'll be in touch."

She handed the floor plans back to Chris.

"Keep them, since you'll be doing the work." He turned on his heel.

"It was you, wasn't it?" Teddy blurted before he left the house.

"Huh?"

"That picture of the eagles. In that special frame." It had shown up on her porch one afternoon. She intended to move it to her studio as soon as it was completed. The framing had been made by someone who knew how to make mitered corners, took pride in sanding wood until it felt like satin, who cared about wood grains and which sealants revealed and enhanced the colors hidden deep in the wood.

She'd guessed that Chris had made it. But she'd hesitated to thank him. Why, with all the time they'd spent together recently, had she not done so? Would a text do? That seemed too impersonal. On the other hand, he hadn't signed the note that was attached, a note acknowledging the eagles as her first major commissioned work. Chris knew that. Yancy had denied knowing anything about the gift, other than that he'd picked it up off the porch and placed it on the kitchen counter. Val wouldn't have known the mayor's eagles were her first big job. He probably thought the Poindexters' fireplace surround claimed that status.

Before she could chicken out, Teddy said, "Thanks for the article and picture of the mayor's eagles."

Chris smiled, his dimples showing when he gazed back at her. "I thought you might like to have it. Wasn't sure you saved that article." He remained by the open doorway. "Are you going to hang it in your studio or keep it at home? Not that I have a say in where you put it. It's just … I'm curious."

"I'm thinking it would look good in the studio." She stepped closer to Chris, her pulse climbing as she recalled the mental debate she'd been toying with all day. A decision that kept interfering with her concentration.

"Chris. Wait. Before you go."

He turned and faced her.

"You never asked again, so I guess it's up to me." She swallowed, deciding to go with her gut, find out if the chemistry she'd been trying to ignore was for real. "Want to go on a date?"

Chris's eyebrows rose. "You're asking me out?"

She nodded. "You said you wanted to, before. Weeks ago. Maybe we should get it over with." Teddy felt her cheeks flame as her pulse raced. "I mean, so we can see what it's like. You and me. Not that you'd want to repeat it. Since you don't do second dates. And we probably wouldn't—" She felt like she'd tumbled off a social cliff she shouldn't have tried to climb in the first place. He stood there, studying her, as if she was an alien being.

When Chris didn't reply, she shook her head. "Never mind. You're probably right. A bad idea."

"No! I mean, yes." He beamed. "Sure. I'll go out with you. When?"

"Oh. Well, we could go out to dinner. Since I'm your business partner, we could discuss one of the new projects. Then you wouldn't have to call it a date," she added, her pulse rising with each word she uttered.

"Wrong. You asked me out. That makes it a date, Teddy. And *not* because we're in business together." He paused and smiled again. "I'm a man. You're a woman. You asked me out." Chris shifted the weight off his left leg. "Lexi reminded me the other day that women ask men out all the time. I just never thought … Anyway. Sure. Dinner. When?"

"How about on Friday, after work? Is seven too late?"

"Sounds good. You'll pick me up?" His left dimple deepened when he gave her a crooked grin. "Or should I come get you?"

If Teddy had to characterize his expression, she would say it contained the barest hint of a dare. Like he wanted her to say yes to his picking her up, even though she had asked him.

"My car's been acting up lately. Yancy was going to have one of his friends in the auto mechanics class take a look. Maybe you should pick me up." Not that Yancy had said the car repair would occur on Friday, but it was a good enough excuse.

She slid her gaze off her shoes and up at Chris, then sucked in a deep breath and her chest rose as she waited for a reply. She watched Chris's gaze shift downward and focus on her shirt before rising again to stop at her mouth.

"Okay. I'll pick you up at seven. Friday."

To confirm that she'd done her dating homework, she blurted, "I was thinking we might go to The Hatchery. Their fish is good. Is that okay?"

"Sure."

Teddy followed Chris out the door as he put his phone to his ear. "Lambert and Partners. This is Chris."

Were he not already on the phone, Teddy figured he'd be laughing at her pitiful attempt to ask him out. But at least he'd agreed, even though he would probably conclude she was a real doofus as a date. Which he'd find out, because that's what she was. Always had been. Not enough experience to pull it off like she knew what she was doing.

She could count on one hand the dates she'd had since coming home to keep Yancy out of foster care. On Friday, she'd add one more date to her miserable record. A date with Chris, the guy all the cheerleaders had swooned over.

When she arrived home, Teddy clambered out of her car, eager to take a shower and then rummage in her closet for something to wear on Friday night. She unlocked the door to a house unexpectedly quiet.

"Yance?"

No answer. She dropped her wallet, keys and cell phone onto the kitchen table and wandered down the hall to his bedroom. Her knock yielded no response. She opened the door. No kid brother sprawled on the bed or hunched over his desk, doing homework.

She returned to the kitchen and reached for her phone just as it buzzed Yancy's distinctive ring. "Where are you?"

"At Peyton's. I told you this morning we'd be practicing our lines for the play. You forgot?"

"Oh. Right. When—"

"I'll be home around nine. Her mom left us dinner."

"She's not home?"

"Peyton's little brother has a program at the middle school. Her mom went to pick up Peyton's dad so they could have a special dinner with him before he goes on stage."

"Yancy, didn't we—"

"Don't say it, sis. If Peyton's folks trust me, why can't you?"

"I trust you. It's just that—"

"Then stop worrying. Talk to you later."

Teddy doffed her clothes and took a shower, scrubbing to remove paint spots that decorated one arm. After climbing into sweatpants and a tank top, she went through her closet. What did she have that was suitable for a date? *Not that,* she rejected the outfit she'd worn to the partnership business meeting at the fancy restaurant.

The black sheath she'd worn when meeting with Yancy's teachers would work, but it was at the cleaners. Then Teddy spied a pale blue top with a v-neckline and pulled it out. This might work. But what to pair it with? Skinny jeans were too casual and the few skirts she owned were the wrong color for the blouse. She pulled out a pair of dressy black pants with a slight flare at the ankle. She'd bought them because they felt like silk, and looked great with heels, those black strappy ones she'd bought on a whim after the mayor paid her for the eagle sculptures. For this first date —probably the only one— with Chris, it seemed fitting that Teddy should wear them.

Clothing decisions made, she relaxed on the couch with a book, determined not to look at the clock as the hands moved inexorably toward the nine o'clock hour and Yancy's expected arrival home.

~ ~ ~

"You've got a *date*?" Yancy did a double-take while filling his face with the last of the baked chicken he'd made and paired with a green salad. "Since when?"

"Since now." She glanced at the clock. *I should have stayed in my bedroom longer,* but her nerves prevented her from sitting quietly and she feared that lying down would create creases. She did her best to act casual as she strolled into the living room to look out the window.

"I hope it's not that Poindexter dude. Chris said he's a douche bag, that you shouldn't have anything to do with him."

Teddy stared at her brother. "When did he say that?"

"Weeks ago, maybe months. Right after that big open house they had where they crowed to their friends about what you did to their fireplace." He gulped down the last of the milk in his glass. "Or maybe it was when Lawson kept coming around checking on when you'd be able to do that fancy door for them. Yeah, then. I was on the crew next door to their house. 'Member?"

"You should give people the benefit of the doubt unless what you heard is true. Besides, Lawson was never douchy with me."

"It's not him?"

"No." A car pulled up in the driveway and Teddy grabbed her clutch. "See you later."

"How much later?" Yancy followed her to the door.

The doorbell hadn't finished ringing before Teddy opened the door.

Chris glanced at Teddy. "I see you're ready."

She nodded.

Yancy leaned against Teddy's shoulder, and pushed her to the side, enough to see who stood on the porch.

"Yance. Hey, man." Chris was dressed in a white shirt, and a pin-striped vest that matched the pattern in his dress pants.

"Just a minute, sis." Yancy pulled her away from the door and shut it in Chris's face.

"That wasn't very nice," Teddy objected.

"*He's* your date?" His brows beetled.

"What about it?"

"He dates *everybody*," Yancy protested, his brow furrowed. "And now you?"

Teddy felt her cheeks flame. "Yeah, me. What's your point?"

"It's just that—" He gave Teddy a quick up-down appraisal. "You better not kiss him. Not on the first date, anyway." His neck and cheeks were stained the same shade Teddy was feeling on her cheeks. "What *you* told *me* on *my* first date," he reminded her.

"Relax, Yance. I doubt there'll be another one. Or that he'll even try." She opened the door and stepped outside. When she saw Chris waiting expectantly on the porch, she said, "Sorry about that."

"You forgot this." Yancy held up her small clutch. "Your phone's inside. I checked." One eyebrow rose as if he was giving her some kind of signal.

She snatched the clutch from her brother and trotted down the stairs next to Chris, determined to calm her nerves, hoping that in doing so, her cheeks would cool, too.

"You look gr—date-like," he said when they'd reached the red sports car.

"We're not taking your truck?"

"This seemed more … fitting," he said. He opened her door and waited for her to enter. "Borrowed it from Todd."

Teddy fumed. "Your whole family knows we're on a date?"

"Just Todd." He smiled. "Why should that matter? One look at you and he'd probably give me a high-five." With that he trotted around the car, climbed in and headed for the restaurant.

Dinner was more relaxed, mostly because Chris seemed to know what hot buttons to avoid. He didn't mention work issues, which convinced Teddy that he was trying to make this a real date, something she was still trying to get her head around. A date with her. Not some other woman, any woman in town who was the right age and not married.

After they left the restaurant, Chris drove to a park halfway to Teddy's house. He stopped the car.

"Why are we stopping?" Teddy stiffened. "You thinking of trying something?" She dared to cast a quick glance to her left.

Chris seemed to clear his throat. "Of course not. You're safe with me, Teddy. And you have a karate black belt. You could cripple me for life if I tried anything." He unclipped his seat belt and turned toward her. "I just thought we might take a few minutes and talk. Or if you prefer, we could take a walk, check out the stars. People do that on dates."

"Huh." She kept her hands in her lap, alternately clenching and unclenching her fists. "Okay, talk. We did a lot of that over dinner."

"You didn't like what we talked about? I just wanted to get to know you better. Those years you weren't living here were mostly a blank—until you filled me in. I knew some of what you had to deal with before your mom … before she died. I understand better now why Yancy acted out at school. Why the two of you are so close."

"Of course, we're close. He's my only family."

"Because you took responsibility for him, which meant you had to grow up fast. Faster than other people your age. Which you did. Another thing I admire about you."

At her frown, he added, "I like that you're pretty, too." He reached up and tugged on one of her curls. "You look nice when you wear your hair down. Not that I'd expect you to do that on the job. I'm glad you don't. It would distract the men."

She allowed herself to stare at Chris, previously her boss, now her business partner. And tonight her date. How was she to take that statement? She'd never felt any of the guys staring at her. Like Chris was right now. Only Axel had acted like he was checking her out, leering. Which had made her mad. Probably why she'd fired him.

"Yeah, well. We can't have *that*," she said. "Do we have to talk about work?"

"Forget I mentioned it." He buckled his belt and started the car. "Time to get you home so Yancy doesn't worry."

"Fat chance of that happening," she muttered under her breath.

Chris chuckled. "Hey, I heard what he said." He grinned at Teddy. "The window next to your door was open."

Her cheeks heated again. "He talks too much."

"He loves his big sister. Which is right. Like I love mine. Even Elaine, who's currently being a real pain in my ass."

"What's her problem?"

"Her fiancé broke off their engagement—after too many years to count. It's all she talks about and I'm tired of the tears and accusations that she should have been the one to call it off. Not that she didn't have good reason."

"You liked him?"

"Used to. Not so much now."

He pulled the car into Teddy's driveway. "Here you are. Home, safe and sound. Be sure to tell Yancy that." Chris grinned, jumped out and trotted around the front of the car to open her door.

"You practice that old-fashioned gentleman thing with all your dates?" Teddy gave him her hand when he helped her out of the car.

"My dad taught us guys how to act with girls. Women. Even with my sisters."

Chris preceded her two steps up the porch, turned and faced her. "There. Now we're eye-to-eye with you in those heels." He smiled and grasped both of her hands. "Remember what you said to me in middle school?"

"Probably lots of things. Mostly swear words when you tripped me on the playground or that time you borrowed my bat and broke it when you hit a home run."

"Didn't I say I was sorry? I bought you a new one."

"But it wasn't a Louisville Slugger," she retorted, as if her words belied the small grin she couldn't prevent from forming.

One corner of his mouth crooked upward. "In those killer shoes, you're taller than me. Not that I mind." He leaned forward and brushed his lips against hers before pulling her forward as he leaned in her direction. When his lips meshed with hers, he held her in position as he wrapped one arm around her back, only releasing her hand when she pressed it against his chest.

Teddy felt his heart beating, almost as rapidly as her own. In fact, for a moment, their heartbeats seemed to be in sync so that she felt a single rapid thudding. She wasn't sure she should have let him kiss her good-night, but she couldn't help herself. At that first touch of his lips to hers, she realized this kiss was as mind-blowing as the first one weeks earlier. The tingles she felt urged her to keep kissing him, to stroke his nape and the muscles of his back, adding to the sensations she was intent on memorizing, if only to recall them later when Chris was dating other women. Women that he didn't see on the jobsite or when he called a business meeting. Women who wouldn't be sharing shop space with him as soon as the building was completed. Women who hadn't known him since kindergarten or played basketball with him.

The night air had been cool, but Teddy felt almost too hot with his arms around her, with his body, chest to hip, against her, and—oh! More than his chest when he stepped even closer. She thought she heard a soft moan and wondered if he'd been about to say something when the porch light flicked on, then off, and on again. Even with her eyes closed, she knew what that meant.

Chris released Teddy, a look of regret in his eyes before he turned to grasp the doorknob, reaching for her hand as he did so.

The door opened, and Yancy stood there glaring first at Chris and then at his sister.

She chose to smile at Chris. "Thanks for dinner."

"Sure." He backed out of the way when Yancy reached up to close the door in his face for the second time that evening. Chris's last words, "I'll call you," were barely discernible over the slamming of the door.

"Sheesh, Yance. That was rude." Teddy tossed her clutch onto the couch.

"I told you not to, sis. You didn't listen," Yancy fumed.

She glared back at him. "Hey, Chris and I are consenting adults. Besides, it's not likely to happen again. You know he doesn't do second dates."

She glanced out the window and watched Chris walking slowly toward Todd's sports car. But she wanted to think Chris would ask her out. Not wait for her to do it. She'd lost that bet with herself that a kiss from Chris would be forgettable, less than epic. His kisses? She'd never forget them. Ever. Even if they never had another date.

Sixteen

Teddy signed the partnership agreement and slid it toward Val, who nodded and passed it to Chris.

He grinned and handed it to Fletcher.

"Thank you. Chat among yourselves while I get copies for each of you." Fletcher left the conference room.

Teddy glanced at Val. "Happy now?"

He beamed. "Only if you are. The girls on the crew will be tickled. They were worried you weren't coming back."

"Women, Val," Chris corrected.

Teddy felt Chris's gaze on her. She shoved her chair back and stood up. "Since we're done here, I have an appointment."

Chris objected, "But Fletch said to wait."

"Oh. Right." She sat back down and stared at the door, as if doing so would hurry Fletcher along.

"Here you are." He handed copies of the agreement to all three partners in the newly formed construction business, renamed Lambert and Partners, LLC. "As soon as I have the business license from the state, I'll be in touch. For now, congratulations." He shook each person's hand, lingering slightly when he grasped Teddy's hand and smiled. "With you on board, I know you'll keep these guys in line." He winked.

Teddy nodded and left the office, eager to get away. She had a carving to finish and had given herself a deadline of six more days to complete it before shipping it off to the State senator's office in Olympia. He'd asked if she could deliver it before the end of the legislative session. Securing that contract had made her day. The politician had seen the eagles she'd done for the mayor and contacted her, wanting something similar, and willing to wait until Teddy had time to create the piece.

Tomorrow she'd return to Chris's jobsite as an official partner, something he would probably announce to the rest of the crew. When she'd received the revised contract, she hadn't been surprised that Chris had included his furniture business under the umbrella of regular construction work.

Knowing that, she'd reconsidered how she might secure her own future as a partner and also reserve time to work on her own art. Two phone calls with Fletcher to clarify certain details had convinced her that she would maintain control over not only her own customer list, but also her artwork and the income it derived. The only connection between her carving and stained-glass projects and the construction company was a digital link that appeared on Chris's website, which she agreed to maintain as part of her partnership responsibility.

Shortly thereafter, Chris sent her the final blueprints of the workshop he was rebuilding. He was as good as his word regarding space for her to do her thing. She'd insisted on paying rent, and his agreement sealed her decision to become a partner in the construction part of the business, which would provide her regular income.

Val wanted to expand the crew again to cover new building contracts they'd obtained. And to prove his point that he'd manage that portion of the business, he began regular visits to tech schools in the area in addition to the places he and Teddy had visited after Chris's accident.

Teddy stopped the car in Chris's driveway and watched the progress on the workshop. Now that the metal roof was in place, it wouldn't be long before the walls went up, enclosing a small office area that would house a fax machine, hook-ups for a laptop and other electronics, in addition to Chris's work area and her own, providing them space to stay in touch with Val,

Chris's furniture clients and Teddy's customers, too, without having to enter his house.

He'd transported the stained-glass windows he'd rescued before the old church was torn down to Teddy's house. She'd agreed with him that the glass in those windows would replace some of the pieces she'd lost in the fire. While sifting through the ashes, she'd come upon two glass pieces from her original collection. She retrieved them and intended to hang them in front of the window of her new workshop space as a reminder of the fire.

Chris had asked her for another date. Part of her wanted to tell him no, if only to make him realize that not every woman fell at his feet. Figuratively, of course.

Another part of her wanted to say yes, if only to enjoy another one of his fabulous kisses. And feel his body in that most personal way when he'd pulled her close, proving to her that he desired her. But focusing on her imaginings wasn't getting her work done.

She turned the car around and headed home. *Time to finish the carving,* she thought, hoping that the work would push out of her head Chris's kiss, the feel of his arms around her, and his body telegraphing his arousal …

~ ~ ~

Another date, and another after that, had Teddy wanting to see Chris every day. To avoid having to explain things to Yancy, who wasn't yet convinced that being with Chris was a good idea, she resorted to texting him before Yancy showed up at the jobsite after school.

Chris's texts usually consisted of suggestions about where to meet him for lunch unless a meeting including Val was scheduled. But twice, Chris had held her hand under the table, causing her body to heat, even in those places she'd previously been able to ignore. Val had given her a quizzical look a couple of times. She hoped he hadn't suspected that she and Chris considered themselves a couple. "Privately," she'd insisted and he'd agreed, at least as it related to work.

Trouble was, she had difficulty not returning his kiss when he stole one in a house under construction, or another at the knitting shop where she was managing the renovations. Teddy sensed it was only a matter of time before one of the crew spotted them. Then their secret would be out.

She showered and pulled on a clean tank top and pair of jeans. Chris had convinced her to meet him at the landing where his dad sometimes put a boat into the water.

"I want to watch the sun go down at high tide tonight. There's fish and chips in it for you if you'll join me," he urged.

She'd laughed, her body tingling at the thought—which had little to do with a fish dinner. How could she keep her hands off Chris and his hard muscles? His hard everything, actually.

Teddy texted Yancy, knowing Huey would give him a ride home. *I'll be home late tonight. Get your homework done.* She hoped her brother wouldn't ask questions. His silent treatment after dates two and three had been difficult to take. Was that what Dad would have done were he still living with them? *Nah. He wouldn't have cared.* Like Yancy, Grandpop would have cared. But would he have stood in her way, or just cautioned her to take things slow?

Minutes after parking near the beach, Teddy spied Chris, waving at her.

They walked the beach, holding hands, and she allowed herself to feel wanted, desired, maybe even loved by a man. Chris's deep voice, with that edge of honey when he laughed, warmed her as they faced into the freshening breeze.

They ate the fish and chips he'd promised and then climbed into his truck. He drove back to his house and she didn't object when he invited her inside. And straight to his bedroom. She was aware now, more than ever, that this was what she had wanted for a long time.

He made quick work of her clothes, and she of his. And when he reached for a condom, a question on his lips, she nodded.

Their first lovemaking was intense, over faster than she would have preferred, but a prelude to a second, slower time that left her boneless and sated, wondering why she hadn't asked him out years earlier, even if it meant she'd interrupt

Chris's series of one-off dates with every other woman in town.

"So that's why everyone wanted to date you," she murmured drowsily.

"My reputation isn't as bad as that," he insisted with an embarrassed laugh. He brushed strands of hair off her cheeks and brow and pulled her close, spooning with her. "I was saving the best for you. No woman comes close to how you make me feel, Teddy. Don't you know that?" And he kissed her for emphasis, a kiss that led to more lovemaking.

They fell asleep in each other's arms that night, their hours together broken only by two phones, one on his dresser, the other in her purse on the kitchen counter, each going off within seconds of each other. At least they didn't sound off until eight o'clock in the morning.

Yancy had left a text for Teddy. *I'm guessing you're with Chris. I hope he wore a condom.*

Chris's message was from Val. *Call this guy. He wants to meet with us about redoing the old Bannister house on Ocean Shore Drive.* The phone number had followed in a second text.

"I guess it's time we got to work," he said. "I'll start breakfast."

"While I hit the shower," she replied and slid her hand down Chris's back as she climbed out of bed.

After she dressed, she called Yancy.

"Yeah?" He sounded miffed.

"I just wanted to let you know I'll pick you up at the job-site this afternoon."

"You're not going back to Chris's for another late night?" he demanded.

"I'm coming home to eat dinner with you," she replied, between clenched teeth. "And I'd appreciate you at least being civil, Yancy."

He hung up on her.

"Damn!"

"Trouble?" Chris asked. "Maybe I should talk to Yance."

"No. I'll do it. Besides, it's none of his business." She crossed her arms across her chest.

Chris kissed her forehead, the tip of her nose and then her lips. "Your brother's just looking out for you. It means he cares, doesn't want you hurt. He should know by now that's something I'd never do."

"Oh, yeah?"

He grinned. "We've already talked. He and I."

"About you and me having sex?"

"Making love is what we did, babe." Chris chuckled. "And that's not what I said or what he asked. I just told him, months ago, that I would never hurt you. Never ever."

Mollified, Teddy sat down with Chris to eat breakfast. She decided not to dwell on whatever Yancy might be thinking about what her relationship with Chris. "Let me know how your meeting goes."

"You know I will. This kind of job would be a real feather in our cap. The Bannister mansion has been an eyesore for years. I heard the city was going to tear it down until this guy bought it and trucked it to its new location."

"If we get it, I'd like to create a 'here's how it's going' story with pictures of the renovation. Maybe post it on Facebook or Instagram, in addition to adding it to the company website. You know, show people how we save old buildings, and make them new again. You think the owner would let us do that?"

Chris put down his fork and reached for Teddy's empty plate. "I'll ask. You going to the knitting shop today?"

She nodded. "That and talk to Yancy when I get home."

"Good luck with that." He rinsed the dishes and set them in the dishwasher. "Come on. I'll drop you off at your car."

~ ~ ~

Teddy parked in front of the knitting shop and waved at the owner, who was creating a display in the larger of the two front windows. Zoya had asked Teddy to look over her plans for expanding the yarn shop. She had appreciated Teddy's suggestions and hired Chris's company to do the work, but only if Teddy was in charge.

Zoya claimed, with a smile at Chris, that a woman's touch was necessary. He'd turned the work over to Teddy, telling her to pick three crew members to help her. She'd chosen one of the women, Huey, and one of her best painters, and had spent most of the last two weeks on site. The store would be finished in another few days. Teddy planned to take "after" shots for the company website to add to those she'd taken before the demolition of the interior of the adjoining storefront. She looked for-ward to hanging the new sign right before the grand re-opening Zoya had planned.

"I'm so pleased with what you've done, Teddy," Zoya enthused. "My shop's name—'Zoya's Needles and Yarns' in extra huge letters. Makes me feel important."

Teddy hugged her. "Because you are. Now you'll be able to hold classes like you've been wanting. And have more room for the supplies you carry, plus the two knitting corners that your customers can use during the day."

"You must come to my opening, your whole team. Or rather, *re*opening." The shop had never closed. Teddy had left the ugly old wall up while doing most of the work, so that Zoya wouldn't lose sales during the redesign.

Zoya looked at Huey. "I can hardly wait for you to take down the wall this weekend. Such a brilliant stroke. I never would have thought of that."

Huey winked at Zoya and assured her that he'd let her knock the wall down if she felt up to using a sledge hammer. The tiny woman, who barely topped five feet tall, craned her neck to smile up at six-foot-seven-inch Huey. Teddy was certain that Huey could easily span Zoya's waist with his ham-like hands.

Partnership in Lambert and Partners Construction had its perks, Teddy realized later that day. Being in charge of certain construction projects was one. Being able to work at home two days a week was another. She used some of those hours to update the construction website. The rest of the time, she carved or visited the rental space where she'd begun work on a new stained-glass project. She looked forward to moving her studio into Chris's shop as soon as the building was completed.

Teddy glanced at the framed article and the photo of the mayor's eagles that hung in her bedroom. Chris's gift to her, his acknowledgement of that first important commission. Wouldn't be her last.

She reached for a carving knife and turned her attention to the design that was nearly finished. Maybe she could call it done before picking up Yancy at the jobsite.

Seventeen

Six weeks later, Chris entered his shop. He grinned as the smell of fresh-cut wood welcomed him. He strode over to the door into Teddy's glassworks studio and hit the switch that automatically flashed lights to get her attention.

"Enter!"

Chris opened the door and watched Teddy lift up her safety glasses after turning off the blow torch. She smiled at him. "What do you think?" She pointed to a narrow sidelight nearly four feet tall, propped against a nearby wall. "When I finish this piece, these two windows can go into the house farthest away from the Poindexters'. I'll bet they're glad the neighborhood's almost finished."

"All but the landscaping on the last two. Those sidelights look great." He leaned over her and planted a kiss before gathering her in his arms.

His mind carried him back to the last two times he and Teddy had made love. He hadn't expected how quickly they'd move from that first date to seeing each other almost every evening after work and then her sleeping over at his place, even if Yancy wasn't at an out-of-town baseball game. He thought they'd succeeded in keeping their evolving couplehood under wraps until Val's comment that several crew members had noticed what he had characterized as "cow eyes." Chris had asked his partner to keep it to himself.

Val smirked. "That particular cat's already out of the bag. But I'll talk to Huey, who happens to think it's about time Teddy had a nice boyfriend."

"Is he the one who spread the word?"

"No. Flint said something, too."

When Chris talked to Huey, the big guy beamed and told him he was glad it was him. But he still made his point that he'd take down any guy who might hurt Teddy. Which Chris would never do. Teddy was his business partner. *And my lover.* The kind of woman he wanted in his life for the long haul, though he hadn't said as much to her.

To cut down on the rumors, Teddy was happy to work on job sites that Chris rarely visited. But when he did, he couldn't resist pulling her into a clinch for stolen kisses.

Their recent activity in bed was working out spectacularly, something he intended to repeat as often as possible. He couldn't seem to get Teddy out of his head, and his bodily reactions, even to the thought of her, whether at a partners' meeting or when he was miles away from her. He wanted her near him. And he wanted his family to acknowledge what he had finally realized—that he was ready for a permanent relationship with a woman. Not just any woman. Theodora Jameson. Only her. It was time his family showed their support, and ack-nowledged that they believed he'd grown up, was no longer a serial dater, scared to death of the C word. Teddy had cured him of that. The more time he spent with her, the more he wanted to spend with her.

Thus far, only Fletcher knew what was going on, and he'd cautioned him about bringing Teddy to a Sunday dinner, even though the sisters weren't going to be a problem. Neither would Hale or Todd. And Logan was probably too young to care. Fletcher didn't have to remind him that their mother had never taken to Teddy, that maybe Chris should mention her to Iona privately to allow his mother time to get used to the idea, maybe even to extend the invitation herself, which would ensure that the elder Mrs. Lambert would be pleasant.

Chris wanted the world to know he'd found the woman he'd been looking for all his life. He admitted to himself, and to Fletch, that he should have recognized Teddy for what she was —the woman he needed, the woman he wanted— years earlier, but he hadn't been ready then.

"Not smart enough, either," Fletcher had countered with a grin.

But he was smart now. And if he could convince Yancy— after several scowling sessions and one meeting at Chris's shop that began with shouted recriminations from Yancy before he finally calmed down and listened —he should be able to convince his own family. Happily, his confrontation with Yancy had ended with a handshake and the teen's acknowledgement that he trusted that Chris's intentions were honorable.

Now that Yancy had backed off, it was time to talk to his mother. Which Chris planned to do this weekend. He sucked in his breath in hopes his rising pulse was the result of seeing Teddy and not a reflection of his fears that she might turn down his invitation to accompany him to his parents' place.

Chris activated the laptop and hit the calendar icon. "I was right. Remembered it."

Teddy swiveled on her stool. "What're you checking?"

"Dates. That award ceremony at the high school is a week from Friday night. And Yancy's graduation is in two more weeks. Hard to believe your kid brother is graduating high school."

She pointed to the calendar. "So?"

"I have an idea." He followed his words with kisses, hoping the desire he detected in Teddy's gaze would result in her taking a break from her work, preferably in his bedroom.

She kissed him back, amping up his hopes. "What's that?"

Chris brushed errant strands of her red hair off her cheek. "We should have a showing of some of your new carvings and stained-glass pieces. And I want to display the new furniture I just finished. Maybe even the ones that're already sold but not yet delivered."

"Weren't we going to buy a booth at the craft fair over the Fourth of July weekend?"

"Don't want to wait that long. Let's do it this coming Sunday. Weather's supposed to be good. And the booth at the craft fair is expensive. We could hold our own show right here. At the shop. For about three hours. It'll give people a chance to see where we work, not just what we work on. And you won't be competing with other carvers at the fair."

He pointed to the completed sidelight. "You could put a 'sold' sign on this one and its mate if both are finished by then. Seeing signs like that might generate more commission work because people are sure to want something they can't have."

She laughed. "Great marketing strategy, Chris. Okay. I'll post an announcement on our web page and send out some social media blurbs, too."

Teddy reached behind Chris to the table where she'd placed three different glass chimes. Their twinkling tones accompanied her smile. "What do you think of these pieces? They're easy to make. I use the left-over pieces from my other designs. They just take sanding to smooth off the sharp edges. I could probably put close to a dozen of these chimes together by Sunday."

"Think Yancy'd be willing to help us out by taking orders and maybe even handling the sales? So we can concentrate on talking to the people who stop by?"

"Probably." Teddy resumed her seat. "Are you going to invite your family? Or have they already stopped by to see how well you've recovered from the fire?" Her smile declined to the point that her lips formed a thin white line and worry lines began to mar her forehead.

"Elaine showed up the other day. Fletcher, too, when he came over to ask for my help installing play equipment in his backyard. A swing set and a tree house like Hale and Eden's kids have in their yard."

"What about your folks?"

"Dad isn't in town right now and my mom probably won't come by herself. She knows Dad isn't in the market for furniture."

He pointed to his portion of the large building. "Before you leave, I want you to check out the butcher block table I put together for Debra and Todd. I used your idea of making a braid-like pattern in the center of the block. Those pieces of alder contrasted nicely with the oak and maple pieces."

"You should show that off, too. Unless you were planning to take it over to them beforehand."

"Deb will probably wait until after the show. If we ask, Lexi might make us some of those mini-cupcakes."

"Ah. The better to keep customers around longer by feeding them." Teddy grinned. "Ask her to bring brochures from Monet's bakery to advertise where she works."

Chris nodded. "If we have sweets, we'll also need coffee and maybe some soft drinks. We can fill a chest with ice to keep the sodas cold. I'll borrow one of those thirty-cup pots that my mom uses for coffee when her bridge club comes over." He clapped his hands together. "Now that we're geared up for the big day, I'm ready for a break. What about you?"

But Teddy resumed her seat and plucked two pieces of glass from a box on the table and held them up to the light.

Chris pushed at one of the glass chimes strung in front of the windows and listened to its musical tinkling. "What you're making is going to be beautiful. Just like you."

Teddy grinned at him. "Give me ten minutes to finish up this corner piece and I'll come find you."

"You got it." Chris left Teddy, and gazed with satisfaction around his shop. Life was definitely looking up, business-wise. Personally, too.

If only Teddy wasn't so skittish about his parents. Not that she didn't have her reasons. Chris recalled what his mother had said about the Jamesons' years earlier. Words that were probably burned into Teddy's brain. But he preferred to think that his mother's attitude about who she thought were the "right people," the "kind of people" her children should associate with, had broadened since then. After all, she'd accepted Lexi, had even apologized to her. Surely that meant she'd softened her views.

He'd remind Teddy that his dad was pleased Val was now a partner in the construction business. Had he mentioned that Teddy, too, was a partner? Their conversation had occurred before his father had taken off for another research trip to Boise, before Teddy had finally agreed to join the partnership. *I'll tell Teddy Dad finally admitted that I proved a college education wasn't necessary to be successful. That should make her feel better.*

He took a seat on the porch and glanced around at the front yard. Other than keeping it mowed, Chris realized it looked empty, needed additional color. *I'll talk to Deb about flowers. Shrubs that don't take much work.*

He looked up when the main shop door slammed shut. As Teddy walked toward him, his pulse picked up. Her smile radiated happiness. When she reached him, he pulled Teddy onto his lap, wanting to feel her curves, her warmth, to catch a whiff of that body wash she used. "You didn't need ten minutes."

"No." Teddy's arms slid from Chris's shoulders to his waist. She squeezed him then took a step back. "I decided to finish that sidelight tomorrow."

"Good."

She followed him into the house and made a beeline for his coffeemaker. "I hope you have something to eat, too. I'm starved."

He pulled out the canister and pried off the lid, releasing the flavor of peanut butter cookies. "Will these do?"

"Oh, yum. Yes."

Deciding to take a chance, Chris said, "My mom's in hog heaven these days with three grandkids to spoil. Eden's two insist that she keep a full cookie jar. And Chance, Lexi's kid, makes her laugh. He's like an old soul in a kid's body. So smart. Which makes Fletcher proud."

"I'm glad she likes them. Your mom was never very smiley whenever I was around."

"That was years ago, water under the bridge. If she saw your work, she'd be impressed as hell. And when she's impressed, she tells everyone she knows—which can only mean you'll be busy taking lots of new orders. Carving as well as stained glass. My mom knows everyone who's anyone in this town. You'll see." He pressed his lips to Teddy's forehead then used two fingers to lift her chin to angle her mouth just so. "You don't have to worry about her, Teddy Bear. She's mellowed. A lot. And this show of ours is going to work out great. I know it."

Teddy kissed him back, then sighed as she moved out of his arms. "You're probably right. It's just that … As long as she doesn't say anything nasty that Yancy might hear. He's likely to take offense and do something about it, like pop her in the nose. Even if she is a woman."

While they nibbled on cookies and sipped coffee, Chris imagined nibbling on Teddy, especially the parts that made her purr and snuggle closer.

Chris reached for Teddy's hand and feigned a yawn. "I'm suddenly in need of a nap. Want to join me?"

She laughed. "Only if you promise not to snore."

"Fat chance of that happening." He waggled his eyebrows at her and they headed for the bedroom.

Two hours later, Chris rolled over, surprised that he'd fallen asleep. Teddy's side of the bed was cool. He pressed his face into her pillow, taking in the scent he loved. Her scent.

When his cell phone buzzed on the dresser, he climbed out of bed and read the message.

Just talked to Lexi. She'll make cupcakes for our workshop show and something else, too. Refused to tell me what the something special is, but that you'd like it. ☺

Chris texted back a smiley face emoji. Teddy was thinking positively, planning for their big day. He hoped it meant that his furniture business would really take off, that Teddy would obtain more commissions for her carvings and stained-glass work. And that his mother would welcome Teddy like she had Lexi, Fletcher's wife.

~ ~ ~

"Wow! You've been busy!" Chris scanned Teddy's studio when she opened the door. Numerous wind chimes hung from a wire in front of the two large windows through which sunlight poured. As if trying to emulate the greens of four of the glass chimes, she was wearing an emerald green sleeveless dress with a flared hem that stopped at her knees. On her feet was a pair of stilettos dyed to match. Her long wavy strands of thick red hair hung loose down her back, the way Chris liked it.

"What is it about women and those sky-high heels?"

She smirked. "They give me courage, and a reminder, in case I need one, that I can hold my own with anyone, even guys. Something my mother told me once. Besides, I love these shoes and they should also make me just about as tall as your big brother if he stops by. So I can look him in the eye." She giggled. "I love being able to look down on you." Her eyes twinkled, softening her goading message.

"Hey, do I care? After what I made for Lexi after she lost the baby, Fletcher claims you can do no wrong."

"You told him I suggested it? But you were the one who came up with that gift."

He nodded and reached for the black pashmina shawl lying next to Teddy's purse. "You're not going to need this today. It's already warm in here."

"The wind was stronger when I left the house. It used to be my mom's. One of the only things I have from her, since the explosion burned up everything else."

Chris nodded. "I'm going to start calling you my wild Irish lass. That's what you remind me of. All that bright red hair in that green outfit. You ready for the hordes coming to check out what we've made? I think I'll open both big doors."

"Go for it." Teddy tucked the shawl and her purse into a closet that usually housed cutting tools. "I'm eager to see who shows."

Chris returned to his portion of the shop, pleased at the number of people who soon were streaming through the place, many of whom also entered Teddy's studio. Eden and Fletcher stopped by, their spouses and children in tow. Lexi carried in several dozen mini-cupcakes and a pair of flat cakes, one frosted to resemble an antique table, and one whose decorations mimicked a stained-glass window. Toward the end of the day, even Elaine put in an appearance.

The photos Teddy had copied from their website called attention to other pieces of furniture Chris had sold and to three large carvings she'd managed to complete along with several smaller ones, including mirror frames, the glass of which she'd scrounged from a second-hand shop.

Chris insisted that she give pride of place to the two stained-glass sidelights she'd recently completed. He considered them a terrific way to point out that special touches could be added to regular construction jobs, something he knew Val would be happy about. Teddy placed a lamp behind them to draw attention to the colors she'd used for the swirling abstract designs. The sold signs he'd insisted on placing on items already spoken for generated several new requests for work.

Four hours after he opened the workshop doors to allow the breeze to circulate, the last of the visitors finally departed. Chris closed the doors and strolled back into Teddy's studio. He glanced around at the space which now looked empty. Her photos of their work had been taken down and no wind chimes hung on those wires she'd strung. All but one of the carvings she had displayed were gone.

"You made lots of sales." Chris plucked a lone mini-cupcake off a plate and popped it into his mouth.

Teddy beamed. "Yancy kept track on my laptop. He says you did well, too. Flint said you even snagged some appointments to talk about custom construction in the Highlands. Did he mention that before he left?"

Chris nodded. "That and five other requests for furniture. I'm glad we did this gig. Now we can concentrate on what we most want to do—my furniture and your carving and glass work." He reached for her hand and pulled her close. "Let's grab some pizza and celebrate."

Teddy sighed. "No can do. Yancy's making dinner, practicing his chef duties. He wants to show off what he might have to cook when he applies for a place next year. He'll probably demand that you give him what he calls a man's point of view—meaning presentation as well as how your taste buds react. He's big into spicy combinations I would never think of."

"I'm for that. Let's go." He kissed her and added, "And after we eat, we'll come back here and celebrate privately."

Teddy smiled. She hit the light switch, locked the door behind her and followed him outside.

~ ~ ~

Chris sat with Teddy in the last row of the auditorium of Pacific Knoll High School, and watched as scholarships and letters of commendation were awarded to the graduating seniors. Chris spotted Yancy seated between two girls in the second row.

Teddy had expressed surprise when Chris said he wanted to go with her to the high school awards ceremony. He wanted her to know that he cared about her little family of two. Something he intended to do something about, after all the graduation activities were over.

"One of the best decisions I made was hiring Yance as a grunt. Who knew he'd turn into a great crew member, too? I hope he gets an award, maybe even a scholarship."

"You know something I don't?"

"No, but you said he pulled up his grades after you came home."

"He'll probably be embarrassed if he gets something and you clap."

"Doesn't matter. Do you know what he's up for?"

"No idea. The principal's letter said only that I should attend. I hope it's something good. Even a small scholarship would be nice."

Chris straightened in his seat when Monet Durham accompanied the principal to the microphone. The tiny baker cleared her throat and pulled out some papers from the voluminous purse slung over her shoulder.

After being introduced, Monet beamed and said, "Good evening, almost-graduates. I remember how I felt at a similar gathering. Let me tell you! If you're a recipient of something good, it can be the start of making at least one of your dreams come true. That's what happened to me. And it could happen to you, which is why I'm here—to pay it forward.

"You see, I had a dream. I wanted to own my own business, a bakery. And the scholarship I received put me on the path to what I have now. Some of you have even visited my place, bought our pastries and cakes. Thank you, everyone, for your support, even when it's as small a purchase as one little doughnut hole. Every sale of our baked goods means that you like what we do. And that makes me happy—along with padding my bottom line." She paused to allow laughter from the audience to die down.

"Tonight, it is my honor and privilege to announce a new scholarship, one to be given to a student who has taken both of the culinary classes offered here. It's not a big scholarship, and I knew that the recipients over the years will need additional monies to achieve their dreams. But I'm a believer in the value of hard work, and that a person who *works* for their dream values it more than someone who doesn't have to struggle.

"I asked the teacher who runs your culinary classes to tell me who she would recommend. But she didn't want to choose. Instead, she shared with me what her students wrote about how they intend to use the skills they've learned in her classes. Let me read part of the winning essay so that you can see why I chose the first recipient of this scholarship. Oh, and by the way, to keep growing the scholarship, we've set up a big glass jar at the bakery. Anyone who wishes can donate to the scholarship fund throughout the year. Those funds—in their entirety—will be added to what we provide each year, thus increasing the size of the scholarship and making it last long after I've retired or gone to that great big bakery in the sky." Monet beamed and waited for the audience to settle down.

Chris leaned forward. *Come on, Monet. Get to the name. Is it Yancy? Make it Yancy.*

"Here's what this student wrote: 'Bread has been called the staff of life. Without it, a person will die. But I prefer to think of all kinds of good food as the staff of life and not just carbs.'"

Monet looked up and chuckled before continuing. "'Food well-prepared isn't always easy to find. Well-made dishes feed not only the body but also the mind. Flavors tickle the palate and remind the diner of the people with whom they're sharing their meal. I want to use what I've learned in this class to make exceptional meals, using as many locally grown products as possible. Maybe even growing my own spices and herbs behind the restaurant I hope to own one day. But if I can't own my own place, I want to work at a restaurant that shares my values and supports what I want to provide to the community.'" Monet stopped speaking and wiped a finger across her cheek. "Sorry. How this person thinks is exactly how I feel about what baking means to me."

"Lexi?" Monet waved a hand. "Lexi is my partner in my bakery," she announced to the audience. "Will you come out here and do the honors?"

Lexi joined her at the podium. She waved an envelope in the air and leaned toward the microphone. "The recipient of this first culinary scholarship is Yancy Jameson. Yancy, are you here? Please come up."

Chris bumped Teddy's shoulder as Yancy rose from the group of students sitting near the stage. "Did you know?"

"No." Teddy gulped and wiped her eyes. "He told me about the assignment, but he refused to show it to me. This is so cool. And to think I was afraid Yancy would end up like Dad. Or Mom. Even if that check's small, it means people have recognized his gift. That has to make him feel good about himself."

Applause accompanied Yancy as he walked on stage.

"He's blushing. I'll bet he's embarrassed at all the attention," Teddy whispered as she stood and clapped. "Wonder what Lexi just whispered to him when she gave him that envelope."

His voice low, Chris said, "He has every right to be proud—turning his life around like he did after you came home, stepping up when I needed him." He rose to his feet and cheered, "Way to go, Yance!"

The young man, who towered over the two women, shook the principal's hand vigorously. He then shook hands with Lexi, who beamed, and Monet, who slapped his hand away and pulled him into a hug that generated laughter and hoots from the students.

Lexi gestured for him to take the mike as she and Monet stepped away and left the stage.

"Um, thanks; thank you. I never thought anything like this would ever happen to me." He squinted at the audience. "It wouldn't have if I didn't have a big sister who kicked my a— er, butt and made sure I kept coming to school, even when I was thinking of quitting." He glanced down at the envelope. "I want you all to know I'll use this money wisely. So I can become a chef. It's what I want to be."

He shook the principal's hand again and bounded off the stage to more applause. After the last two scholarships were awarded, Yancy joined Teddy. He accepted a big hug from Teddy, and shook hands with Chris.

"Good for you, Yance. You deserve it."

The trio walked out of the auditorium. Not caring who saw him, Chris gave Teddy a quick kiss. He leaned close to her nearest ear. "We're still on for later?"

"Yancy is going over to Peyton's. He and I need to talk about who gets the car for the night and for how long. I'll call you." She grinned, and her cheeks turned pink.

Chris nodded. "Hey, Yance. We should talk about changing up your hours so you can make more money for when you start college in the fall."

"I was going to ask you about that," Yancy said.

"Glad we're on the same page."

Minutes after leaving the high school, Chris pulled his truck into the garage and texted Teddy.

Don't worry about coming here. Let Yancy have the car tonight. I'll come to your place. He smiled to himself and thought, *Now's the right time.*

Chris thought of Fletcher's comments about commitment and "the right woman." His brother was right. Especially as it related to Teddy. Not that he intended to tell Fletch, who'd probably gloat and say "I told you so."

~ ~ ~

After changing into his best suit, Chris knocked on Teddy's door, his heart galloping as if he'd just run a mile.

She opened the door and smiled before sliding into his arms for a kiss, which speedily went from a casual *hi* to a much more passionate *well, hello. I've missed you so much.*

Teddy was the first one to speak. "You're looking spiffy. Why'd you change?"

He glanced down at the knife-sharp crease in his pant legs. "Felt like it. Should have got a haircut, too." He ran a hand along the nape of his neck, aware his hair was caressing the neck of his suit coat. An example of his not having fully planned out what he wanted to do, how he wanted this night to end.

"Does this mean, since you're in a suit, that you don't want us to go to Brewskers for a drink to celebrate Yancy's scholarship? He called a few minutes ago from Peyton's to say they were having a late dinner with her folks."

"Good to know. That gives us more time together. And, no. Brewskers is out. I'd rather we go someplace else." Where, he couldn't say. Eating wasn't what was on his mind as he allowed his gaze to scan Teddy's form. She still wore the dress she'd donned to attend the high school gathering for seniors. A dress that showed off her mile-long legs, which he loved, which he wanted wrapped around him later tonight.

He felt his neck and cheeks warm even as his pulse continued to climb. At the rate his heart was racing, he'd soon have trouble talking. "I was hoping we could celebrate here first. Then go out. Or maybe stay in. Do you still have that bottle of wine we didn't finish the other night?"

She turned on her heel and walked over to the refrigerator. "Yep. Still here, but you didn't have to wear a suit for us to finish off the bottle. I mean, I've seen you—"

"Naked?" He finished her thought and laughed. Her cheeks were stained a deep rose color.

"But you've never heard me say what I came here to say." He stepped back onto the porch and grabbed the bouquet of multihued flowers he'd hurriedly picked from Debra's front yard. "These flowers remind me of those stained-glass chimes you make, the windows, too, and the sidelights for that house on the bluff."

Teddy took the flowers and grinned. "Wow. This is turning out to be a red-letter day. A real first. Never received flowers before. First Yancy gets a scholarship that will help him go to cooking school, then you bring me flowers. Thank you."

He watched as she lowered her nose to take in the fragrance of the lilies in the collection. "Then I'll have to do it more often."

"Let me put them in water."

She returned to stand next to him. "Want that wine now?"

"Sure." While she filled two glasses, he slid his hand into his pants pocket and gripped the tiny box he'd stared at every night for more than a week.

Teddy cocked her head and handed a glass to him. "What did you want to talk about, other than Yancy and his scholarship? You look like something's on your mind."

"I'm thrilled Yancy got that recognition. But I'm here—that is, what I wanted—actually it's me, us. I want to talk about us." He clinked his glass against hers and took a sip.

"Cheers," she murmured.

"Cheers," Chris followed suit, then set his glass down.

"Yancy says you told Val if it wasn't for me, we wouldn't be doing so well. Because of our new, expanded website." Teddy grinned. "Just goes to show that going digital was a smart way to market the company. I told him that was all I was shooting for with all those pictures, the ones with the guys at the different construction sites that I posted earlier this week. But I knew at least some of the crew would send their pictures to all their friends, which would expand who knew about what they do every day."

"Your little brother is wise beyond his years."

"Can't call him little anymore, Chris," Teddy huffed. "He's taller than we are."

Chris nodded. "I noticed."

The warmth in her gaze as she again brought her wine glass to her lips sent heat spiraling through Chris's veins.

He reached for her hand. "Teddy. If your dad was still alive, I would have talked to him first about this. I thought about talking to Yancy, but then I figured you wouldn't want me to." He shuffled his feet. "But you have to know. Or maybe you've already guessed what I'm going to say."

Teddy's expression sobered. "Now you're scaring me. Am I fired? Is that what this is about, that you're trying to let me down easy?"

"No, of course not." He grasped her other hand, and a zing of familiar electricity shot through his arm and straight through to his heart before zooming downward. "I love you, Teddy. Probably always have. And I've been going crazy, seeing you every day, wanting to hold you and kiss you, and worrying that people might think the wrong thing about us. You know, like I used to be, or at least what people *used* to think about me."

He stepped closer. "I can't live without you. And I don't want to." He pulled Teddy closer, the better to touch her. He brushed his fingers along her cheek.

"I go to bed every night thinking about you, wanting to touch you, make love to you. When you're not in my bed, I can't stand that I'm alone. It's all I can do not to jump out of bed and race over to your house to make love to you here. Even though Yancy'd probably kill me if I tried."

He stopped talking when tears seemed to well in her eyes, their sea-blue color darkening even as her cheeks took on a deep pink hue. "You're surprised that I feel this way? Maybe I should have told you before, but I figured you already knew. That I love you, I mean. More than life itself." He punctuated his words with kisses on both cheeks before homing in on her lips.

When they came up for air, he continued, "Don't you see? I knew we were meant for each other from the very first time we met."

When she shook her head, dislodging tears from under her lashes, he said, "You knocked me off my first two-wheeler, the one with the training wheels. We were four, or maybe five, I think. My mom stopped you from climbing on and yelled at you to go home. I knew you were the woman for me when you stood right there and stared her down with your hands on your hips. You told her "no, I won't," and she didn't know what to do, so she grabbed my hand and hauled me and Elaine home. We both cried, because we didn't want to go. The next time I went to the park, I looked for you. You were on the jungle gym, and I was so glad, because I wanted to play with you again." He chuckled. "The way little kids play." He wet his throat with another quick sip of wine. "Still do, only now we can play adult games."

He pulled her close again, hoping that the feel of his thumping heart would confirm that he loved her, that he wanted to hold her this way every day, every night. He imagined the warmth of her body blending with his heat, creating a fire of longing and desire that she couldn't resist.

"I love you so much. Marry me, Teddy. Will you, please?" He kissed her forehead then lifted her chin so that he could gaze directly into her eyes. "Want me to get down on one knee? Almost forgot I was going to do that."

Teddy smiled. "Oh, Chris," she murmured, right before she kissed him.

"Is that a yes?" He had to know. "That you want to marry me, too?"

She nodded, then backed up. "Does Yancy know you were going to ask me?"

"No, but if you want me to call him, I will. Maybe I should have talked to him first—since he's kind of the man in your house."

She smirked. "Not necessary. After our last talk, he gets it. That he can trust that you do love me. I told him I thought you did, and that I love you, too. I don't think he'll mind if we get married. Or even if we just move in together. You know, after he goes off to college. Whatever." She huffed out a quick laugh. "I mean. He'd have to be around for us to get married. No way am I walking down the aisle by myself."

"Fine by me. As far as I'm concerned, Yance is already a brother. You and Yancy are *my* family, the family I choose."

"You don't think of him as a son? Even though that's kind of how you were with Yancy at the jobsite when he first came on—when you were teaching him what to do."

"No. He's a brother. I know how to deal with them," he laughed. "A lot more than I know how to deal with kids."

"Does that mean you don't want kids?" She straightened his tie as she gazed at him. "I always wondered what it might be like to have kids. Probably better than being a big sister to Yancy when I first came home and he was all attitude and not very nice."

"You want kids? You mean *our* kids?" Chris's pulse, after settling down, took another giant leap upward.

"I guess I do."

"I'd like that, too. But I want time with you first. When we're ready, we'll have kids." Chris tightened his arms around her and his next kiss seemed to explode with desire as he pressed her against the back of the couch on which they'd been sitting.

When they finally came up for air, both were panting. He angled his face and kissed her again, aching to do more.

She slid her hands up Chris's back to his shoulders, then stroked his cheeks in a move he recognized from a previous night, after they'd made love. But she stepped back and grabbed her glass, still half-filled with wine. "Where's your glass?" She picked hers up, her hands shaking slightly. 'We're going to celebrate."

He grasped his and held it between them. "But we already toasted Yancy."

"Now it's our turn. To celebrate us," Teddy declared.

He nodded. "Okay. I, Christopher James Lambert, love you, Theodora Jameson. I hereby propose that we get married. As soon as possible. And since you already said yes, I refuse to take no for an answer." He bobbed his glass in her direction. "Your turn." He took a sip.

She laughed. "And I, Theodora Jameson, love you, Christopher James Lambert. I always have, even though I didn't always show it except by punching you or trying to steal your two-wheeler. Because I didn't have one and yours was really neat. Bright red and all. I want to live happily ever after with you—as long as you let me do my thing." She laughed and sipped from her glass.

Chris set his glass down again and pulled the box out of his pocket. "Kind of out of order, but here." He went down on one knee, remembering Fletcher's comment, "first the knee, then the ring."

"I hope you like it. But if you want something else, we'll go back to the jewelry store. Together. That way you can pick out anything you want if this one isn't right. It might be too big. I wasn't sure of your ring size."

Teddy reached for the unopened box. "Can I see it?"

"Oh! I'm making a mess of things," he declared to more laughter.

Teddy opened the box and stared down at the diamond solitaire that winked at her. "You got this for me? For real?" She shifted her gaze back to Chris's face, her blue eyes reminding him of a moonlit sea.

He nodded. "Didn't even ask for help from my sisters."

"Will you put it on my finger?"

He did so.

She let out a long breathy sigh. "Beautiful. It's perfect." She pulled Chris to his feet. "Does anyone else know?"

"I think Fletcher may have guessed. We talked a couple times." Chris slid one hand around her waist and grabbed her other hand before swinging her around, dancing her past the kitchen table and down the hall toward her bedroom. "He invited us to come to his place for dinner."

"When?"

"The Sunday after high school graduation. I know you and Yance will be busy with all his parties and stuff. And he deserves to have your full attention. But don't tell him. The guys in our crew are going to throw him a graduation party of our own."

Teddy beamed. "Really? He'd like that. Where?"

"Flint's house, I think. Huey said he'd let me know. Doesn't want us to lift a finger."

"Then I should probably not wear your ring until after graduation, so it doesn't detract from what Yancy's accomplished."

"A good plan. Wear it when we tell everyone at Fletcher's."

"Your whole family will be there?"

"Just my brothers and sisters, and the niece and nephews. My folks are in Boise. Even though Dad's on a research gig again, and Mom doesn't like having to hang around while he's neck deep in dusty library stacks, he insisted she come with him this time."

Teddy pressed her lips to his. "You think they'll approve, be okay with it, with me becoming your fiancée, I mean?" She held up her left hand, on which the ring sparkled.

"Of course. I want you to bring Yancy, too. He's part of your family, which makes him part of my family, too. *Our* family." He returned her kiss as he pushed her onto the bed and fell next to her, laughing as they bounced.

She rolled toward him. "Don't you think we should get out of these clothes?"

"Good idea, but first I want to kiss you again." He angled one leg over her knees and pulled her close.

Eighteen

Chris trotted up the steps to pick up Teddy and Yancy.

"Is my tie straight?" Yancy asked. "Want to make a good impression with your folks."

"Spiffy, and grown-up. How'd your meeting go with the restaurant owner?" He grabbed Yancy's hand and pulled him into a man-hug.

"He isn't ready to take a chance on me yet. Says to come back after my first year in culinary school." Yancy brushed a hand down on side of his suit coat. "At least this suit feels more broken in after two wearings. I'm just glad all that graduation hoo-ha is over with."

Chris nodded. "Forget about the restaurant. Summer's the best time for you to rake in the money working on Val's team. With the work we have lined up, you're sure to make enough to cover your first year."

"And my scholarship will help. Your sister, Ms. Lambert, already knows, since she's a counselor at school, but what about the rest of your family? Will they ask me if I'm going to college? I know your folks think that's important." He brushed a lock of hair off his forehead.

"Probably not Lexi. She already knows your plans. My parents are out of town, but my mom will be impressed you won that scholarship. Besides, that's not why we're going to Fletcher's place."

"Right." Yancy beamed. "Never thought Teddy'd ever get engaged. One surprise after another this year."

Teddy came into the room, wearing a cream-colored dress festooned with bright red flowers.

Chris smiled approvingly. "You look spectacular. Where'd you get that dress?"

"At the second-hand store, if you must know. I like the way it swirls when I move." She demonstrated and the fluted edge of her dress floated away from her knees before settling again, emphasizing her curves when she brushed the fabric into place at her waist. "Ready, Yance?"

"Let's do it." He held open the door and waved Chris and Teddy through. "Did you ever dream you'd be getting married, sis?"

"When I was little. Not something I thought much about after Dad left." She gazed at her brother. "But I'm glad you're okay with it. Doesn't mean your opinion would stop me, but if you weren't happy, it would make things harder."

"Because it's Chris you're engaged to. Not that tool, Mr. Junior Judge. Him, I wouldn't approve of." Yancy grinned at Chris. "Right, boss? As long as Teddy marries you, I totally approve." Yancy chortled.

Teddy glanced at Chris. "You told him that's what you call Lawson?"

Chris looked chagrined, but only for an instant. "Hey, kid. I thought that was between me and you."

"Sorry. Guess I forgot." But his lopsided grin suggested he hadn't.

Chris closed the door. "Let's go. We don't want to be late. I know for a fact that Lexi is laying on some great desserts. And if Todd's manning Fletcher's grill, we're going to eat well."

As they walked to his truck, Chris leaned toward Teddy and kissed her on the lips.

"Do you guys have to get mushy?" Yancy complained, though with a grin.

"Get used to it, kid. She's my woman now. Wearing my ring. And I intend to kiss her as often as possible."

"Then I'll be glad when I've got enough money to live on my own," Yancy groused good-naturedly.

Teddy gave his shoulder a playful punch. "You'll be too busy at school and at work to pay attention to us."

"Are you two going to move in together?" Yancy held open the door of Chris's truck and stood aside when he helped Teddy into the seat.

Chris motioned for Yancy to climb in next to his sister. "That's not something we plan to announce. Besides, your sister and I haven't decided that yet."

"Right. Mum's the word." Yancy made a zipping motion near his lips.

Minutes later, they pulled into the driveway at Fletcher's house.

"I remember this place," Teddy said. "Didn't you update the bathrooms a couple years ago, right after I started working for you?"

"You have a great memory," Chris replied. "And the kitchen, which was one thing that sold the place to Lexi when she saw it and Fletcher decided to sell his other house."

"How many bedrooms does it have?" Teddy asked.

"Lexi'll give you a tour if you want. Three now. They're thinking of adding on in the back, so every kid can have their own space."

"How many do they have?" Yancy asked.

"Just Chance at the moment, but they want more." Chris glanced at Teddy and smiled. "Maybe they'll have good news on the baby front soon." He pulled his truck to the side of a sporty car that Teddy recognized.

"Looks like Todd and Lexi are here already."

"Yep. That SUV is Hale's and Eden's buggy, which means the little kids are all here." As if conjured by Chris's comment, two young boys, followed by a smaller girl, screaming happily, careened around the corner of the house. Behind her came an older boy.

"The big kid's Logan. He's twelve. Reminds me of you, Yance. Interested in all kinds of stuff. He helped me deliver some finished furniture pieces the other day. He's staying with Eden at the moment. She sometimes has him watch her kids when she and Hale have a date night."

"Convenient. A built-in babysitter in the family." Teddy chuckled.

"Eden doesn't abuse the privilege, and she always pays him, which keeps Logan in video games." Chris grinned. "Let's go meet everybody." As he helped Teddy out of the truck, he leaned closer and whispered, "Relax. They're all going to love you, *and* that I'm no longer living up to that rep I got in high school."

Teddy rolled her eyes and reached for Chris's hand.

"You're still okay with Fletcher making the announcement?" He held up her left hand.

"Sure, since I'm wearing your ring." Teddy grinned.

The door opened, and Fletcher stepped out. "Welcome! Come on in and meet the rest of the clan." He pointed to the children who clambered up the steps after Yancy. "Don't mind these little savages. Two of them are Eden's. I claim only Chance." He gave a mock-stern look to the blond-haired boy who stopped near him, panting to catch his breath. "You three need to take a breather. Why don't you go in and get washed up? We'll be eating soon."

Chance looked up at his father. "Good. I'm starved." He led the other children into the house.

Fletcher reached out to shake Yancy's hand. "Are you the scholarship winner? Lexi told me about your talents. Congratulations."

"She ate some of what we cooked at school."

Fletcher chuckled. "So she says. Was yours that salad with all the nuts? And the cranberries? She tried to copy it today but wasn't sure she recalled all the ingredients. You may want to help out. She's in the kitchen with the sisters."

Yancy preceded Teddy and Chris into the house. Teddy stopped in the entry and looked around. The high-ceilinged living room held two different conversation areas, one of which faced a large fireplace. Near the two leather occasional chairs sat a table with natural wood branches for legs. And on its top rested a graceful pair of wooden candlesticks.

"You made them, didn't you?" she asked Chris. "That table, too?"

He nodded. "Lexi said she wanted something other than straight legs, so I used tree branches instead. Like the effect?"

"I do."

Lexi approached, wiping her hands on a towel. "Teddy, so glad you're here. Your brother is fixing my salad. I forgot two key elements." She laughed. "I don't want the rest of the family laughing at me for not bothering to write down the ingredients when I sampled those dishes at school."

The two women hugged.

"I'm honored to be invited."

Chris led her to the table and pulled out a chair. "I'll introduce you as soon as everyone is seated." Which he did, beginning with Eden and Hale, their two children; then Todd and Debra, who smiled. She waggled her fingers at Teddy. Fletcher sat at one end of the table with Chance between him and Elaine. Logan took a seat next to Yancy.

"Good to see you again," Teddy said to Elaine. "You're always shorter than I remembered, though."

"Probably because you and Chris both kept growing and I didn't," Elaine quipped to grins and chuckles around the table.

Chris sat down next to Teddy just as Lexi took her seat at the other end of the table.

Fletcher raised his wine glass and waited for the other adults to do the same. "To Chris and his fiancée. At last he's been tamed," to laughter and cheers from everyone. "We want you to know, Teddy. Some of us concluded years ago that you and Chris were destined to be a couple. And your timing—what with all the problems he had to deal with this year with his business and the loss of his old shop—was impeccable." He gave her a wink, then turned to Yancy. "Bringing a future chef into the family is a real coup, Chris, although I attribute it to Teddy. With Lexi as our personal baker, there's no excuse for the Lambert family to ever eat poorly. But don't tell Mom I said that." More laughter.

Fletcher started a dish around the table and Lexi did the same. It wasn't long before all plates were full and silence was interspersed by complimentary comments about the food.

Chris smiled at Teddy and Yancy, pleased that his sibs had made them feel welcome. Not that he'd expected anything less, but he suspected Teddy was comparing this dinner to those anger-filled meals with her parents, or others that followed after Teddy's dad disappeared. When their mother was too drunk to cook. When the meals Teddy had shared with Yancy were thrown together with whatever leftovers they'd managed to scrounge from the refrigerator or Lord knew where else.

When conversation began again, Teddy raised her voice and clinked a spoon on her glass to get everyone's attention. "Thank you all for inviting us. I'm happy to be here. It's not that I didn't know some of you before—when we were all a lot younger—but …" Her voice trailed off. She seemed to gulp back tears that were forming.

Chris's brothers and sisters stared somberly at her. Were they recalling how unwelcome their mother had made Teddy feel years earlier? He had yet to decide how best to talk to his mother. Something on his must-do list.

"Anyway," Teddy continued, "I love Chris." She huffed out a quick cough. "I guess I always have—even when he broke my bat when the girls' softball team played for the City Championship."

Elaine laughed. "I remember that. Didn't you haul off and slug him?"

"No," Chris countered. "But she refused to let me walk her home after the game, which her team lost by only one run. And she wouldn't accept the new bat, either. Insisted on never being beholden to anyone." He leaned over and kissed her cheek.

"Because it wasn't the right kind of bat," Teddy clarified, her cheeks reddened.

"Chris, you should have insisted that she take it," Eden said.

Teddy shook her head. "Now that we're partners in the construction business, he and Val and I have agreed that whatever decisions are made must be by consensus."

"Then I'm sure you'll keep those two men from making bad ones," Debra added. "Yancy, are you ready to walk your sister down the aisle?"

"I guess, but she hasn't mentioned a date yet."

"What's holding things up?" Hale asked with a grin. "Now that you're business partners, tying the marital knot ought to be easy, Chris."

"Hey, I'm for that. But it's Teddy's call. No long engagement, like Elaine had." Chris waggled his eyebrows at his twin sister, who stuck her tongue out at him.

The men around the table laughed.

"Hey, I just got engaged," Teddy replied. "I want to revel in that status for a while." Her cheeks flamed.

"Totally understandable," Deb agreed. "Enjoy it. I'm gues--sing you have lots on your mind right now, what with Yancy gearing up to go to college, and the business being so new."

Teddy nodded. "You're right. Plus, Chris and I want to move forward with his furniture-making and my carving and stained-glass businesses. We did really well that day we open-ed the shop, and this summer seems like the perfect time to take advantage of the new clients we picked up. And I expect we'll be busy every hour of our long summer days building houses."

Teddy glanced at Eden. "You had a winter wedding, didn't you?"

"And it was beautiful." She smiled at Hale, who squeezed her hand.

"I've been thinking late fall or winter might be a good time for us, too. When we're not so busy." She glanced at Chris, who was looking down at his empty plate.

"Sounds like a plan," he said before looking around the table. "Something *we'll* decide. When we do, we'll let you all know. Okay?"

The sound of a door closing and soft footfalls approaching preceded Nathan Lambert's question. "You'll let us know what?"

Eden's two children and Chance, slid out of their seats and ran toward the older couple.

"Grandma, Grandpa!" they squealed.

"You're back!" Chance added.

Teddy watched as the adults rose from their seats, half smiles on some faces, full-blown grins on others. She looked at Chris, who turned more slowly than his siblings to greet his parents. He grasped her hand and muttered, "It'll be okay."

He turned to face his mother, who'd never hidden her disdain for Teddy.

But the woman seemed not to have noticed that she was in the room. Instead, she stared, goggle-eyed at Yancy.

"What's *he* doing here?" She pointed with a trembling finger. "You! Get out! Fletcher, why is that boy here? He—he—" She stumbled backward against her husband, who caught his wife and eased her into a chair as she gasped for air.

"What's going on?" Chris asked Teddy in a whisper, who shook her head.

Yancy's red cheeks paled to ivory as he bumped into the table. To no one in particular, he muttered, "Oh, cripes. Maybe I should leave."

Fletcher turned. "No. You're our guest. Please stay."

He went to his mother and knelt down next to her chair. "What's this all about? Do you know him? Yancy Jameson? He's Teddy's kid brother."

Iona nodded then shook her head, her mouth opening and closing like a fish desperate for water.

Yancy's head bobbed and he whispered to Teddy. "I remember her."

Fletcher looked his way and approached Yancy. "You do? How?"

"I—she came to our house a couple times." Under his breath, he added, "Before Mom died. For drugs."

Fletcher stared back at his mother, shock evident in his expression.

Debra's face paled. She looked at her father, as if he could explain.

Nathan stepped forward. "That'll be enough. I'll take care of this." He reached down and pulled Iona to her feet. "You need to lie down. How about on Lexi's bed or the guest room?"

Lexi stepped forward. "Of course. The guest room's closer." She preceded Iona, who leaned heavily on her husband, as she entered the main floor bedroom.

When Lexi and Nathan returned, all eyes were on him.

"What's going on, Dad?"

Nathan shook his head. He glared at Yancy. "You'd better explain yourself, young man."

Yancy's face was pallid, his lips a thin white line. "I didn't know she was your mom, Chris. Honest."

Chris stared at his father. "Go ahead, Yance. Tell us why my mom reacted like that."

Yancy gulped, shot a quick look toward his sister before replying. "The last months before my mom's ... accident, I knew she was selling drugs."

The room fell silent. No one breathed or uttered a word.

"Go on." Chris encouraged.

Teddy gripped her brother's hand and gave it a squeeze, her expression bleak.

"A few times, people came to the house. Customers. She made me swear I wouldn't tell anyone, especially not Teddy."

Under her breath, she groaned. "Oh, Yance. Does that mean—those nights she went out..."

He nodded. "She was probably dealing. She made me stay home, wouldn't tell me where she was going. But I figured out what she was doing, since she always came home with cash. Sometimes groceries, too. I tried to follow her a couple times, but she always took the car, and I couldn't keep up on my bike."

He gulped and stared wide-eyed at the elder Mr. Lambert, then at his sister. "Those times I skipped school? It was mostly because I was worried about Mom. One of those days, I saw *her*." He pointed down the hall. "She parked right next to the back door, like she didn't want anyone to see her in her fancy car. When Mom saw who it was, she told me to go to my room, but I saw her hand over a plastic bag of stuff."

"Why did you assume it was drugs?" Nathan demanded, his voice cracking. "This is craziness! Iona would never do such a thing."

Fletcher spoke up. He laid a hand on his father's arm. "Dad, Yancy wouldn't make up such a story. We need to hear him out." He nodded at Yancy. "Go on."

The teen took a deep breath. "When the lady drove off, Mom had bills in her hands. She said to forget what I saw, that I couldn't say a word or bad things would happen." He stared pleadingly at Teddy. "I wanted to tell you, sis, but Mom made me promise. She said she didn't want you to worry. That you needed to stay in school." He looked down at his shoes before again pointing in the direction of Lexi's guest room. "After that, whenever her car pulled up at our house, I went into my room. Didn't want to get in the middle of it with Mom."

He looked around the room, avoiding Teddy's searching gaze before settling on Chris. "I'm really sorry, Chris. If I'd known she was your mom, I'd have told you."

Fletcher crossed his arms over his chest. "You never called the police?"

"Would *you* rat out your own *mom*?" Yancy snapped, his eyes filling.

Chris glared at his brother, then focused on Yancy. "It's okay, kid. Go on. You knew your mother was dealing at home, sometimes, but mostly when she went out at night? Gotta admit that had to be a heavy burden to carry."

"I was scared. Kept thinking, what if she got arrested? What if they arrested me, too, 'cause if they'd asked, I'd have had to admit I knew?"

"Did you ever look for your mom's stash?" Todd asked.

Yancy nodded. "I tore her closet apart one night, and her bedroom, under the bed, under the mattress, everywhere I could think of where she might hide stuff. I was going to flush it down the toilet. But I never came up with anything but the usual stuff. You know, aspirin and vitamins. And I never knew she was cooking meth, either, until she blew up the house."

Yancy's chin trembled. "If she hadn't died, I was going to tell Teddy when she came home for spring break."

He glanced at his sister. "I'm really sorry. I didn't know. You want me to leave now?"

Teddy, tears in her eyes, hugged Yancy. "We'll both go."

When Chris started toward the front door, she said, "No, you stay. Talk to your mom. She's probably wondering why we were here in the first place."

Nathan spoke up. "Why *are* you here?"

Chris reached for Teddy's left hand, displaying the engagement ring on her finger. "To celebrate, Dad," his voice steady, firm, as if he were intent on proving himself strong enough to weather whatever parental storm might follow. "I proposed two weeks ago. And Teddy said yes."

Nathan Lambert's face took on a pained expression. "You never told us? Never warned us? Your mother and I?"

Chris glanced at his father. "How could I? You guys were out of town. Besides, it's not your decision. I knew Mom wouldn't like it, but tough shit. She'll just have to get used to it, like she did with Lexi. I love Teddy, always have." He brushed a bright red curl off her forehead. "She's my business partner, too. Which makes it even better."

Nathan's frown turned to shocked surprise. "What? I thought you asked Val to go in with you."

"I did, and he agreed. Teddy, too, but she had issues that had to be ironed out first. Why she didn't sign on the same day as Val."

Nathan Lambert slumped into a seat in the living room. "This is almost too much to contemplate. You'll have to give me time to absorb it all."

"Don't bother. I'm getting married to the love of my life. And you and Mom are not going to stop me. So don't even try. Let's go, Teddy. Yancy, you coming?"

Before Fletcher could stop them, Chris walked out with Teddy, her brother right behind them. When they reached his truck, Chris pulled her into his arms.

"Go ahead, let it out," he murmured as she began to sob. "Get in, Yance. Maybe you could squeeze into that backseat?"

"Sure." Yancy climbed in and sat sideways, stretching out his long legs.

At Teddy's house, Chris listened as Yancy talked about his mother and how things had gone from bad to worse, assuring Teddy more than once that their mother had been okay until after their grandfather died.

"That's when she really started to lose it. I wanted to tell you. She was always reminding me about Grandpop saying how important it was that you get your degree so you could become a famous artist. That I needed to get good grades, too, so I could go to college after you were done." He ran a hand through his auburn hair, causing it to spike upward through his fingers. "Only you quit after she died. Because of me."

His eyes welled. "It was bad enough that she was selling pills and stuff. If I'd known Mom was cooking meth, I swear I would have gone to the cops. Only I didn't know. Maybe that's what she was doing wherever she went at night. She told me she was helping out at the pharmacy with their audits and stuff." He scoffed. "Sure she was."

Chris stood aside as Teddy hugged Yancy.

"It wasn't your fault Mom was dealing. She was probably desperate for cash. Her job at the pharmacy never paid all that well." She gasped. "Do you suppose she was stealing from her boss? Maybe that's how she got her hands on those pills she was peddling."

"I don't know." Yancy shook his head, looking miserable. "Maybe. But her boss never said anything. He even came to the funeral. Remember? He gave you a check for Mom's last couple of weeks' pay."

"That's right. He did."

Chris interrupted. "If you guys are going to be okay, I need to talk to Fletch and my dad."

Teddy returned his kiss, looking bereft.

Yancy followed Chris to the door. "I'm sorry I messed things up."

"Don't worry about it. Fletch'll get things straightened out," Chris assured him.

Yancy grimaced. "Seeing your mom, Chris. A total shock. Nearly fell over when she walked in. I guess I shouldn't have said anything about the ... you know, drugs."

"You were just telling the truth, Yance." He paused on the porch. "Are you working with Val on Monday?"

Yancy nodded.

"I'll see you then. Take care of your sister tonight. What I have to do may take a while."

~ ~ ~

Chris's head pounded. Three days had passed since the aborted engagement dinner. His bleary gaze settled on the whiskey bottle sitting on the coffee table, now almost empty. The table was one of the first pieces of furniture he'd put his name on. He'd been pleased with how it turned out and refused to sell it when a customer made him an offer. Instead, he built another one, and two side tables to match. So began his furniture-making business.

He glanced at the Post-it pasted to his refrigerator with the date by which he intended to focus exclusively on creating high-quality furniture and restoring worthy older pieces. A date five years into the future. Would he make it? He hoped so, even as he thought about the construction business that was paying most of the bills these days.

Thank God it was going well. Chris had no doubts that it would continue to grow as long as Val was in charge. Chris intended to reward him with a bonus at the completion of the multi-house neighborhood they were close to finishing in record time. Val was right. If they continued to increase their custom home building, they'd be able to do more year-round work, which would give Chris the freedom to cultivate clients for his furniture business.

But what about Teddy? She'd listened to him earlier in the day, but had said little, and left, telling him only that she needed to focus on Yancy and getting him into culinary school. Did that mean they wouldn't be getting married?

Imagining life without Teddy blanketed Chris in a dull gray patina of loneliness. She was staying busy at the construction sites he'd assigned her. She said little about

Yancy's unexpected confrontation with Chris's parents, asking only that he give her some space.

"I need to figure things out, Chris. On my own," she'd insisted.

He'd nodded, but worried that he might end up seeing her even less than those short encounters over the past three days. At least she was spending time in her art studio on the far side of his shop. But yesterday, when he stopped in to talk, she'd said she was too busy, that she had to finish what she was working on.

He knew what it was like to want to focus on a project, so he hadn't argued. But what worried him was how she'd stiffened at his approach, as if the kiss he'd deposited on the nape of her neck was no longer wanted, maybe even resented.

He reached for the whiskey bottle. Might as well kill it and stumble off to bed. He grabbed the neck of the bottle. *No sense pouring a shot.* The way his hand shook, he'd probably miss the shot glass and mess up the carpet. He raised the bottle to his lips just as someone pounded on his door. Chris jerked at the sound, missing his mouth and hitting his cheek. What had been in the bottle was now a cold and sticky stain spreading down his neck and onto his shirt.

"Shit!" He rose and shuffled to the door, unsure of his footing. He squinted when the last rays of the setting sun blasted into his brain.

"Whadda you want, Fletch?"

His brother pushed the door open, nearly sending Chris crashing to the floor. Fletcher grabbed Chris's arm and hauled him upright.

"Since when do you drown your sorrows in booze, little brother?"

"Shince when is it your bishiness?" Chris slurred, before slumping back onto the couch.

"I talked to Dad."

"Good for you."

"He's worried about you."

Chris snorted. "That's a goddamn lie! He never has before—except when I refused to go to his goddamn college and get a goddamn degree. So I could be a goddamn engineer like he goddamn wanted."

Silence ensued, broken only by Chris's harsh breathing.

Fletcher looked in the direction of the empty whiskey bottle before pointing to Chris's chest. "I'm going to take a wild stab and conclude that this pity party of one is about Teddy."

"Bingo."

"You're going to have the hangover from hell tomorrow."

"So what? I'll sleep in if I want to."

"It's a workday."

"What about it? Val's working. He'll keep on keepin' on. Teddy, too."

Fletcher lifted a shoulder in the direction of Chris's workshop and relaxed into a chair. "You convinced her to stay business partners?"

"Wasn't hard. She needs the money." Chris ran a hand through his hair, mussing it further. He licked his hand. "I need a shower. Shticky." He pulled at his T-shirt where it adhered to his chest. "She won't talk to me about it. Really talk, I mean."

"You're a big boy. Do something about that. Although you've always been a bit slow on the draw with her. Took you long enough to wake up and realize Teddy's the only woman who could put up with you for more than a one-off." Fletcher smirked.

When Chris did not reply, Fletcher frowned. "Are you saying you two are no longer engaged?"

Chris reached for the side table lamp to turn it off. When he couldn't find the switch, he squinted up at Fletcher. "I figure that's next." Chris belched then sighed.

"She gave your ring back?" Fletcher's left brow rose.

"Not yet, but she's not wearin' it."

"Because of all those sneers and nasty comments from Mom when you were in high school, no doubt."

Chris rolled his eyes. "Said I was slumming, spending time with a girl from across the tracks."

"Well, I doubt many mothers would have found the Jameson family worthy of their son," Fletcher pointed out. "A drunk for a father and a mother whose drug habit we now know killed her. You realize Teddy's mom would have killed Yancy, too, if he'd been home that day?"

"I know." Chris groaned. "I just wish Dad hadn't sided with Mom, refusing to believe Yancy's story about her. He just made matters worse."

"What do you mean?"

"Because of him, the day after we were at your place, Yancy enlisted in the army. According to Val, Teddy totally freaked. She's convinced Yancy's going to get himself killed."

Fletcher sat up straight. "What? I thought he was going to culinary school."

"Yeah, well, not anymore. Dad's reaction at your place convinced Yancy that the only way for me and Teddy to be together was for him to leave town." Chris leaned his head back and closed his eyes, hoping to stop the pounding in his temples.

"The day Yancy came over to get his paycheck, he said Teddy was mad as hell. She kept going on about how he was *destroying* their family. What she kept calling their 'little family of two,' the only family they had." He air-quoted.

Fletcher's eyes widened. "Oh boy. She should blame Dad and Mom, not Yancy. Our fucking *parents*." He leaned back in the chair then shifted forward again, his elbows on his knees. "What do you think she would do if I told Dad about Yancy joining the army? He knows General Thompson. Plays golf with him. Maybe he could pull strings and make Yancy a stove captain."

Chris grimaced. "Are you kidding? If Teddy found out, she'd probably slap the General silly for interfering. And you, too, if she suspected you had anything to do with it." Chris pushed himself into a semi sitting position. "The general can do that?"

He shook his head and immediately regretted the action as a wave of dizziness descended. "No. Bad idea. Besides, if Yance found out, he'd probably be mad as hell. Don't tell Dad. He's made enough trouble." Chris's voice rose and he stifled a groan. Too many whiskey shots. "I don't want Teddy hauling ass over here just to yell at me!"

"Want me to talk to her?"

"No!" Chris forced himself to stand up. He wobbled for a moment then focused on Fletcher when his brother rose and steadied him. "Any Lambert talking to her right now is sure to make things worse."

Fletcher nodded. "I get it. You love her. You two deserve to be together. Which means it's time to change her mind about her thinking she has to go it alone. Make her see that you've got her back. Yancy's, too."

"Whadda you know about it?" Chris pushed a hand against Fletcher's chest, as if that would get his older brother to leave, to shut the hell up.

"Hey, I've got eyes. I've seen the two of you together, when neither of you happened to notice anyone else. Val sees it. Your entire crew, too." He backed away from Chris's hand.

"No, they don't. Only guys who know about us are Flint and Val. Teddy and I, we've been careful." Chris's sodden brain registered those times when he'd sought Teddy out, mostly at one of the custom houses for a quick kiss and an invitation to meet at her place or his after work.

Fletcher chuckled. "Don't kid yourself. When you look at her like you want to lick the sweat off her neck and she'd let you do it, it doesn't take sneaking around for other people to know how you feel about her." He backed toward the door. "Teddy's hurting right now. And you're the only one who can fix that."

Chris shook his head, regretting it again. *Gawd. Why'd I finish that bottle?* "Can't fix what Yancy did. Can't keep him safe."

"No, but you can let Teddy know that you love her, and always will. She'll feel better about Yancy, knowing you're not deserting her. Tell her he'll come out of boot camp in one piece and return home safe and sound. Maybe with less hair," he added with a soft chuckle, "but safe. Don't let her scare you off. Be the friend you've always been."

Chris followed Fletcher to the door. "Was Mom into drugs, like Yancy claims? Is that why Dad came on so strong, trying to protect her reputation?"

Fletcher's eyes narrowed. "It's possible. That time she fell and wrenched her knee, she was in a lot of pain. I suppose she might have tried to get something stronger than the doctor prescribed. Or more of it. What I can't fathom is how she knew Teddy's mom might be a source. Assuming what he said was correct."

"Yancy doesn't lie, Fletch."

"Not saying he did. But he may have misinterpreted what was in those bags his mom handed out."

"I doubt they held cookies," Chris muttered.

Fletcher opened the door. "One more thing. Eden and Deb and I, even Elaine— with her own romance troubles —we want you and Teddy to get back together." His lips quirked upward. "To quote Elaine, 'you're made for each other.' Go see Teddy and grovel big-time."

He pulled the door shut behind him, leaving Chris to wander down the hall, trying to decide what to hit first, the shower or his bed. Bed won.

Nineteen

Another week after the blowup at Fletcher's house crept by. Since the last time she'd told him she wasn't ready to talk, Teddy hadn't heard from Chris. She suspected he was locked in some kind of verbal battle with his parents. She'd been so busy with the final details at Zoya's knitting store that she chose to go straight home instead of touching base with any of the Lamberts'. Even when Lexi called, she'd put off her offers of help.

With no news on the Lambert family front, and the silence getting to her, Teddy sat in the car waiting for Yancy. He'd refused to tell her more about their mother's last days, saying only that there was no point rehashing what she had done. Mom was dead and buried. And, as for Mrs. Lambert, he remained arms-crossed-over-his-chest silent and frowning.

And just as stubbornly silent about his decision to join the army, even after Teddy called the recruiting office and demanded that the sergeant *do* something. That man, too, had simply replied that the decision to enlist was her brother's.

Yancy emerged from Monet's bakery with two cake boxes in his hands. He opened the car door and slid inside. "Okay. We can go."

"You got *two* cakes for Peyton's birthday?"

"One's for us. We could use something sweet, don't you think?"

His first reference in days to all the nastiness that had swirled around them.

"You're right." She pulled away from the curb.

Yancy remained silent until a stoplight prevented their forward progress. "You never guessed Mom was cooking meth after Grandpop died, or who her customers might be?"

Teddy glanced at her brother. "Of course not. If I'd suspected, I never would have left you alone with her. I had no idea what Mom was doing until the police called, after the explosion." She gave his nearest hand a pat before driving through the intersection. "I still feel guilty about leaving you. Stuck in a situation like that."

"Grandpop used to grouse about her drinking. But he probably would have hauled me out of there if he had known about the drugs, especially the meth."

"But you knew. About the drugs, I mean, not the meth."

"Only after Grandpop died and I was skipping school, seeing things. Those nights she was gone until after midnight? I'd lie awake wondering if she was just going to up and leave like Dad did. You know, no warning. But when she came home and wasn't into the booze as much, I figured that whoever she was seeing was helping her stay sober. I wanted to tell you. Wish I had."

"Not your fault. Besides, I was so caught up in art school and working to pay the bills that I didn't pay attention to anything else." She stared at Yancy who seemed intent on studying the kids walking across the street.

"You going over to the studio at Chris's after dinner?" he asked. "After we sample *our* dessert?" He briefly lifted the boxes off his lap.

"No." She pulled into the driveway. "You and I, we need to talk about this army thing."

His look told her nothing she said would change his mind, and it sent her pulse climbing.

In the house, Teddy opened the cake box Yancy pointed to. She cut two pieces from the three-layered cake with chocolate frosting, noting that the interior included a pudding-like creamy filling between the layers. She handed a piece to Yancy and took a seat at the table.

Yancy sucked in a breath, ate a couple of bites and set his fork down. "Go ahead. Have your say."

"Don't you remember what Grandpop said about Dad? That his time in the army messed up his mind? There's no reason for you to join up. I'll deal with old lady Lambert. Even the professor."

"But you haven't. You didn't. Where's Chris these days? I'll bet he'd help if you asked. Besides, his mom's pissed at *me,* not you! Way I figure it, if I'm not around, you and Chris can be together. Like you want. At least you *used* to. 'Sides, I already agreed to sign the papers, sis! You don't need to protect me anymore."

Tears slid down Teddy's face. She wiped them away. "I can't believe you're going to be eighteen. When Mom brought you home from the hospital, she plopped you into my lap and said I'd be your other mother." She snorted. "What kind of mother am I not to try to keep my kid brother safe?" She reached out to fluff his hair like she had when he was younger.

Yancy leaned away from her fingers and shoved another bite of cake into his mouth.

Teddy's heart thudded in her chest, her brother's silence sending an ominous chill through her.

Without warning, he shot out of his seat, went into his bedroom and returned, clutching a folder which he thrust at Teddy. "Here. Read this."

The logo of the US Army adorned the top of the first document.

"They'll pay me to go to college after I've done my eight years—and I won't have to deal with any shit face who dares to talk bad about me, or you, or Mom!" Tears bloomed in Yancy's eyes, as startling a response as the words he'd used.

"What Chris's dad said? How his mom acted, like it was *my* fault that she was doing drugs? I knew she never liked *you,* but you were always saying it didn't matter 'cause his dad was so cool. Never talked bad to you. You were right about his brothers and sisters being nice. But after that night at Fletcher's, they probably all hate me." Yancy sucked in a breath as he stood next to Teddy's chair.

"I know you want to marry Chris. And he wants to marry you. If I'm not around, it'll make things easier for you guys. His folks won't have as much of a reason to be nasty to you."

"But what about your scholarship? I thought you wanted to go to culinary school." Teddy knew she was grasping at straws.

Yancy shook his head. "I tried to give it back. Monet's partners with Lexi, and she's married to Fletcher. I thought the scholarship was really *Lambert* money and I don't want any part of it!" He swiped his forearm across his eyes. "But Monet wouldn't take it back. Said it was *her* money and Lexi's, *not* Fletcher's, and that she wouldn't insult her partner by telling her I didn't want it."

Teddy stood up. "Didn't you hear Monet when she talked about paying it forward?" She pulled out her phone. "Let me talk to her."

Yancy placed his hand on her arm. "No need. She made me promise I'd keep it and use it *after* I get out of the army."

"But, Yance, you're barely out of high school."

For the first time since she'd sat down across from him, Yancy grinned. "Doesn't matter. I signed what's called a DEP, Delayed Entry Program. It's all in that paperwork. Means I don't go to boot camp until after I turn eighteen. Next week. The sergeant said my high school grades were good enough. Even told me to bulk up so I can get through what they make recruits do without looking like a wuss."

She appraised her brother, now three inches taller than her, with added muscle on his previously thin frame. He was no longer the skinny, too-tall kid with big shoes that she'd come home to over a year earlier. "You already have muscles. From your work at the jobsite."

"I know. But Flint says he'll show me what he does to stay fit. He used to be in the army."

"He told you war stories while hanging sheetrock? I'll bet he made it sound glamorous. He shouldn't have. You could get killed!"

"You're wrong, sis. He said it was the hardest work he ever did. Besides, I told the recruiter I want to be a chef. He said maybe he could recommend me for that."

"Ha! Fat chance! You'll be lucky if he assigns you to KP duty, which means you'll be cleaning up garbage in the mess hall. Not exactly the same as cooking."

"Doesn't matter. I report for duty the Monday after my birthday." He reached for the cake and cut himself another piece.

"What about Peyton? Does she know?"

Yancy nodded. "She cried, said I was stupid."

"You're not stupid, but you're my only family, Yance. What if what happened to Dad—?"

"Don't say it. And I'm not Dad. Not your only family now, either. You have Chris. You're already sleeping with him."

Her cheeks flushed at his words.

"Like you said." Yancy chuckled. "I'm not stupid. I can tell when you come home all happy and everything. I figured if Chris and you don't get married before I leave for basic training, you two can at least live together. Since I won't be around. He makes you happy, sis. That's what's important."

"But, Yancy, you could be sent to a war zone."

"Maybe. Why do you think they teach us how to use a gun? So we can shoot back. Besides, if I'm in charge of a mess hall, the enemy won't be shooting at me."

"Please don't do this." Teddy squeezed her eyes shut, trying not to cry.

"It's already done. You don't have to take care of me any-more. Take care of Chris. He's the one who needs you." Yancy's neck took on a pinkish hue. He sat down next to her and put an arm around her shoulders.

"Damn, damn, damn!" she exclaimed, unsure what to say that might get through to her brother.

"Since when do you swear?" he asked.

"Since you joined the army! Don't you need parental permission?" She looked down and flipped through the contents of the file folder.

"Not after I'm eighteen. I'm healthy and a citizen, passed the criminal background search, and I already passed their test, what the recruiter called the Vocational Aptitude Battery. He said I did better than a lot of guys who join up." His chin jutted forward.

"Won't you please reconsider? You don't have to worry about the cost of school. Maybe we could get a bank loan. Now that I'm making more money with my carvings, my glass work, I'm a better risk than when I first came home."

"No. I'm a man now, in charge of my own life." Yancy turned so quickly that the legs of the chair on which he had perched screeched against the floor, giving a credible impression of serious pain, and mimicking perfectly how Teddy's heart felt at the thought that her little brother had taken steps to place himself in harm's way.

Knowing she wasn't likely to change Yancy's mind, she stood up and gave him a hug, no longer able to hold back her tears.

After he retreated to his room, Teddy spent the next hour reading and rereading the brochures he'd picked up at the army recruiting office. Her plan to make dinner floated away like so much smoke from a recently doused campfire.

After showering and changing into clean clothes, Yancy emerged from his room. "Can I borrow the car? I told Peyton I'd come over after you and I talked."

Teddy tossed him the keys. "Don't be too late."

"I won't." He walked out the front door, carrying the unopened cake box.

~ ~ ~

A week later, Teddy smoothed her fingers along the edge of the wing of the angel she was carving for a grieving family. She'd held back her tears while talking with the parents of the young child who died, nodding silently when they described what they wanted. After they left, she'd lost it—big-time—thinking of Yancy, even though he wasn't her child, and not a preschooler, either. Nor was he dead. But she imagined him, after surviving boot camp, being sent on a scouting patrol with other men in some god-forsaken place she couldn't find on a map, stepping on an IED or hiding behind a too-small boulder in a hail of gunfire.

Two days after he'd boarded that bus to South Carolina, Teddy imagined what her brother was doing. Marching with the other recruits? Doing push-ups? She'd watched a comedy that brought tears to her eyes. Yancy had texted her to assure her he was fine, that South Carolina was hotter'n hell, that he'd already made a couple friends. But she missed his first call home.

He'd followed up with a too-short text including his mailing address and replied to her first letter with three short notes: that boot camp wasn't bad, that Flint's advice had been good, and to please thank him for suggesting those extra gym work-outs, because they'd paid off. He ended the first two notes with the same admonition. "Don't worry about me." The third note urged her to talk to Chris. She'd bitten her lip so hard when she read it that she'd nearly drawn blood.

Hadn't their father's PTSD sent him over the edge into manic behavior, followed by depression? Each episode he'd unsuccessfully fought off with a drinking binge. And, finally, he'd deserted his family. Teddy clung to the thought that Yancy was stronger than Dad. She knew he was, but still she worried.

She set the angel aside to look over her notes and sketches for another fireplace surround. She would use alder wood this time, the preference of the homeowners, who'd chosen it for the big central staircase and the window frames and doors of their home that overlooked Puget Sound in one of the priciest neighborhoods in Pacific Knoll. A carving in that neighborhood might be Teddy's entry into doing more custom projects for homeowners there. As soon as she completed the angel, this new design would become her primary project.

Concentrating on construction in the morning, usually as soon as the sun came up, enabled her to avoid questions about Yancy that the crew members raised. His talk with Flint must have alerted the other guys of his plan to join the army. Thinking about him boarding that bus still made her cry.

Staying busy helped to keep her sane. She met with Val and Chris when he called a partnership meeting to go over bonuses for the month. And she agreed to supervise the renovation of a pair of townhomes on the south side of town while Val and Chris concentrated on other work sites.

Even though they hadn't been together since the blow-up with his parents, Teddy had come to believe that she and Chris had a true and lasting love, not just friendship love. Lover love, too, the adult kind she'd often wondered if she'd ever be lucky enough to experience, but which she'd always wanted to have with Chris. If he loved her back. And he had, at least for a little while.

And, as much as she wanted to talk to Chris, to tell him what she felt she had to do, her heart ached that in doing so, she would lose him for good. After all, he loved his mother. His dad, too, although she knew Professor Lambert and Chris had never agreed on certain things, like attending college, getting a degree.

That night, she sat at her kitchen table, determined to face up to the two people she felt she had to confront. *For Yancy. For me and Chris.* But the thought sent shivers down her spine. Which meant she was the weak one.

Ever since she and Chris had been friends, the adult Lamberts' and Jamesons' had never liked one another. Back then, Chris hadn't cared; nor had she. He'd crossed that invisible line, the line his family— his mother, anyway —had drawn be-tween her children and all others who weren't the "right kind" of people. She'd simply ignored his mother's comments, but Teddy couldn't ignore what Chris's parents had implied about her kid brother. It was past time to act. But in reviewing what she felt compelled to do, she worried. Would Chris understand? Would he still love her?

Tomorrow. I'll do it tomorrow.

~ ~ ~

From its position hanging from the edge of the porch railing, a bamboo wind chime swayed slightly, its tones sonorous and soothing as it swayed back and forth. Teddy closed her eyes, leaned back in her chair and stretched out her legs. Without

Yancy, the house was too quiet. On the porch, she was soothed by the susurration of the breeze through the leaves of the trees bordering the property, by the chime and occasional birdcalls. She relaxed into the quiet. She'd be talking to Yancy tonight, a connection, even if long distance, that she dared not miss.

The sound of a car pulling into her driveway caught her attention. *Please don't be Chris. I don't know what I'll do if it's him.* She kept her eyes closed, hoping whoever had happened by would think she was asleep and leave.

"You look comfortable." Val said, his voice soft. "Don't move, Teddy. Just wanted to come over and see if you've heard from Yancy."

She opened her eyes and straightened in her seat. "He says he's doing fine."

"And you believe him?"

She squeezed her eyes shut, determined not to cry in front of Val. "I'm trying."

A gentle pat on her arm told her Val had heard what she hadn't said. "I have every confidence he's sailing through boot camp. He's smart and strong and knows to keep his mouth shut when the DI gets testy."

"DI?"

"Drill instructor," Val chuckled. "Someone Yancy'll remember all his days. Not always with a smile on his face. Sort of like when Chris or Huey have to get tough when a grunt doesn't measure up. Not like Yance. Always followed orders to the letter. I'm guessing you're counting the days before he comes home."

She scooted into a more upright position. "That's why you stopped over?"

Val grinned. "You always were kind of psychic." He took a seat on the top porch step. "I'm going to just say it. Chris isn't doing so well right now."

Her pulse took a sudden plunge, then soared. "What do you mean? Is he sick?"

"Heartsick is my guess. That's Paula's diagnosis. We had him over for dinner the other night. He barely said two words, in between deep breaths. He looked sadder than when our dog wants a snack of people food, knows he shouldn't beg, and just sits there looking at you. Me, anyway. Old Benjy's given up on Paula. Knows she won't cave to his big brown eyes."

Val leaned against the upright. "I'm guessing you and he have yet to clear the air."

"We've talked. Mostly, I talked and he listened."

"So you broke things off with him?"

She startled and stared at Val. "Not exactly. It's just that … Let's just say I have something I have to do first. Before I, we—" What could she say that would even *sound* right?

"Your left hand's bare again. All the guys have noticed. Huey's really bummed. The crew had a pool going. Two actually. One on the date of the wedding. He was sure the date he picked would be the winner." Val's head bobbed. "The other one was about who you'd pick to give you away if Yancy isn't back in time."

"Well, you can tell them to just stop! The only person giving me away is Yance!" She felt chagrined for having yelled at Val, who'd never been anything but nice to her. Softening her tone, she added, "And I never wear my ring when I'm working. Don't want to ruin it."

He nodded acknowledgement. "Makes sense. What I suspected." His eyes twinkled. "About your wedding. Maybe you could make the crew your bridesmaids, or brides gentlemen, or something."

Teddy stood up, her hands on her hips. "That's the most ridiculous thing I ever heard of." But she burst out laughing at the image of Chris's mostly male workers marching down a white satin wedding aisle in front of her.

Val stood up and hauled her in for a quick hug. "If you don't mind my saying so, why don't you go see Chris? He needs you, Teddy. He told me about that nasty business with his folks. I can understand why you might be angry about that … and then Yancy joining the army. Even if he was just trying to make things easier for you and Chris. Yancy's eager to show he's a man. Able to take care of himself."

"You talked to him a lot, didn't you?"

Val nodded. "Reminds me of my cousin, the one who died in that car accident a few years ago. He'd be about Yancy's age now. When your brother needed to talk guy stuff, I listened. And gave him my opinion. Mostly, though, I just listened. Me and Flint."

"Did he tell you he was going to join the army?"

"Did that all on his own. Took account of what he thought was best for you and Chris. Totally his own decision."

Val glanced up at the bamboo chime. "That thing another one of your creations?"

"Yes. I made it as an experiment, to see what was possible with bamboo."

Val unhooked the chime from where it dangled above Teddy's head. "Hmm. You carved Chris's name in the longest piece." The corners of Val's mouth quirked upward. "You going to keep it?"

"The other longest one spells my name, too," she countered, as her pulse climbed.

"I'll bet you could sell a bunch of these the next time you have one of those studio showings."

He rehung the chime. "If you decide to add another name to this one, use mine, since we're partners." He grinned. "Maybe you could hang it over at Chris's workshop, since it's now the company office."

Val reached for Teddy's hand and tugged her into a standing position. "Show it to Chris. He'd like how those two chimes hang together."

"Maybe." She gave him a sidelong squint.

"Or you could ask Yancy what he thinks about these bamboo chimes, when he shows up here all tall and handsome in his Army greens. He was always talking up your art work." Val gave her a smart salute and walked away.

~ ~ ~

Something about Val's words galvanized Teddy into action. Hadn't she decided she'd have it out with Chris's parents? Wasn't "tomorrow" today? *No more stalling,* she thought. *Just do it!* Even if Chris never spoke to her again, she had to have her say. She'd never be able to live with herself if she didn't.

She went inside and changed clothes, opting for a dress she wore at her mother's funeral. The charcoal gray color seemed to fit her mood. But to break up the somber color, she added a pale blue scarf around her neck, opting to let her hair lie free. Today was not the day for braids or a ponytail. She slid her feet into a pair of black ballet flats and grabbed her purse.

At the front door, she suddenly turned and retreated to her bedroom, slipped off the flats and placed her feet into the one pair of five-inch stilettos she owned. She'd worn them only a couple of times, having concluded that she felt more comfortable in the four-inch ones. But today seemed to demand as much height, as much strength, as she could muster. An extra five inches seemed fitting for confronting the devil incarnate, Mrs. Iona Lambert, and her officious professor husband.

Teddy gunned the motor as she swung out of her driveway. She didn't hit a single red light as she drove across town to the upscale neighborhood of older homes, mostly Colonials scattered among three painted-lady Victorians. She swung into the Lamberts' circular driveway and stopped in front of the porch.

Each of those seven steps now resembled a mountain she had to climb. When she reached the top step and ventured close to the front door, she was breathing hard. For a moment, she closed her eyes, swaying slightly as she tried to remember exactly what she'd planned to say. When her mind went blank, she raised her hand to touch the door bell, changed her mind and instead, clanged the old-fashioned door knocker. Chris had told her it was a relic from his great-grandparents' last house.

After three thunderous bangs on the door, silence descended. Even the birds had stopped singing.

I should have called first. Teddy turned to leave, both disappointed and relieved that the confrontation would not happen today.

The door opened, the breeze it created ruffling the edges of her skirt. Teddy turned and stared at Chris's mother.

"Oh. It's you." Iona was dressed as if to go out.

Rather than be put off, Teddy said, "I have something to say to you. This won't take long, so wherever you're going, you can still make it. Shall we go inside?" She stepped closer and Iona backed up.

Teddy walked into a living room she hadn't seen in years. The furniture was the same, although the room seemed smaller than what she remembered. Then again, she'd been in middle school the last time she'd been ushered inside by Chris, who'd hustled her directly to the kitchen to rummage for a treat after a summer ball game. She'd been shorter then, and not wearing heels.

"Whatever you have to say, I, we … what is it? My husband isn't here. Just me." Iona Lambert looked past Teddy, as if wishing she wasn't alone.

"Doesn't matter. I'll talk to him later." Teddy sucked in a deep breath and let it out slowly. Her heart was pounding so forcefully, she was sure Chris's mother could hear it.

"I'll just cut to the chase. You've never liked me, never thought I was good enough for Chris. But I am. Because I love him"—she held up her hand when Iona opened her mouth to interrupt—"and there's nothing that you can do or say that will stop me from loving him. I don't know if we'll ever get married—"

Iona gasped.

"But we *are* engaged. Something he wanted, something I want, too. I don't know why you can't see that Chris is a grown man who knows his own mind, who owns a business he's built with his own two hands without any help from you or your husband. Just him in the beginning and now with a crew." Teddy glanced down at her own hands: she was still a member of that crew. "You need to stop trying to make him live his life like *you* want. Because if you don't, you're going to *lose* him. He'll *never* come back for your precious Sunday dinners, where you lord it over his brothers and sisters." On a roll, she couldn't seem to stop talking, even as Iona's face gradually lost color and her hands moved upward, stopping when they covered her mouth.

"Lexi told me how nasty you were to her. But she stood up to you. Well, I'm with her. Just like her in a lot of ways, in fact. Strong. The kind of women your sons love and want. You should be *proud* of them for picking us instead of milquetoast girls who don't have minds of their own. Lexi and I don't *need* your sons. We love them for the wonderful men they are and want them in our lives and would never do anything to hurt them." Teddy stopped talking, in favor of getting air.

Iona opened her mouth as if to respond, but Teddy had more to say.

"About my brother and what he saw. He never gave you away, never told a soul until you forced him to relive a really bad time in his life. You owe him big-time for keeping your secret."

What else could she say to make Iona understand? *Nothing.* She'd said enough. It had to be. She was all talked out.

Teddy turned and walked out the door.

As she drove home, her fingers trembled on the steering wheel, and the mantra that kept repeating in her brain was, *Done. I did it.* She had to tell Chris before he heard from his mother. Iona Lambert was perfectly capable of twisting Teddy's words into something ugly.

But when she called Chris, his phone clicked over into voice mail, and what she had to say deserved more than a text or even a quick voice message.

She drove to the jobsite and asked Val where she might find Chris. He shrugged his shoulders, saying he'd left for a meeting downtown with a big corporate guy.

"I'm not sure when he'll be back, Teddy, but I'll tell him you asked. Everything okay?"

She nodded. "I'm going to the studio. Will you ask him to meet me there?"

"Sure."

Twenty

Teddy changed into a pair of sweats and a tank top before driving to her studio. She toyed with sending Chris a text, but decided against it. Val would pass along her message. If Chris was downtown, he was probably negotiating a new contract. No way did she want to disturb him.

But as if to bedevil her, errant thoughts of Chris kept coming to mind. She saw him in his work clothes hefting drywall; his sleeves rolled up as he bent over a piece of furniture he was restoring; better yet, shirtless on a hot day. He'd reminded her of a modern-day Adonis when they'd gone swimming at the local pool one evening after work. Her brain kept scrolling through that memory of water droplets sliding down his chest, past his abs and into the waistband of his trunks.

He and Teddy had closed down the pool that evening, enjoying the water until the lifeguard finally whistled them out so that he could go home. As if those images weren't enough torture, she imagined Chris naked, after they'd made love and he'd oh-so-casually climbed out of bed and headed for the shower, inviting her to join him.

A text pinged into her phone. *Chris loves you. You love him. Talked to him yet?* Why couldn't Yancy stop asking?

No, but soon. She added an emoticon to emphasize her reply. Then, in hopes of getting Yancy to stop asking about Chris, she pointed her phone at the angel she was carving and clicked a photo. *My latest commission. Like it?*

Nice.

She straightened in her chair, rubbed the nape of her neck. She lifted her hair off her neck and let it fall, up and down, feeling more relaxed with each rise and fall of her heavy mane.

The blinking light that signaled that someone was at the door startled her. *Chris? Already?*

"Can I come in?" That sexy-as-melting-caramel-sliding-down-the-sides-of-an-ice-cream-cone voice of his. Her pulse jumped and certain girl parts came to attention.

"Val said you wanted to see me." He paused and picked up a shaving of wood that lay next to the leg of her chair. "I've missed you, Teddy. Yancy, too."

She swiveled in her seat, the better to look at Chris, knowing he was taking up too much space, sucking up all the oxygen in the room by standing so close. If he touched her, she was a goner. But did he know about her little *chat* with his mother? "You know Yancy left for boot camp."

He nodded. "I tried to call you, but you weren't answering your phone that day. So I called Lexi for news and she told me when he was leaving. I went to the bus station to tell him good luck and everything, but you were there with him and I didn't want to interrupt. You had him in a death-clinch. For a minute there, it looked like you weren't going to let him on the bus."

He sucked in an audible breath and handed her an envelope. "Check this out. From the president of the college. He talked to me about making repairs at the student union. They want to replace several windows with stained-glass scenes depicting different activities on campus. Are you interested? It's all there. In his note."

Teddy mentally tallied up how long such a major job might take. "Is this why you were downtown?"

"No. That's another big job we might get. Won't know for another couple of weeks."

Chris shuffled his feet. "My dad stopped by our jobsite, the one along the bluff. You know, those high-end houses next to the one we finished a month ago. He told the president about those sidelights you did."

Teddy stared up at Chris, shocked that the president of Lambert-Knoll College even knew who she was, what she did.

Chris crossed his arms across his chest, then uncrossed them and slid his hands into the pockets of his work pants. "If you don't want the job, I'll tell him you're too busy." He glanced down at his shoes and frowned, looking as if he'd already concluded Teddy would turn down what had to be a major job, one that would keep her busy for months. Was he offering it to her because of the president's relationship with his parents? Was this his father's way of apologizing to her?

Her heart leapt at the thought of what such a big job would mean for her reputation in stained-glass art. Or was it slamming against her ribs because Chris was standing so close, the heat from his body curling around her, tempting her to fly into his arms?

"Looks like a big job," she croaked.

"Yeah." He reached out to touch her, then stopped before his fingers made contact with her shoulder. He cleared his throat. "The president didn't offer because of my dad, Teddy. When he called me, he said he'd checked out your work, first on the website and then I guess he sent out some people to look at what you've done with other windows. He was impressed."

Chris's feet shuffled. "I decided to bring this over personally. So I could see you. So we could talk. Is there a chance you might come over to the house when you're done here? You can get back to the president yourself. Directly. No need to go through me."

Teddy felt caught in the heat of Chris's gaze, his chocolate eyes so warm, so loving, as if he couldn't get enough of her. She wanted to slide into his arms, but didn't dare, not until she told him what she'd said to his mother.

"You're still not wearing your ring," he said.

She glanced down at her bare left hand. "Not when I'm working." But that excuse had worn thin even to her. She'd taken it off because it seemed the only way to distance herself from Chris's family. Even though Yancy had declared that she *deserved* to be with Chris, that he deserved her, too. That she should just ignore Chris's parents and their hateful words.

"How long were you planning to work today?" he asked.

"I haven't been here long, and I'm pretty much done. Concentration's shot." She looked sidelong at him, determined to tell him. "Because I went and talked to your mom today. Did she tell you?"

"No."

"Let's go to your place and I'll fill you in." She hoped he'd understand, but if he didn't, if he stood with his mother … and not her? Then, she'd give him back his ring.

~ ~ ~

Chris listened, nodding, occasionally frowning. Then he leaned over and deposited a quick kiss on her lips. "I'm so proud of you for talking to her, telling her to back off. I was going to do that. Just never got around to it. Call me a coward."

"You're no coward, Chris. It's just that your mom … She doesn't really know you."

"No, she doesn't, and I don't agree with her stupid ideas about who I should be, who I should hang with. Whatever my dad says doesn't matter, either. Not to me. They should know that by now. I want us to forget about them. Like Fletcher does. And Deb and Eden. Even Elaine has stopped listening to them. The only kid they can still control is Logan, but he'll stand up to them soon enough."

Teddy leaned forward, her elbows propped on her thighs. "But you can't just ignore your parents. Can't just cut them out of your life. At least you have parents. If mine hadn't been so messed up, I would still want to have them in my life," she added. "Such as it is."

Chris squeezed her shoulders. "I get what you're saying. Them not being there for you and Yance is probably the reason he was messing up right after your mom died. But you and Yance have each other. That's not going to change. No matter what. I know my parents love me, but they have to back off. I make my own decisions—have been ever since I apprenticed with Old Man Ludlow. If it hadn't been for him, I'm not sure I'd have survived Dad's demands that I go to college. Even when my grades weren't good enough for me to get into L-K."

"He could have pulled strings to get you in," Teddy countered, sensing that Professor Lambert might have done so.

"No way was I going to go, especially if he did that, which I told him. Fletch did, too." He rubbed a palm across his chin and cheeks. "I'm twenty-eight next month. When are they going to learn to accept me for who I am?"

"But even *normal* parents want what's best for their kids." Why was she playing devil's advocate?

"Maybe, but who says they're normal? The bottom line is I love you. I. Love. You. You're what's best for me. I want us to be together."

Tears welled, and Teddy shook her head. As if that would stop the waterworks.

"No? Or are you saying Yancy doesn't want me in your life? I thought he liked me." Chris sounded hurt that he might have misjudged her kid brother.

She huffed out a soft bark. "He likes you. Even said I should make you part of *our* family. Our itty-bitty family of two. At least it will be if he ever makes it home."

"*When* he comes home, hon. He'll be here as soon as he's done with boot camp. And in between deployments. And when he's through with his service. Even if he ends up living somewhere other than Pacific Knoll, he'll always be your brother. Your brother, the chef. Just think. After he makes a name for himself, we'll be able to say 'we knew him when.' You have to know that."

"I hope so," she squeaked, and brushed the tears from her lashes.

"Will you let me talk to him?"

"He said he might call me today or tomorrow. I keep my phone with me every second so I won't miss his calls."

"Then let's grab dinner. You can tell me what you've been working on. That angel sculpture has the makings of a masterpiece."

Teddy's phone buzzed in her pocket. "Yancy." She sat back on the porch swing. "Hey! How're things?"

"Great! Tomorrow we begin marksmanship training. Can hardly wait. What're you doing? Made up with Chris yet?" His voice boomed out of the phone.

Chris grabbed the phone and put it on speaker.

"Not yet, but I'm working on her," Chris replied.

"Hey, Chris. You at our house?"

"No, I convinced your sister to check out the new swing I installed on my porch. We're going for dinner soon. I miss what you can do in the kitchen. Had any MREs yet?"

"Nah, and what we get in the mess hall isn't that great."

"Nobody knows what you can throw together?"

"I'm keeping my mouth shut and my nose clean. Boot camp's no place for making waves. One of the guys had to do fifty more this morning; ended up puking his guts out."

"Hmm. Too bad for him. Here's Teddy." Chris pointed the phone toward Teddy, and she took it from him.

She asked, "You're sure you're okay?" She flicked the phone off speaker.

"Except for the heat. It's brutal here. The humidity, too. Can't wait to leave South Carolina," his voice low. "Am I still on speaker?"

"No."

"I hope you're making up with Chris. Even if his folks are pricks."

"Yance. That's not nice."

"Hey, the truth I speak," he uttered, trying to sound like Yoda. "Gotta go. My bunkmate wants to use the booth."

"Love you, Yance. Stay safe."

"Always, sis. Write me."

She shoved her phone into her pocket and wiped her eyes.

"Yancy sounds great." Chris motioned for her to follow him and they took his truck to the Greek restaurant, where they'd eaten after he gave Teddy her ring.

After they were seated and their order taken, she asked, "You heard what Yancy said, didn't you?"

"About the fifty pushups?"

"What he said about me making up with you."

"Smart man, that Yancy." Chris grinned crookedly.

"I needed time, Chris. Time to figure out what to do about your folks, about us."

She stared at Chris, whose mouth curved up into a hopeful smile.

"You're cool now? About us? I want us to go to my brother's house again. For dessert as well as dinner." He brought a hand to the nape of her neck and pulled her forward so that he could kiss her. "Does this mean we're a couple again?"

Her cheeks flamed. "I've missed you, Chris. Really badly. I just wish your folks didn't hate me and Yancy."

"That's a little strong. My mom has her own ideas about people. But my dad? He'll come around. Fletch told me he was shocked at what Yance said. That's why he went all protective of Mom. I told both of them that they'll never see me again unless they can accept that you and I are together." He stood up and pushed her deeper into the booth so that he could sit next to her. "We are, you know. A couple, I mean."

She allowed her gaze to settle on his face, his cheeks deeply tanned. "You still want us to live together?"

"I'm willing to do whatever you want, as long as you want it. I want us to get married, but if you're not ready for that, living together's a great compromise."

Teddy's mind filled with images of sharing breakfast with Chris, sleeping together, working together, laughing at silly jokes, picking up Yancy when he came home from boot camp. Each image ramped her pulse higher.

"Where? Your house or mine?"

"You pick. Mine's a little bigger and I own it. Or," he quipped with a grin, "the bank does. But you'll save rent if you move in with me, and be closer to the studio."

She couldn't prevent her lips from quirking upward at that dig about saving money, something she was always telling him and Val whenever they speculated about the difference between projected and actual business income and expenses.

Yancy's words came back to her, almost a dare to move in with Chris, to test the couple waters with him. "Then I pick your house, but I'm not going to break my lease. What if you don't like that I take up too much space in your closet or—"

Chris stopped whatever objections she was going to raise with a firm kiss that quickly amped into overriding passion and left her trembling.

He waved to their server. "Mind if we just pack up this food and take it with us?"

She nodded and brought several boxes to their table.

Minutes later, Chris raced her up the steps of the porch, but halted her forward motion when he swung her into his arms and kicked open the unlocked door.

"You never locked the door?"

"Guess I forgot. Had other things on my mind. Mostly you."

"I love you, Chris," Teddy murmured. "That's never going to change. I think I've loved you forever."

"Hey, I was going to say that."

"So, say it." She allowed her eyes to close as she snuggled closer, resting her head on his shoulder.

He preceded each word with multiple kisses that began on her lips and descended slowly downward with several detours to both breasts and other parts. Teddy encouraged Chris with sighs and moans as her pulse soared.

"Oh, yes," Teddy murmured right before she handed him a condom.

He slid home, filling her.

~ ~ ~

"You think you'll like it here?" Chris asked as he stroked Teddy's cheek the next morning.

She nodded. Her stomach growled. "But I'm hungry. I'll start breakfast while you shower. Just don't use up all the hot water." She climbed out of bed and reached for his high school jersey, draped over the only chair in the room.

"You look better in that than I do," he remarked as he headed for the bathroom.

"Ha ha." She entered the kitchen and rummaged in the refrigerator for breakfast fixings.

Minutes later, Chris took over while she cleaned up and got dressed.

They had just sat down to a breakfast of orange juice and French toast when Nathan Lambert knocked once, opened the kitchen door and entered.

"Dad!" Chris stood up, knocking his chair against the wall.

Nathan's eyes widened when he saw Teddy. "Didn't expect you to have company, son."

"I'll let you two talk." Teddy rose from her seat and angled toward the front door, intent on putting distance between herself and the retired professor.

"No. Don't go. I have something to say to you, too." Nathan softened his voice. "I was hoping I might learn how to reach your brother."

"He's at boot camp," Teddy said. "Gets family calls only. And I doubt he'd take your call."

"Then perhaps you might give me his address. I recall how important letters were when I was in the service."

"Why do you want to write Yancy?" Chris joined Teddy in the living room where she stood, rubbing her hands together as if she was chilled.

"I owe him an apology. For not realizing ..." Nathan glanced down at his shoes before focusing on Teddy and then his son. "I have no intention of interfering with your business, or your life, Christopher." The older man's cheeks turned ruddy. "Or with you, Theodora. You and Chris have had a special relationship for more years than most married couples—"

"Dad—"

"Don't interrupt me, son. Your mother has her own view of things, and people. They don't always coincide with mine. I want you both to know that you'll always be welcome in our home. Your brother, too, Theodora. I'll bet when he shows up in his Class As, my wife will welcome him with open arms. She's always had a hankering for men in uniform." His lips curved upward into a crooked smile. "At least she did where I was concerned."

"You got to the bottom of things with Mom?"

"I did. My times away have allowed her to hide certain activities from me. I'm just happy that Logan was not affected after she took that nasty fall and had so much trouble with her knee." He let out a whoosh of air.

"She took it upon herself after Mrs. Jameson's death to seek help from our family doctor, whom she swore to secrecy. She's no longer taking those pills she was fast becoming addicted to. I hope you'll agree, Christopher, that your mother showed remarkable strength of character doing that."

Nathan stepped closer and reached for Teddy's hand. "Your mother's untimely accident was the wake-up call my wife needed. I'm sorry it took such a terrible accident for her to see what she was doing. And I want you to know that I'm deeply grateful. Even though it took your mother's death to force Iona to seek help. Not that she was willing to admit it until seeing your brother brought it all back. Which is why she reacted as she did. Not her best behavior. But it forced her to tell me what happened. And I wasn't my best, either."

"You want Yancy to know you're sorry for what you and your wife said?" Teddy asked.

"In a nutshell."

"What makes you think he'll even read your letter?"

"I can only take ownership of my actions, young woman. And my wife's, on her behalf." He stepped back. "Having known you for so many years, I have a feeling Yancy is very much like you. A strong character with a big heart and a forgiving nature. And that he wants *you* and my son to be happy. Which is in jeopardy right now if you continue to think we might stand in your way."

Nathan turned his gaze on Chris. "We aren't, son. We won't. We're inordinately proud of you and your business. And in your choice of friends and partners." He glanced down at Teddy's left hand, now gripped in Chris's. "I would imagine that ring you were wearing the other day is ample evidence of your plans for the future. Which I approve. Chris's mother does, too."

His left eyebrow rose when he smiled at Chris. "If you don't believe me, you can ask her yourself."

Nathan walked back through the kitchen. "You'd best sit down and finish your breakfast, before it gets cold," he admonished.

After his father left, Chris stared at Teddy. "Wow! Never thought I'd ever hear him say that."

"He's an honorable man." She returned to her seat then gave her forehead a light slap. "I forgot to give him Yancy's address."

"I'll do it." Chris pulled out his phone.

"No. Let me. He asked me. Send me his email address." But on receiving it, she refilled her coffee cup.

"If you want me to move in, could we get some of my things?"

Chris beamed. "I'm for that."

# # #

Thank you for reading this book. My characters reflect the life experiences of people I know. Perhaps also, people you know, or even yourself! A reader's greatest gift to an author is a review. If you enjoyed this story, please post a brief review on Goodreads.com and/or your other favorite social media sites.

Questions for Book Clubs and Reading Groups

1. How would a single twenty-something man you know react if he was accused of getting a woman pregnant when neither was committed to the other?

2. After Fletcher agrees to look into Bambi's background causes Chris and Fletcher to doubt that she is telling the truth?

3. Teddy and Chris have been friends for years. What about Teddy would encourage you to be friends with her?

4. How is her strength of character a role model for Yancy?

5. Would you, if asked, meet with the deans assessing your boyfriend's qualifications for tenure? Why or why not?

6. How would you describe Teddy's relationship with Val at the jobsite? With the other constructions workers? With Axel?

7. How would you describe Chris's relationship with his niece, his nephews? When Chris takes Lexi to the hospital, what does that say about his character?

8. What do you think of Lawson Poindexter? Would you trust him if he asked you to dinner? Is Chris right to be jealous of him?

9. Why do you suppose Chris is so clueless when it comes to Teddy and her feelings for him?

10. Is Teddy right to ask Chris out? Why? If you were advising her, would you have suggested that she do so?

11. What do you think about Chris's gift to Lexi, his gift to Teddy?

12. Why do you suppose Iona Lambert is so antagonistic to Teddy? To Yancy? What does this say about her?

13. When in the story would you have preferred Chris to make his interest in Teddy obvious?

14. What do you think about Teddy's decision not to wear Chris's engagement ring? At work? Elsewhere?

15. If you were Teddy, would you confront Iona Lambert? Why or why not?

16. What would you like Chris and Teddy to experience in a future story in this series?

About the Author

Kate Vale lives in the beautiful fourth corner of northwestern Washington state. She enjoys the slower pace of a small city located between Vancouver BC, and Seattle WA. Her stories reflect the many different careers she has experienced and some of the challenges that confront real men and women. Helping her characters get to a happily-ever-after is a continuing goal.

Reviews, a link to her blog and first announcements of new titles appear on her webpage: http://katevale.com. Feel free to visit it.

You can contact Kate at katevale@sent.com, or find her on Facebook: https://www.facebook.com/kate.vale.127,
on Twitter: http://twitter.com/katevalewriter; or
on Google+ at katevalewriter@gmail.com

www.ingramcontent.com/pod-product-compliance
Lightning Source LLC
Chambersburg PA
CBHW051423170626
46809CB00006B/2293